Jane E. Murphy studied A-level English and Art. After leaving Art College she sidetracked as a civil servant before leaving to become a full time parent. Jane then began writing her first novel after being inspired by a waking thought; this epiphany led to a fully-fledged book along with complementary art work.

JAUNT

'An excursion of enjoyment, happiness, contentment and revelation'

Dedication

For Mum who ensured my love of not only the written word but the tactile rapture of holding and flicking through the book itself. Her nonjudgmental support and belief in everything I do will always be an inspiration to me – it paid off in the end!

Jane E Murphy

JAUNT

'An excursion of enjoyment, happiness, contentment and revelation'

AUSTIN MACAULEY
PUBLISHERS LTD.

A CIP catalogue record for this title is available from the British Library.

ISBN 978 184963 543 1

www.austinmacauley.com

First Published (2013)
Austin Macauley Publishers Ltd.
25 Canada Square
Canary Wharf
London
E14 5LB

Printed and Bound in Great Britain

Acknowledgments

My dear friend Jane for her totally unselfish assistance.
Thanks Philthy for your friendship, honesty and technical expertise; you've been there even when exasperated, don't think I haven't noticed the metaphoric head shaking and eye rolling whilst remaining unconditionally helpful - I love you for that.
Thanks little sis, Stella, for helping me to nurture my faith.
To all songwriters, musicians and musical performers I have ever loved, admired, seen and listened to – without these supreme beings I would have quietly lost my mind a long time ago and would never have written this book.
And.
My oldest and dearest friend Sarah who makes me laugh when there's no laughter left.

Rachel's Overture

Music mirrors her life and summons the past, reflects a moment, magnifies the present and persuades her future.

Chapter 1

Do something that scares you

"I am not doing work today!"

I say this out loud as though it's an inevitability.

My spoken words are mingling with the air we all breathe making them organic and 'out there'; they can't be taken back and that feeling is comforting.

Complete defiance and resolve, that's my 8 a.m. condition; the peaceful release of all obligations and responsibilities.

'I'm not doing work today' is the consequence of a myriad of rehearsed imaginary excuses to stay at home, the same meaningless perfunctory thoughts every morning make that initial bleary eyed, waking work-day moment a more bearable transition into full consciousness.

I gradually pull open my eyes, so slowly I have to peer through the blurry mesh of eye lashes trimming my blackout blind lids, while my uncontrolled thoughts snake through the smoky rings of a gentle but powerful, haunting medley – Philip Glass - still on repeat from the night before.

Staring emotively at the beautiful Art Nouveau silvered ceiling rose seared onto the pale blue satin expanse above tempts me out of sleepiness; its well defined shadow, painted by an unusually intense sun forcing its way through the haphazard opening in the curtains, dramatically parachutes directly to the back of the room out of sight behind my head and I'm happily led into a false sense of relaxation and contentment.

I can just hear the snapping twang from the ropes on the sash window through the heavy velvet drapes, billowing from the draught that's gusting through the considerable gap in the old decrepit wooden window frames.

My body is warmed to a perfect temperature under the covers as a cold current of air skims my face, neck and shoulders like a soft summer breeze; I'm then transported to a lazy, warm, Saturday afternoon.

From a great height the ceiling rose's ring of voluptuous silver spoon shaped petals converge in the middle and slope toward me into a seemingly unending tubular point, an imaginary umbilical leads directly from that tip straight down to my navel. There are four giant hooks, one on every other convex section, which I assume once suspended a chandelier; this possibly, in the history of this building, may not have been the bedroom.

Trying to work out how this apartment would once have played its part in the whole majestic yet quaint and intimate house with all its nooks and crannies helps me organise my thought processes toward the ultimate goal of getting out of bed – not an easy task!

The notion of the static outer husk of this old house containing the ever evolving compartments within intrigues me every morning when I first wake up. I don't think I could actually start the day without pondering the internal mysteries from the little clues left over from all the previous occupants. I hope I will also make an inspired and long lasting addition to this collection of personal absurdities and quirkisms, or at least leave an imprint of myself for others to ponder over – whatever that may be!

The whole flat contained within this large Georgian building is a mishmash of different periods from Art Nouveau, Baroque and Gothic styles to Retro and all the previous tenants' diverse avant-garde ideas – a mix of histories and genres, this for me is the appeal and why I love it so much.

The only thing I would change are the carpets, each room is having its own Purple, Green or Orange psychedelic 'rave'. You don't need to bring drugs or alcohol to this party; the spectral aromas rising up from the floor like a bad smell, will get you high without the need for hallucinogens – there's a thick shimmering desert haze of bad taste hanging a foot above floor level!

I've seen this very same purple swirls carpet that dominates my bedroom at the local Indian takeaway which makes me think either the takeaway owners lived here for a while and used a remnant for this room, or vice versa, or it's just a very disturbing coincidence. Surely no two individuals would have had the same liking for this putrid pattern! Even by the swinging sixties 'anything goes, drug induced' standards, or the 'bad taste' decade of the seventies, it would be revolting.

I suspect no one since then has had the finance or inclination to replace any of the floor coverings, as ironically they are extremely good quality and indestructible – I could unleash a whole bottle of red wine and the fluid would mercurially slither away to find more to join with or effervesce into the atmosphere. No amount of military style traipsing about in hobnail boots will wear through this Kevlar like material. I won't be any different, I will put up with the annoyance until I just don't notice anymore.

*

Of course, I will get up and do the work thing! Delaying things ultimately helps me with the prospect of getting out of my safe cosiness and easies me into the must have routines of everyday life. I don't have OCD but I definitely aspire to it!

On shifting focus from thoughts to gaze, something catches my eye to the right of the ceiling rose – a tiny tear in the paper, from the days when people used to wallpaper their ceilings. Tearing down the many layers of paper might cause the whole ceiling to crash so it's just been repainted over and over again.

A small unlikely triangular rip reveals the bare smooth ceiling skin underneath and after staring at it intently for what seems an eternity I feel as though I can actually reach out and pick at it a little, an uncontrollable urge to reveal more of what lies beneath, a little scab that itches and needs to be removed.

It now seems to be inches from my nose and I can inspect every little flaw and angle surrounding the tiny imperfection on an otherwise perfect canvas ... my clock alarm breaks the flawless silence and literally brings me back down to earth. I'm suddenly many feet away from the ceiling again; such a vivid delusion!

*

Back to Priorities – change the music. The player is right next to my head teetering on top of four huge columns of books, one of my many imperfect improvisations to reduce stress and effort. Reading is my most expensive vice, music comes a close second and is the reason for a lack of remaining finance. I don't buy expensive books; it's the volume that's my downfall!

I need a different mood, last night I buried myself deep and indulged in melancholy, this morning some gentle waking up music would be appropriate to make a gentle transition from drowsy bottom step to the more precarious midway corner landing! The dulcet tones of 'Nick Drake' – Road will revive me sympathetically although given my reluctance to get up I should choose music that will stun me and have me racing straight to the bracing top floor summit.

I need something invigorating that will have me cavorting enthusiastically; starting with an anthemic build up – an oldie but goodie, 'New Gold Dream' – Simple Minds with its pulsating and increasing rhythm, maybe followed by 'the Foo Fighters' – The Pretender or the more potent German band, Rammstein; they get me off my backside and stomping into my clothes with unconscious energy. I haven't a clue what Rammstein's Till Lindemann is singing about, to me it's a lot of counting and marching instructions when really their Germanic pounding is probably very gratuitous and disturbing – I'm happy in my ignorance, but I love industrial music with its raw kinetic operatic energy. All in all it's a very eclectic mix that does the trick. They're all on one playlist entitled 'Motivational getting up in the morning music!'

I live by music, my whole life seems to have had its own soundtrack mirroring my mood or experiences and if I don't have some electronic gismo continuously pumping out tunes, including the radio, then the music inside my head more than compensates. It's embarrassing how vivid and loud it gets. Sometimes I wonder if anyone else can hear it radiating out of me from invisible speakers hidden under my hair or see cartoon crotchets and quavers flowing out of my ears, floating up into the sky like lost balloons.

Music for me is the measure of a person; it's the best quick way of understanding someone's character without having to delve too far. We all have a different combination, a musical fingerprint which defines us, everyone, whether you like their taste in music or not, has a different mix of songs and styles of music they like which makes them unique.

Gift or curse, my uninvited but welcome organic, internal jukebox has given me reassurance and salvation throughout my life.

All my music is alphabetised and catalogued, including all downloads, so I can find whatever I want at a moment's notice. I would be lost without the comfort of my index cards and logbooks!

By the time I finally shove back the covers, and the strings that control my limbs have thrown the lower half of my legs out of the bed, while my upper body is still completely static, my head resting defiantly on the pillow, there won't be enough time to work out what to wear.

I will put on the same clothes I had on yesterday and I'll wear these every day until they are spectacularly unwearable then I may one evening spend hours going through my wardrobe deciding what I will wear for the next four days.

Personal hygiene is not the issue here; it's a matter of prioritising. I take an interest in my appearance but I'm not fanatical about it. I don't like up-to-date fashions unless they're used unconventionally. I'm not a modern conventional person – it just so happens I can't relate to the masses.

Not having much money left over after essentials due to my passions, or vices depending on which perspective you take, means charity shops, second-hand clothing agencies and eBay are my preferred boutiques.

Generally I love vintage clothes from the 20s right through to the 60s and I like to mix things and come up with something different; stylish and chic clothes mixed with a hard edge, lots of layers, light pretty frocks or chic short evening dresses with biker boots but I can't always be bothered or have the time to work it all out ... and why is it that whenever I have enough money to buy the latest look, something that suits my sensibilities, new, expensive and of good quality, a new addition to my collection, there's nothing that inspires me? I always see something I really like and want, that beautiful garment I think I can't possibly live without, when I'm destitute; bad management I suppose. I don't get into debt but I'm no good at saving so I stay on this continuous cycle of buying second hand clothes or utterly bad new buys.

I don't do makeup. I gave up trying to cover my mass of freckles some time ago. Just a little mascara and a light lip gloss to make me look like I'm actually awake.

My hair is always a mess for work but if I'm going out I will do something different with it, pile it up precariously with strategically placed wild bits hanging around my face, big hair with rock-chic backcombing or carefully arranged and tied back in a pre-Raphaelite style.

*

My next mission after toothbrushing and desperately trying to organise my mass of long waves into a uniform collective, is to rush around like a woman possessed; I should have had this feeling of urgency twenty minutes ago. 'Maniac' by Michael Sembello seems too obvious; maybe The Killers version of 'Shadowplay' on repeat will do for that. I love Joy Division's original but it depends on my mood. The Killers version is 'popier' – less intense. If I need something real then Ian Curtis is the choice.

I'll get my stuff together whilst grabbing some toast and rush out of the door in time to catch the bus, all within about ten minutes (I'd been smacking the snooze button on my little cheap digital clock every ten minutes for an hour before I started to come around) in order to get to a boring office mainly full of middle-aged ladies twice my age They talk about their kids or grandchildren a lot, have what they would consider as an in-depth scene by scene analytical discussion about *Eastenders* and ponder their culinary masterpiece for tea that night.

After bouncing dangerously down the long, narrow, steep, dark, deep red, luxuriously carpeted stairs from my flat to the ground floor, I'm out of the modern mediocre side door which is next to the back entrance of the hairdressing salon.

I'm now in the passage, between my building and next door's less grandiose and slightly intimidated abode, which leads onto the glorious tree filled Lime Grove in picturesque Butterfield; a lovely, 'too good to be true', idyllic, lazy, affluent, leafy area with a large park used by everyone and a winding river with rickety bridge nearby. It's on the outskirts of a large industrial market town – Brailsford.

I was lucky to get this place. A work colleague and mentor Diane, a sophisticated older lady nearing retirement who I adore, is a friend of the landlord Paul Channing. She knew I was fed up with all the travelling and that he was looking to rent again – she introduced us. I sacrificed my beloved Mini to pay the bond and first month's rent.

Paul owns the whole building and is head barber of the hairdressers/barbers in the rooms below mine. I like him. As the older man, he's handsome with that reserved distinguished gentlemanly look about him but there is a naughty twinkle in his eye; he reminds me of Peter Cook, one of my heroes. He definitely has some sort of intellectual sex appeal; I can't quite put my finger on what it is. He obviously looks after himself; works out or runs, he has a magnificent sturdy posture all contained within a six foot two statuesque physique, very becoming in a man of his advancing years.

He's given me a good deal on the rent so that also makes him kindly and charitable.

I don't currently have a partner; I broke up with Simon two years ago. He was a teenage sweetheart and once we got together we were 'together' quite a long time.

We broke up because we both realised we were in the relationship for the sake of it and in all honesty there never was any passion there. Like any new relationship, in the beginning there was the constant need to be touching and kissing and to be together but that fizzled out quite quickly and we didn't then naturally move on to the next level.

We knew each other so well when we started to go out and then the physical side of things happened and it was disappointing; more a matter of going through the motions. There wasn't as much passion as I'd hoped there would be. We seemed to be constantly striving and failing at having that something special!

In the films or on the TV programmes you see a couple building up to something over a period of time, then when they finally have that first highly anticipated kiss or touch intimately for the first time they are in raptures and become hooked! That didn't happen to us, it was a bit of an anti-climax for me; for him too I suspect.

Maybe for me he just didn't live up to my first, very brief love, a school holiday romance with a much older boy – Alan.

He was in the sixth form, I was only fifteen. I would spy on him from a distance on the other side of the tennis courts, womanising, making out with any girl he wanted; wrapping himself around them in a cape of lust and self-gratification. Or I'd watch him, whilst daydreaming from my classroom window, on the cricket pitch showing off his skills in front of the other hungry, attention seeking boys. But despite all this I adored him; I could see through all the boyish bravado to his brightness, energy and potential for depth and deference. I suppose I had a sort of inexplicable empathy and care for him.

I didn't imagine for one second he would come down from that pedestal and notice or actually be interested in me.

Then during the last term before the summer holidays we weirdly and surprisingly ended up together (I was in the right place at the right time and I must have drawn out some of the qualities I had vaguely seen in him – my quietness and subservience complemented his gregarious personality and he must have seen that and liked it.) and I was on cloud nine.

I had that surge of tingling and tugging of the stomach lining when he was near me or holding my hand and I physically ached when we weren't together. Then he treated me abysmally and broke my heart, but that's another story and unfortunately if I ever see Alan now, even in the distance, I get those same urgent, intense feelings even though I should hate him, and then I try to hide so he won't see me. Snow Patrol's 'Spitting Games' pops into my head as soon as I think of him or see him, reminding me of that whole long period of admiring him from afar.

Maybe I was and am still 'in-love' with him but I don't know; I haven't experienced anything like it since to compare it to. I have had a couple of very brief intense liaisons since Simon but they don't come remotely close to the lingering emotions I can't shake off for Alan.

It was nice with Simon though. He taught me so much about music, new and old, the arts, current affairs and my undying, passionate love of all things culinary including fine wine and real ale. We joined the 'Campaign for Real Ale' – 'CAMRA'- together, as soon as we were eighteen and I have remained a member ever since; one of the ever increasing numbers of young women to appreciate the many qualities of an ancient and modernised craft. Apart from that it's one of the cheapest value for money tasty drinks a young person can order in a public house which is a must when you're on a budget and still want to socialise in an environment other than your own home. I have a lot to thank Simon for; he helped to mould the woman I am today!

We went for long bonding walks in the countryside; I loved just being with him and talking. I remember him with such fondness and wonder what he's doing now; he moved away and I haven't seen him for years, not even to just say hello to. Whenever I listen to timeless classics like Pink Floyd – 'Wish you Were Here' (which is my all-time favourite piece of emotion inducing music) or Peter Gabriel's memorising soft intelligent entrancing music 'In Your Eyes', I get quite emotional and I think of him sat cross-legged on the floor looking intense with his young Paul McCartney face surrounded by abundant blond waves and vinyl record sleeves lying all around him; meditating in the middle of a tile factory explosion. He's John Cusack in 'Hi Fidelity' – completely obsessed with his music and narrating his life with it.

He had such a deepness and intellect about him but he was unable to transfer that intensity into a physical emotional relationship with me.

The music that sums us up as a couple though is the never out of date The The – Matt Johnson and Sinéad O'Connor's singing of the very beautiful but sad 'Kingdom of Rain'. The melody is so evocative and makes me remember him with vivid affection, but on the other hand the lyrics remind me of our failed relationship; an intense irony! We broke up by mutual agreement and although he readily accepted my reasons he tried to reunite us on several occasions. He just liked being with someone he knew so well; secure, which I suppose can be a strong motivator, directing you away from your better instincts.

I'm not outgoing and have not met anyone I could even vaguely consider having a relationship with since then. I have spied a couple of men I quite liked the look of but I'm too shy to do anything about it. I probably give off bad vibes due to my self-conscious demeanour so have rarely been approached. I would rather grow an intimate relationship from the seedling of a friendship – safe! Do I ever learn?

I don't consider myself a 'looker' although Roxanne is constantly telling me kindly that I have a 'natural beauty'; I'm sure she's just trying to build my confidence. She says I remind her of a tall and freckly Anna Friel but I don't see myself like that at all.

Despite living alone with my angst and constant self-deprecation I actually have a fairly full life. I go out with friends to the pub, cinema and theatre, do some half-hearted running and swimming by myself every other week, read a lot and love my music. I just barely have enough money to do these things but what I currently desire most is mystery and spontaneity. Something that will make me challenge myself; give me the opportunity to break out of my shell and express myself without worrying about the consequences.

I long for something unexpected to happen, sometimes even to the extreme of it being something terrible. I actually hope for some horrible disaster to happen in the world, not for people or animals to die but an impending threat that could create havoc but ultimately doesn't, like a meteor hurtling to earth. We all need to instantly run for cover or take drastic action to save ourselves, then it turns out to be a false alarm; just so there is something interesting to think about or do that's real and not something I read in a book. I love the snow. Whenever it falls I want it to stay forever; the disruption and chaos it causes me satisfies the spontaneity and excitement I crave without me having to actually do anything to achieve it.

Is that sad? ... no, more like desperation or boredom. Am I sick? ... probably, but at least I know I need something more than the shallowness that seems to surround me at the moment and the emptiness that I feel most of the time.

You could put it down to laziness but don't we all crave unexpected excitement in the day to day running of our lives. We can't all go scooting off looking for adventure, someone has to stay behind, do the housekeeping, feed the fish and keep the world running smoothly.

I prefer being alone as I find it difficult to get to know people, I find them frightening or they aggravate and irritate me. I am not an egotistical person who looks down on everyone else; I'm the complete opposite of that. I generally like my work colleagues and love my small and close family and few special friends. I actually think everyone is superior to me whether its looks, brains or personality.

I have a relatively good life for a twenty five year old, it's just something is missing, something meaningful and relevant to me, it's not a depression, I'm just shy with self-esteem issues and all those phrases that are sub headed under 'insecurities'. I wish I wasn't. (Another one of my heroes is Woody Allen who really shouldn't be considering my own constant self-analysing but at least he makes me laugh at myself.)

I saw a film last night '*Defending Your Life*' with Albert Brooks and Meryl Streep. A charming little comedy but with quite a powerful message – 'Don't always do what your head dictates, don't take the easy route or do the 'done thing', be inspired and brave and have the passion and courage to do something out of the ordinary'. Sounds clichéd but it made me think – I need to do something scary and unpredictable!

*

The bus journey into the heart of Brailsford, the nearby industrial town, is just long enough for me to enjoy the trip, the warm pleasurable foreplay of Butterfield before the rougher serious intercourse of the town centre which sadly always results in the disappointing anti – 'climax' of work!

Listening to my iPod on shuffle, Roxy Music plays 'Oh Yeah' which always reminds me of my best friend Sarah – it's her favourite 'Roxy' track, followed appropriately by Justin Hayward and 'Forever Autumn'; I gaze out at the tall stabbing trees on either side of the road, criss-crossing the sky. My own personal 'sword arch' ironically celebrating and welcoming me to the world of work which I try so hard to avoid each morning but never do. I'm a single home bird and don't want to be congratulated for my supposed commitment to marrying into a conformed lifestyle, leaving family life and stability to be thrown into the uncompromising big wide world and told to get on with it, 'you're on your own' – you've had the wedding breakfast, now it's time to get down to basics!

The road reflects the river for a time and flecks of the sun's shallow rays bounce off the water creating a mosaic on the bus windows. I love Autumn, low suns, cooler misty weather, transforming shades and shape shifting nature, the winding down of life, it's enchanting and mysterious for me.

I find this time of year strangely uplifting when others start to get the winter blues. Maybe it reflects my general attitude to life that everything shouldn't always be 'pert' and 'jolly', that quietness is reassuring or perhaps I'm just contrary to everyone else because it's easier than trying to fit in and positive all the time.

Losing myself in the environment's slow transformation, I vacillate through the whole spectrum of emotions; nature's talented illusions morph into a cleverly sculptured, man-made chimney-potted skyline where every home is different to its neighbour; Then we gradually move on to the intensive, dramatic, industrialised landscape and I'm held transfixed, a captive audience. Each frame tells a different story in the flipper book of someone's life.

By the time we get to the compliant droning bustle of retail and the precision built cubed shops and offices – my moods, the feelings that prove I'm still living, have gone. I'm now resolute, my anxiety has ignited and pulses through my circuits; I'm therefore prepped for work, mechanical and predictable.

I get into the office bang on ten, the latest you can get into work under the flexible working hours scheme, much to the chagrin of my fellow employees as they have already done all the donkey work and heavy duty filing required each morning before we can get down to the slightly more interesting 'pen-pushing' and keyboard tapping of the day. They seem to forget I gather everything together the night before, when they have all gone, ready for them the following day. I'm a night person.

"Hi Rachel," spouts Roxanne loudly in her sunny sarcastic tone, which I just ignore whilst trying to creep in unnoticed. You would think she of all people wouldn't aggravate the situation by magnifying an already tense atmosphere; a small but significant hardcore of people here like something to complain about –

Roxanne, who only yesterday confided in me that despite her demonstrative, overbearing personality had never been able to talk and open up to anyone like she could to me about really personal things, but then I suppose I should expect it from someone I have nicknamed 'Madame Whiplash!' She has serious dominatrix personality traits!

I'm not aggressive; I don't swear at all or have violent thoughts but feel at this frustrating moment I could quite easily verbally abuse her. Nothing in particular springs to mind but if pushed I'm sure I could come up with something vaguely malicious.

Roxanne very freely uses expletives much of the time and it makes me laugh the amount of swear words she can fit into one sentence. Despite her free and easy mix of tactless quips with profane and lewd remarks she is an intelligent, intuitive young woman but likes to be the centre of attention – the complete antithesis of me.

She is also abrupt, but I'm glad there is someone here who can expose themselves so blatantly without shame; there have been many times her demonstrative behaviours have got me through the day. I see her flicking out her long lizard tongue, reeling in her victim then spitting out what's left with disdain. If I told her about this image she would probably like it. Strangely, despite her questionable attributes she is very likeable … to me!

I quickly slither off to the ladies to check my dishevelled hair, and overall general appearance, hoping I don't look too much of a mess before I knuckle down and get myself that first necessary cup of tea.

I will be truly amazed if I haven't got the buttons aligned incorrectly on the little grey mohair cardigan or there isn't some sort of light coloured food stuff stained on my extremely wide-legged dark jeans. I love my big trousers, they go so well with snug top things but they are not the best choice for me, it just means more acreage to catch those drips that always seem to fall so precisely in the wrong place.

At least the pretty little silk flower brooch placed centrally right over the top button on my cardy is still in place and the slide on the right side of my head hasn't slipped. As I suspected my wild mass of unruly long hair, which has a mind of its own, has once again disobeyed and instead of staying in one flat shiny sheet, has metamorphosed into lots of individual medusa strands like the before picture in a shampoo ad.

Roxanne constantly tells me she envies my extensive chestnut locks and she prefers that natural look to the perfect salon finish. I then tell her she can buy them from me, bleach them then add them to her own hair extensions when I get round to lopping them off. She talks me into keeping my hair as it is and although I sort of understand what she's saying, it's a constant source of irritation. My wild untameable hair doesn't reflect my quiet personality.

Trying to get to my desk unnoticed I don't see Jason crossing the corridor in front of me and we bump into each other like one of those comedy duos in an old black and white film trying to avoid the baddie when they back into each other scaring themselves stupid.

He whispers, "Oh my God… I thought you weren't in yet. I'm trying to avoid Karen." He takes in a deep breath and sheepishly looks left and right while holding onto both my shoulders.

I put my hands round his beautiful face in sympathy.

"You're just not cut out to deal with women on heat. Can't you do something to minimise your hunkiness, it's wasted here. You know your 'Gaydom' doesn't come across at all to those women who don't want to see it. All they see is this confident, handsome man with amazing style and sophistication." My soft empathising is tinged with sarcasm!

He throws his head back while his hands descend to his hips.

"What do you suggest?" he replies reluctantly knowing full well what my suggestion will be.

I bring my hands down and use them to emphasise my point.

"Flatten your hair and wear tank tops. Cut out that 'I'm available' spring in your step and walk around with your chin on your chest like you've just lost something. Alternatively, you could just be honest and tell her she's not your type instead of all this pussyfooting around, and then we can all relax."

I state the obvious to him, yet again, and try to sound pitiful about Karen's behaviour but I can so see why she acts like she does. Jason is stunning and given that this office contains mainly women I am still perplexed by his completely intentional manly thrusting.

In his case there aren't many women that wouldn't be turned on by him but in general it always fascinates me how the unobtainable becomes even more attractive, sexy and desirable even if the initial attraction is fairly innocuous. Karen is still quite immature though and can't get a grip on her emotions yet or see the obvious.

"I don't want to hurt her feelings. She is too extreme, can you imagine trying to work alongside her when she's in a bad mood … all crying and overreacting, it's hard enough when she's happy, all that constant chatter and giggling."

"We cope alright with you, don't we!" I joke but he's not seeing the funny side today. "Look I know, it gets a bit much sometimes but she's young and excited by everything like a little puppy. She means well and hasn't become cynical and worldly wise like us, she hasn't been hurt yet. Weren't we like that once? Try to be more laid back about it, enjoy it even!"

I appeal to him with a cajoling smile on my face. I like trying to calm him down, it helps me pull myself together.

"I think you must have been born clutching a certificate in diplomacy in one hand and an honorary degree in 'I know best' in the other! Anyway I am quite accommodating with her," he snaps whilst giving me a reproachful look.

He turns on a sixpence with a perfect pivot on the balls of his feet, down to all that club gyrating I think, and just walks away. I can hear the especially camp and enticing Quincy Jones – 'Soul Bossa Nova' and I'm left smiling and watching his graceful gait while he shimmies along the corridor on his own personal catwalk. His trousers just hang a little on his perfectly formed round bottom so the crease in the material from his waist band moves a little from one cheek to the other when he walks. Not too tight … I must stop staring, it's definitely too early for this sort of thing; is it getting hot in here?

It's nice having something pretty to look at, at work; he's a welcome distraction, a sort of Italian style Russell Crow. If he was food he'd be a robust German sausage with a pungent French mustard on the side.

Jason knows how good looking he is and when we go out to the gay clubs, whenever I need lifting out of myself, he loves to show me how he can flirt and get any man he wants. I so enjoy people watching and gay clubs are the perfect voyeuristic arena for that – lots going on.

He is one of those colourful people that contributes to my surroundings as that special little 'knick-knack' on an otherwise plain mantelpiece. He adds a certain *je ne sais quoi* to my life.

At my desk Roxanne wants to talk about her bloke but I'm not in the mood so I just let her drone on and try to rearrange my desk.

I like Roxanne, she is up front and you know she won't simply fob you off. The only downside is she has no consideration of other people's feelings at all. She takes the concept of being honest a bit too far. Whenever I stare open-jawed at her after an incredibly insensitive statement she simply says in that immature, sing song manner,

"If they don't want to know the truth then they shouldn't ask for my opinion."

People like that usually only have one or two friends who have endeavoured to get to know them and realise deep down that he/she is a genuine person with other great attributes. She doesn't get asked to many functions!

Finally at the end of an especially tedious long day I realise I will have to go and get some shopping. There's no food at home and I'm running out of all the usual day to day bits and pieces, toiletries and cleaning stuff.

I have been trying for days to live off concoctions of odds and ends, I'm now officially sick of pasta or rice mixed with a variation of half rotting vegetables and either chopped chicken or bacon or neither, and would so like a more complex dish to devour.

I love cooking but hate shopping, too many people and enclosed spaces, so I will manage with what I have until I absolutely have to replenish the cupboards, then I end up buying way too much and glut out on everything in a short space of time. It's feast or famine!

I will have to leave work a bit earlier than I intended which therefore means I'll have to be in early tomorrow to help with the filing. My life won't be worth living if I haven't done my bit tonight and then on top of that arrive after the event tomorrow!

*

The supermarket isn't too full tonight so it's quite a pleasant undertaking and I have treated myself to a not so cheap bottle of 'Shiraz'.

Having paid, I stagger from the packing area with my heavy load thinking about bus times when something catches my eye on the notice board to the left of the automatic doors. It's only a small ad but it's the word "EXPERIMENT" that's so interesting. That intriguing word infers so much and conveys so little. My stomach does a little summersault as I put down my bags and read;

Are you aged between 20 and 35?
Would you like to take part in a
Psychology Research Experiment
and be paid for your time?

For more information please call Anna Paisley
on 201824.
(Student at Brailsford College)

This looks interesting and maybe 'the bit scary' that's been so prevalent in my mind recently.

I would never normally put myself forward for something like this. It could be something horrible, why am I even considering this? But the seed has been sewn and it's an opportunity to be spontaneous, my current ambition in life. Anyway I could just find out what it's all about and then decide.

I jot down the details and then quickly gather myself to hurry for the bus.

While struggling down the high street to the bus station my mind is going round and round trying to imagine what the experiment might be. Is it just looking at weird patterns trying to give them meaning or is it talking in a group or role play even – hope not, that won't appeal to me at all. Or do I really hope it is something like that which then gives me an excuse not to do it?

I'll ring straight away when I get in; I won't be able to eat until I've satisfied my curiosity.

The bus ride is long and for a first I do not put on my earphones! I'm too wrapped up in my thoughts at the moment and besides, my personal soundtrack is playing – Bowie's 'Heroes'!

*

After putting away the shopping I sit staring at the phone knowing I'm going to pick it up and press the keypad. The message is leaving my brain 'goodbye message' but it's not reaching my fingertips. The impulses that make things happen naturally have been seduced by fear, blocking the easily swayed instruction by questioning its motives. While my outstretched hand quivers over the plastic of the handset the sincerity in Bowie's voice holds back the fear letting my impulse take back control, then finally I've made the call.

It's ringing and I am in two minds, shall I hang up or be brave? Just then a pleasant perky voice answers and makes my decision for me,

"Anna Paisley."

"… Oh hi, err … I'm ringing in regard to the ad for the experiment?"

That word sounds so stupid when I say it out loud. My voice goes up at the end of the sentence with a questioning tone like I'm really trying to say, 'what is this thing and I don't know what the hell I'm doing!'

"Would you like to come for an interview? You can find out what my research is all about and see what you think."

"Oh … yes … good, thanks. What … errrr … when shall I come?" desperately trying to sound equally perky but probably coming across as ditsy and inept.

"I have a few other interested parties so I'll put you at the end, tomorrow evening, say 8.00 p.m., just arrive at the college and ask for me at reception."

"Err, ok then." I say hesitantly … already regretting doing this.

"What name shall I put here on my list?"

"Rachel Fleetwood Look … err … can I ask what the basics of your research are, you know, what sort of things will we be doing?"

"I don't want to say on the phone, I would rather explain face to face and judge your response. Don't let that worry you though, it's all part of the work I'm doing. It will all be very informal. Does that sound alright?"

"Yes I suppose, I'll treat it as an adventure then!"

"It really will be, especially if you embrace the concept! I'll see you tomorrow then, cheers."

Oh no, she shouldn't have said that, especially with that 'let's just run and jump' tone in her voice.

"Bye." I blurt, after the phone has already gone dead. What on earth am I getting into? A momentary blankness spreads through my brain like a drop of ink on still water, then as always I flit from one opinion to the other – I'm only going to see what it's about, what's the harm in that?

I start to shiver from a combination of excitement and fear. Do some people really thrive on this feeling? I think I would have a nervous breakdown dealing with this level of adrenaline on a regular basis, or do I produce more because of the kind of person I am and that's why I try to avoid situations – too confusing.

What am I going to be like when I actually go there tomorrow night? I usually feel sick just with the thought of an appointment at the doctors or going shopping. Should I ring my best friend Sarah and share my trepidation? Best not until I know what's involved. It's the sort of mad thing she would do. She will be supportive no matter what but it's got to be totally my decision though. I'll bear the nerves by myself. Hopefully I won't back down now, after all what's the worst that can happen? Where's that wine?

I wake up the next morning and I'm uncharacteristically wearing a hangover, then I remember I drank a whole bottle of wine to myself, on my own and that's not like me.

I routinely gaze at the ceiling and don't know if I'm hallucinating, with a brain that's been chopped up into bits, blanched then pickled, but I could swear the little rip I imagined I toyed with yesterday on the ceiling is a little larger.

I stare at the gash for what seems an eternity and then once again I'm picking at it but with a little more vigour. The alarm brings me back down and in a slow hazy return to reality I put my elevated aberration down to an unusual one off drunken indulgence and shrug it off.

Today I am a hopeless case in every respect. I can't eat, work, concentrate or hold a conversation. The hangover effect hasn't dulled the senses enough for me to deal with the trauma of what I did yesterday or of what lies ahead.

"You are definitely away with the fairies today Rachel. Why are you so distracted?"

Roxanne picks up on my moods quite easily which isn't a simple feat as I usually hide my frailties and emotions quite well from most people, staying well under the radar. I have a general look of dismay, complete strangers do that annoying thing of saying "cheer up, it might never happen" to me a lot even when I think I'm beaming.

Sometimes walking through town I must have a disturbed look on my face, a mixture of badly disguised sad eyes and forced grin in order to deter those predictable comments. I probably look madder than a box of frogs! An overused but effective saying, it makes me laugh every time I think of how mad a box of frogs would be and how a person looking at a box of frogs is an even more absurd image!

I have already decided I'm not going to tell Roxanne about 'the thing', don't think it would be prudent at this point in time; she may well talk me out of it. Roxanne is aware of her beauty and is outgoing and vivacious, her over-confident head rocks unpredictably on her shoulders but she doesn't let 'the crazies' dominate her. Every now and again she shows signs of maturity so she would surely question everything about it and wouldn't let it go until she thought she knew the best course of action. I just need to do this and think about the consequences later.

"Sorry Rox, I'm just tired and the weekend's looming. Think I'm winding down too soon."

She leans across the desk on her fists and looks me straight in the eye.

"You sound more like one of the apron brigade over there. For God's sake Rachel, you're young and stuff's got to happen to you yet. You shouldn't be feeling like that at your age!"

As usual her voice is a little too loud, despite how close she is to me, and she gets some looks. I just shrug and roll my eyes at the offended onlookers, she has got a point but on this occasion she's wrong.

She's probably putting my mood down to constant anxieties. If she knew I was up to something it would be fodder for her for weeks.

I have had plenty of weird experiences in life to teach me enough about people and certain situations but Roxanne doesn't know much about my past. I thought I would let things unfold in a natural way and tell her if she asks but I haven't known her long enough for that, well not in the grand scheme of things anyway, and the right situation hasn't arisen yet.

I suppose I am a little guarded with her. Thankfully she is out with her boyfriend tonight, cinema or something, so I don't have to make up an excuse not to go out with her.

At the end of the working day, I can finally remove my glasses, which I have to wear for close work, reading and computers, and rub my nose while I surreptitiously look around. I wait until nearly everyone has gone, only a handful of 'diehards' remain so I can now go and try to refresh myself in the ladies without anyone noticing. I had already decided to stay late and go straight to the college from work. It would be a bit much for me to go all the way home first.

As I try to do something with my hair and replenish my lip gloss I notice I'm trembling.

Glancing down at my permanently cold hands I'm taken aback by the long, icy, rust airbrushed, pale, quivering fingers, they remind me of the spidery things that jump out of the giant eggs in *Alien* before clamping onto some poor victim's face.

Now the haunting music from that film is swirling around my brain and that's not a good image to have in my head before I'm due to go to this interview – the unknown … a naive inquisitive victim prey to some violent grotesque beast.

Seeing the humour in the way I'm carried away with myself, I start to laugh, slightly hysterically. I need to calm down.

As I lean forward with a hand on either side of the wash basin and scrutinise myself in the mirror I think about those things Roxanne doesn't know about me.

The time my dad threw my mum, sister and me out of the house and we walked the streets, homeless, till midnight, with a carrier bag each, quickly stuffed with anything we could grab. I was only nine but I distinctly remember, whilst standing right in the centre of the old market square, looking up at the especially clear night sky, seeing all the stars so bright surrounding the church spire. I wasn't unnerved by it, I just remember being surprised at the quietness at that time of night. All the later events that followed that evening are so vivid but I can't attribute any emotion to them. It's more like I was an observer than a participant.

I am now either really scarred by it all and that's why I'm so timid and messed up (I'm not bitter though) or it taught me a lot and I don't like to see anything in black and white which makes me look doleful and indecisive – sitting on the fence! Maybe I'm a mix of all of that but how can I be so scared of this latest undertaking after going through all that …

"Get a grip" I whisper to myself in the mirror.

I realise I've been 'reminiscing' far too long and it's nearly Eight!

Chapter 2

The Interview

On arriving at the huge imposing college sign I become surprisingly excited … in a good way. I have a strong urge to relish it; this is a new sensation for me. It's a bit like the anticipation when first arriving at the cinema or theatre knowing you're treating yourself regardless of whether it's going to be a good or bad experience!

The building is very new and uninspiring, clinical, and the sight of it then, looming above the billboard, takes the edge off my new found enthusiasm. I rarely venture over to this side of town, nothing much that I'm aware of to attract me here. All the museums, theatres etc. are across town.

Sight of the reception desk throws me off balance and brings back all my fears and sensitivities. That confidence boost was short lived … a whole ten seconds!

The girl at the desk is unmoved by my presence.

"My name is Rachel Fleetwood, I'm here to see Anna Paisley?"

Without looking up she mutters, "Just go down that corridor and knock on the first door on the right."

I sarcastically thank her for her pleasant demeanour and my eyes follow the length of her pointing scrawny scarecrow arm and skeletal finger which is just inches from my face. At this point the shiver down my spine gives me a strange foreboding.

There's no one else around and I walk some distance along an unusually wide, bare corridor. I have the sensation that I'm walking but not getting anywhere when I notice I have reached the first door.

The *Alien* soundtrack is spooking me again as my hand grasps the handle and I have to actually shake my head to get rid of it. I knock on the door.

"Yep." A light high pitched welcome is offered so I open the door into a bright well lit room, way too many windows and lights. All the darkness dissipates.

Feeling stupid and sheepish at my Hammer Horror prelude I bleat out a nervous, "Hi, err … hello … I'm Rachel."

A young woman probably four or five years my junior but with quite a mature disposition, sits with one knee bent up under her chin with her foot on the seat of the chair. She has very straight and glossy black bobbed hair, that 'short at the back and slightly longer at the front' look. It swishes as she moves her head like those too beautiful animated heroines in modern computer generated children's films. 'Glossy' and 'Animated' sum her up very well!

A warm Celtic "Hellooo," greets me. "Don't panic. Take a seat … we'll just chat a wee bit and then I'll explain what I'm doing and why I need someone for this position. All will be divulged!"

The emphasis on 'divulged' is expressed in a deep but light hearted way to put me at ease I think! It takes the pressure off.

My facial expression must have been a picture when I walked in the room, like one of those stupid women in those scary films who always go to investigate when they hear a strange sound, then end up being ripped apart by some lunatic with a butcher's knife. If they'd stayed put they could probably have escaped and lived long happy lives.

Alien is buzzing round my head again and I have a strong urge to swat it!

Clumsily I sit down then spit out a fast hopeless explanation.

"Thanks, I'm just really nervous. I've never done anything like this before. I'm quite an introverted person so this is a big deal for me. I get butterflies just at the thought of leaving my flat. I was nearly sick with the idea of walking into that new pub on my own …"

Should I have just garbled all that out? I don't even know what this is about yet. I could have ruined my chances or given the wrong impression with such a protracted meaningless monologue … such an idiot!

"That's really interesting," she exclaims.

She stops writing and looks up; her reaction takes me by surprise.

She has the most amazing eyes, those incredibly clear, translucent pale blue eyes made even more memorising by the contrasting black hair framing her pixie face. I have a feeling her dolly features mask a tempestuous personality. The antithesis of me, and there I go again comparing myself to everyone I meet. Each time I do it I tear off another layer of confidence; there can't be many left, I dread to think what pathetic spineless blob will remain.

"You're the first person to admit that! You're either the only honest person I've seen who also happens to have an inferiority complex or the rest have been over-confident or lying. Everyone else has been chomping at the bit, egotistical, or tried to put on an air of nonchalance, you know – could take it or leave it. I like you already Rachel."

She seems relieved and sits back in her chair, her hands now twiddling the pen she was writing so frantically with a minute ago. Her confidence is striking but it's not overpowering, she's in control of the situation without being controlling.

It would appear she has sussed me out within thirty seconds of meeting me, how annoying but at the same time reassuring, I can be myself. She has put me at ease, there obviously have to be no pretensions here.

Anna is now looking at me differently and actually takes note of my face, it's almost like a double take and now she recognises me.

When I first walked in etiquette dictated and she briefly looked up to acknowledge my presence then looked down again and carried on writing while she was talking, but I feel right now at this moment in time we have made a small but significant connection.

She has a cool intelligent way about her, with a lovely soft and deep faint Scottish accent, which in my nervous state didn't take much notice of on the phone or when I first walked in, not what you'd expect from the first sprightly spoken 'yep'!

"Do you live locally Rachel?"

I like that she uses my name; she's interested in what I have to say. I wonder if that's something specific she's learned to do. I must stop analysing so much!

"No, on the other side of town, Butterfield."

"Oh Butterfield is lovely." Her voice takes on a lighter airy tone. "I have a very old aunt living there. I don't get to see her as much as I'd like, I always enjoy my visits and having links with such a historically relevant place is quite reassuring for me, being so far from home."

"Yes I know what you mean. I don't actually hail from there myself but if I could choose where to set my roots it would be Butterfield. It's like living in another time."

"It reminds me of Scotland, bits of my home town – Galashiels near Glasgow, and of Edinbrough. The brave and the mild, you know beautiful and earthy!"

I notice her Scottish accent gets a little stronger now.

"Yes, it's lovely and quiet, non-invasive, but there's a constant open friendliness. I feel as though I connect more with the world when I'm there. Most people I know feel they can only function if there's civilisation and chaos around them!"

"We seem to have quite a lot in common, like we're peas from different pods but bubbling along in the same old pot...that's quite good. I have the feeling we'll get on really well."

There is a sudden realisation that my being chosen for this maybe a foregone conclusion, although I can't be a 100 percent sure, I'm getting the impression that I am now 'the chosen one'.

If the tables have turned then she is now the interviewee!

For the first time, with a complete stranger, I say my thoughts out loud without scripting them methodically first.

"So do you need to convince me why I would want to do this then?" There's a slight playful defiance in my voice and

I'm wondering how to go forward with this, also some cockiness which is strange for me.

She looks down and chuckles as though she has just read my thoughts.

I wonder why I am so right for this. I suppose it will become obvious once I know what it's about.

"I will just explain the basics and we'll take it from there. I'm conducting this experiment as part of my dissertation and this part is a study on voyeurism and social interaction.

"Ok, this is how it will work – there will be two couples, each couple, consisting of a male and a female. Each pair will be in a separate room sat on a chair facing each other three feet apart.

"One couple will be in what you would call a normal environment i.e. room with lights and windows, books, CD player magazines and a TV, nothing strange or out of the ordinary, a bit like a living room.

"The other couple will be sat in the same way but in a sensory deprived room. It will not have any windows or light, except for an insignificant extremely low night light for safety purposes, the point being they will not be able to see each other or have access to any ice breakers or material to kick start their conversation or to maintain it, they'll be blind to each other and practically imperceptible. There may be just a slight silhouetted image to lock eyes onto but no facial features for reassurance or detectable expressions.

"Each person will have sensors attached to their bodies which monitor and record heart rate, perspiration levels and body temperature. I toyed with the idea of measuring blood pressure but that would be a logistical nightmare and it's not totally necessary anyway. Now this is the point of the whole project:

"Simply put I want to measure how the body reacts to being with a complete stranger in the knowledge that they're being monitored and recorded; how the body reacts to levels of pheromones and testosterone and to touch but particularly in an intimate situation and totally deprived of sight. Are the senses heightened, and so on, compared to the other couple?

"I'm also looking into voyeurism and studying whether the subject has an intensified awareness of themselves when they know they are being monitored. I want to see how or if people create a relationship when intimately thrown together. There's no need for any prolonged physical contact but if it's something that happens naturally then that's fine! You may feel you need to be tactile. There is a requirement for some touch in later sessions but again that is not compulsory and is supposed to be in a very innocuous way, and only if you feel comfortable.

"There will be an audio recording of your exchanges, no visuals obviously, so I can tie up your conversations and subject matter with the physical readings.

"It's a ten week programme of one hour per week, and of course you will then be paid a small but not insubstantial fee funded by myself."

It was then that I realised the money/payment hadn't entered my head, but then more importantly, this is going to challenge every doubt I ever had about myself.

There is a long pause as I am dumbfounded by all the information and my heart is racing at the thought of being alone with a stranger, thrown into the sort of situation I try really hard to avoid. Anna can obviously see I'm in pain and looks at me with an expression of, 'this is going to be so good'.

"As you are the successful candidate you will be in the darkened room as I already have the couple for the alternative control room."

I take a prolonged deep breath.

There it is, confirmation that I have been chosen for the most socially challenging situation I will probably ever experience.

She sees my reaction and offers an explanation,

"The important thing is that I like the people I choose for this, which I do. I have to feel there is a trust and honesty there. I felt an instant rapport when we first spoke and you fit my criteria perfectly. You're everything I need to get the best out of this and you're very like the other woman I have chosen which was also an important prerequisite. The other couple are vaguely acquainted with each other and have not had an intimate relationship and they're willing to follow a programme which includes physical contact. I have to say I was beginning to lose the will to live with all the pretentious money grabbers I have had in here today."

She looks at me waiting for some sort of reaction but I don't know what to ask. I suppose the questions will come when I get the background details – 'rules and regulations'. Reading my mind she continues,

"Don't be concerned, there will be lots of rules to protect you. You can go home and think about all this and ring me and let me know if you're interested. Then you can come back and we'll go over the more intricate details … You're very quiet, do you want to ask me any questions?"

The first thing that pops into my head just blurts out –

"Touching did you say? Who is the man that I will be partnered with?" Oh, wrong choice of words, that supposes we're going to be like 'a couple'. "I mean who will be doing me … I mean doing this with me?" Nope that's not good either, "Err …"

Her mouth curls up on one side while she looks at me through her long eye lashes like a parent trying not to laugh when their child says something naughty but charming.

"Stop right there. I know what you're trying to ask. As you will discover, if you chose to do this, one of the most important rules is complete anonymity. I can't tell you anything about 'him' and you will not be able to ask each other for personal information. I can tell you though he is an extraordinary man!"

She looks at me then as though she's trying to tell me something without actually saying it; it's a look of 'you're in for a treat'. Either that or 'it's going to be a white knuckle ride'. A sort of crooked smile with bright eyes, she looks like she's going to say 'nudge nudge' or wink at me and that makes me laugh. Anna laughs as well but just to make me feel comfortable.

"There is physical contact involved but only if you feel comfortable and that doesn't come until later on anyway.

There is absolutely nothing sexual involved!" She says that very demonstratively and I imagine her underlining it with her finger.

"I certainly wasn't expecting this. The whole thing epitomises the fears and reservations I have about myself and life in general. Considering only a couple of days ago I told myself to do something that scares me and to be spontaneous, I think I would achieve those goals and many more all in one go here!"

"Go home now and give it some thought; I think it will be fascinating and exciting for you. Let me know by six tomorrow night. You can ring me on the same number."

She stands up and offers her petite hand, my cue to leave, a porcelain but firm grip!

"Right ok then, I'll speak to you tomorrow, bye Anna." I pick up my bag and head for the door slightly light headed. I'm 80 per cent sure I'll do it but don't know how I'll approach it or justify that last 20 per cent to myself.

I should do it, it's perfect for me and my situation, I just need to talk to someone who can help me weigh up the pros and cons better. I'll ring my best friend when I get in.

"Hi Sarah, how are you ma' dear? Still at the same address, at the same job?" I drawl with some sarcasm.

I love Sarah but she never sticks to one thing for long. She needs to settle down and start to manage herself better but then I suppose that wouldn't be Sarah. It's a while since I last spoke to her but each time we get in touch there's never any awkwardness – it's as though we only spoke yesterday.

"I'm great." She ignores the question with the contempt it deserves.

Sarah was always an A student in English and History and when she achieved her A levels she wanted to go into journalism. She never takes the easy route though and started at the bottom in telesales working her way up through different newspapers, magazines and radio, making a bit of a name for herself and now does reviews of plays, films, concerts, small gigs, etc. on a local high profile Radio station in the City. I often listen in. I'm so proud of her.

She has a lovely Southern accent, she's not posh or pretentious, she just speaks nicely, is vivacious and full of personality, she's witty and intelligent and she means the world to me because she knows me so well and will always work things out with me if I'm undecided about something. She doesn't judge or criticise, she's good at asking the right questions and that is a rare quality.

I used to wonder what she sees in me or what I have to offer her but after all these years I don't question it any more I just make the most of our inexplicable relationship.

"Please don't move from your current flat, I love it! It's warm and cosy and easy for me to get to …"

I have a constant need to express this opinion and reinforce the importance of her staying put so that she might have a reason to suppress her urge to move again, I can't keep up with her constant address and telephone changes,

"Anyway, listen, I'm ringing you for a reason." If I don't get right to the point we will end up talking about anything and everything in a totally random way, never coming to any conclusions and laughing till the early hours of morning.

"I have sort of got involved in something and I'm not sure about it, I wanted your take on it really."

It feels weird hearing those words come out of my mouth. The word 'involved' suspends over me on faulty wires; the heavy 'd' at the end is going to drop down and poke me in the head!

"How mysterious!"

There's a well-considered pause and I know not to speak again until she has a mind blowing revelation

"Hang on, that's not like you at all. The last time you really surprised me, and I don't mean I think you're boring, far from it, was when you split up with Simon. I thought you would be together forever and the week you announced the break up was the very week I thought you were going to get engaged. Well that was the impression I got from Simon anyway."

"What!" I'm incredulous … "After all this time? You never mentioned this before! I didn't know that was his intention!"

I feel slightly nauseous but I don't know why, maybe because it now seems obvious that everyone knew what was going on but me, either that or my unusually high pitched voice is triggering my vomit reflex!

I can physically feel the backtracking going on while she realises her huge error, she's flipping back desperately through the pages of her life to come up with some justification.

I am shocked, not by this revelation but by her deception. I'm not cross though.

"I know, I thought the timing was all wrong and then the months turned into years; it got harder to approach the subject and then I forgot about it. You wouldn't have married him anyway. I know you loved him but you weren't 'in-love'. Those were your exact words."

Here we go again totally off the subject, but I must make a mental note to go back to that one at a later date! It's just as well I didn't know her when I had that thing with Alan. Who knows how distracted we could get over that.

"Yes, yes I know. Can we change the subject please?" I say spitting out the 'pl' and elongating the 'ea'.

"Oh my God … yes! What is it you've got involved in, it's not a cult or even worse, please tell me you haven't got so low you're now buying Crimplene blouses and nylon belly slappers from mail order catalogues."

I can just imagine her large wild brown eyes widening while she throws her short but thick mass of brown and blond streaked curls back with her free hand.

Sarah is very attractive but not in a conventional way; she's quite masculine, while remaining sexy and pretty. It's not so much her hairy body, she only has it where it should be, it's just more abundant, thicker and darker than most women I know!

She has that earthy gypsy look about her even more defined by her use of large earrings and exotic clothing, her personality shines and is almost tangible; everyone who meets her wants her as a friend. I feel privileged to have her undying loyalty and friendship, although I still can't understand what it is about me that she likes so much.

"No I'm not! Although higher waisted pants are starting to look more appealing!"

I'm trying not to laugh so I can get on with the task at hand.

"To put it in a nutshell, I saw an ad for a science experiment, well psychology research, and after the interview I was offered the position. I'll be paid but it's what's involved that's freaking me out and I'm not sure what to do."

"What's involved?"

"I have to build up a relationship with some guy, but it's all done over a ten week period and well … it's in the dark so I can never see him. I will never know his identity!"

After a long silent pause,

"That's so bloody exciting! I'm completely envious. A dark mysterious man to meet with once a week and no questions asked, all above board and legal, what an opportunity. It's what fantasies are made of! My gut reaction is that you should do it."

Well that was quick!

"But could it be dangerous do you think? Could I end up screwing myself up even more than I am already?"

"Your shyness stops you doing stuff, which is not always a bad thing, but it makes you overly cautious sometimes."

Right! What's coming next I wonder?

"I sometimes wonder what it is that enables a person to discover an amazing hidden talent they have. For example, is everyone born with a natural ability to sing but only a certain number of people have a 'trigger' that enables them to discover it, hone in on it, have the drive and dedication to want to exploit it – is that the real talent? Sometimes it might take someone twenty years for the trigger to kick in and then sometimes it's luck if someone else sets it off. With you Rachel … I know you've always had this brilliant wasted ability to read people. You can understand them from just a few small words and then empathise and even if you fail to do that you way up all the options and never judge. It sounds as though this experiment could be your 'trigger'!"

I immediately know what she means, although I have no idea what the outcome will be, and this is my green light for go!

"Thanks Sarah." I sigh with a comforting resignation. Once again she has helped me make a decision without hand prints on my back, just a gentle nudge in the right direction.

"This is so exciting. When do you start, how old is he, what happens at the end?"

She is going to be so disappointed with my one quiet generic answer to all her frantic questions.

"I have to sign something to say I will never try to find out who he is in case follow up research is done later so therefore I can't discuss the details with anyone. I can't tell you anything about it or him."

"Ok … I have to go now I'm supposed to be meeting Jim at the Hand & Heart … oh err… only about an hour ago."

That sounds like Sarah, not a brilliant time keeper, although normally her dilemma is having arranged to meet two people at the same time and forgetting about one of them. She never says no to anyone.

I quickly interject, "Don't be mad with me. I'll see what direction it takes and then I'll give you hints."

"I'm not cross, just in a rush. Speak to you soon, cheers!"

The phone goes dead but I know she's not mad, maybe a little frustrated. It's a coincidence that she has to go quickly after just hearing she can't have things her way. I'm not too concerned about her sudden departure, it's a Sarah thing. She does it to me all the time.

Chapter 3

Rules and Regulations
The 'Jaunt'

Saturday morning and I'm waking up to the rich, velvety and calming Rosie Vela – 'Magic Smile' which was a must last night – that explains the dreaming about cheap 'drag queens', a source of entertainment I have experienced far too much of for a young, heterosexual woman. Not that Rosie Vela is mannish, far from it – she's gorgeous and feminine.

My brain must have subconsciously mixed her deep voice and big hair, which is quite prominent on the CD cover, with a dollop of my friend Jason and a pinch of Sarah for extra flavour. Yes, that arrangement of features would definitely create a larger than life testosterone filled goddess-like creature with hairy legs and a penchant for nipple tassels – frightening!

At this point I realise after my mental rantings I am once again, after staring at the ceiling, inches from the fissure I recently discovered.

This time it's different. The physical sensation of movement is very real.

As I get closer, then touch the open wound with my nose, my face starts to feed through the hard surface. The feeling is like putting your dry face slowly into a bowl of water and feeling the meniscus rise up the side of your head. The pulling effect is overwhelming and I really need to keep going. The sensation is now spreading along my still body and I can feel the tightness moving down my horizontal length as I elevate just clear of the joists. I am now able to see inside the next unexplored floor.

My eye level is only moving upward very slowly so I am able to take in everything. The wooden floor is very dusty, mixed with desiccated insects and the air is dry. It's a large loft space and light floods in through a well-appointed small round window.

Once again, but more annoyingly this time, the alarm brings me violently back into my bed and I am left rigid, not with fear but with a pleasant adrenalin-fuelled aftershock. I then realise that during the whole experience I didn't question what was happening to me and I actually felt at home with the sensation, like I was completely safe and protected against all the malice, judgements, fear and cruelty of the material world. I had physically combined with a fundamental spiritual Earth. It's probably one of the few times I have actually felt serene.

Do I now investigate what's just happened with a risk of losing this new found ability or do I just accept it and go with it in the hope it will continue and maybe take me further?

With my new found ability to 'Jaunt' (to rip through into happiness, contentment and revelation on a personal level) I'm skimming the froth from each layer/dimension of my own time and space over and over as I move upward. It's the reverse of a sheet of paper gliding from side to side as it falls from a great height. I'm not actually moving side to side but that's the effect I'm having on the air around me, like it's a liquid gel and I'm leaving a pronounced permanent wake. There's a slight resistance from above me but the power beneath gently guides and pushes me through it.

I will turn off the alarm permanently and see what happens tomorrow. Why do I even have it turned on at all at the weekend? Routine!

It would seem this phenomenon has only happened when I've been in a state of total relaxation and my mind is wandering or pondering something trivial while my eyes are focusing on a specific point.

If it happens again I may ask Paul if I can go up there into that loft space and have a look around. The real burning question is why it has started to happen at this point in my life. There wasn't even the slightest inclination or sense of this ability to hover, of an alternate incorporeal existence before a couple of days ago.

More importantly, it now occurs to me, where is my earthly body when the 'Jaunt' happens? What's happening to me and why am I so accepting of it?

As always, my mind turns too quickly to the day ahead. With a wonderful dawning I realise it's Saturday but then like flipping a switch I remember I have to ring Anna and let her know my decision. My heart starts to beat so fast that I'm feeling sick. I need ORDERS – "Get up and do something!"

*

11a.m. – Punching in the numbers on the keypad and my fingers are shaking.

"Hello."

"Hi Anna it's Rachel calling about the position you offered."

"Rachel! Hope you had a good night's sleep?"

I detect her poking fun, knowing I will have been tortured over this.

"Umm! Well I gave it a lot of thought and I want to do it."

"I am so pleased and relieved. Will you be able to come back today and go over a few things and then maybe afterwards we could go for a drink to get to know each other better in a more social environment. Trust and insight are going to be key in all this and I really want to get to understand you better, you know … a bit of background before we start. Is that ok?"

"Yes I'd like that. Where shall I meet you?"

"If you come back to the college for about 2 p.m."

"Don't you ever leave that place?"

"Nope. I practically live here at the moment. This research has taken over my life, but I love being engrossed in something like this, something I strongly believe in. I have high hopes for what I can learn and document."

"No pressure then! This has happened at just the right time for me but whether I'll be right as far as your research goes remains to be seen. I'm a nervous sort."

"I'm so glad you said that, this wouldn't work if you were too confident of yourself, not enough dimensions, but I don't want you to try and fit into a role. Just be yourself. Anyway, I'll see you in a wee while. Cheerio."

She can go from deep and interesting to light and jolly on the flip of coin.

"Bye." I say with some intrepidation.

Plenty of time to work out what to wear!

I wonder what we have to go over in detail. I am really quite excited and for the first time I am positive about the unknown.

Back at the college – I feel more at home this time. Anna is waiting cross-legged on a low sprawling chair in the reception area reading a book.

"Thought I would wait here for you seeing as there's only me and the caretaker knocking about at the moment."

She cocks her head to one side as she looks me up and down.

"You look really good!"

"Thanks. I wasn't sure where we'd be going so I've tried to combine a bohemian, studenty look with a bit of sophistication. Don't want to look like mutton dressed as lamb."

"Are you saying students can't be classy?"

"Not at all, but having been there myself I know what it's like trying to be original and expressive on a budget, I still do to a degree. I just wanted to fit in, not stand out too much. Anyway from our last meeting I could see you have style."

I sound like I'm coming onto her but it's too late to back track now, 'digging myself deeper' springs to mind along with the fact that surprisingly she hasn't asked me about my sexual orientation. Maybe it doesn't matter.

"Thanks very much. I try to do my own thing but I am a bit of a slave to fashion ... money is no obstacle in my case."

She manages to say that without bragging, almost as though she's embarrassed by her affluence.

"What are you reading?"

"*A Dangerous Liason* by Carole Seymour-Jones."

"Wow, heavy stuff, will it help with your research … all that 'high brow' philosophy?"

"Don't know but it can't hurt. I'm quite fascinated by Simone De Beauvoir, you know obsession and control and how even the most intelligent and academic person can be blinded by love and do the most dark and out of character things; this book is supposed to be quite comprehensive and in-depth about her and her weird relationship with Jean-Paul Sartre."

She then stands up with the graceful elegance of a dancer; it's obvious she has breeding without the intimidation that sometimes goes with that. She has a class all her own, she's not so much 'Shabby Chic' as 'Elegant Dissenter'!

As Anna turns away and walks towards the corridor, the one I ventured down last time with such fear – fear of the unknown, she looks down at her side, head tilted towards me which I take as a motion to follow and so I do like a subservient dog desperate for praise and acceptance.

In the same room as last time we sit on a little corner sofa. We face each other and then she hands me some stapled sheets of paper.

"This is a contract you need to sign before we can begin the process proper, but before you do I want to go over a few ground rules; they're for your peace of mind and the protection of all parties involved. I don't want to be seen to be condoning any questionable behaviour!"

I reel back in horror.

"My God what do you think is going to happen?"

Her hands go up defensively, palms facing me.

"Nothing, nothing! I'm just kidding, but I do have to cover myself. Who knows what two people are capable of given the conditions you'll be in? This is unknown territory."

I reply sarcastically, "Ha ha!" whilst trying not to actually laugh at my gullibility, "Ok. So if I don't want to sign then quite simply you look for someone else?"

I don't want her to think I'm a pushover.

"Well, if there is anything you don't like or are unsure of we can modify it or compromise or thrash it out. It's not set in stone, it's more a guide really. Look, 'I' chose 'you'. You are an ideal match for the man I've chosen. I can't tell you much but I think I will get really interesting unpredictable results from you both and the main thing is I like you ... a lot!"

She has looked me straight in the eye the whole time and it's hard to be antagonistic or questioning with her. My instinct is to like her too but I wonder if everyone who meets her feels the same. I need to try and work out whether this is the case. She has the ever changing, adapting nature of a Chameleon, cute and stoic but devious even though the intent probably isn't there. Her complimentary appeal seems to be a natural response to the person she's engaging with.

I try to get an understanding of how she thinks about herself.

"Can I just ask out of interest whether you would have considered someone like yourself for this, I mean you come across as quite confident."

She definitely has, to put it scatalogically, 'BALLS!'

I continue, "You're very different to me but from what you explained before, you're not like any of the interviewees you rejected either."

"I definitely wouldn't have chosen me. I'm one of those people that others don't warm to easily. Whether they think I have ideas above my station or that I'm too involved in myself I don't know but I don't have many friends, which suits me just fine. People don't as a rule exchange general chit chat with me at say the supermarket or waiting for the train, which also suits me. I bet they do with you though."

I suppose I am quite approachable due to my sheepish demeanour. Maybe people see her reservations as a veneer too impenetrable. I personally like that she speaks only when she has something worth saying.

I continue by putting myself down yet again,

"Yes but usually it's lost kids, kidless mums or old men with overactive libidos who like 'the young ones', it's never a young attractive well-adjusted male."

She laughs,

"Well you see it's the direct opposite for me, the attractive people that do go for it and approach me just want a bit of fun and nobody of any substance gives me the time of day. I'm not interested in one night stands no matter how gorgeous they happen to be!"

Looking the way she does I find her abstinence hard to believe, but why should she lie? I'm probably pigeon holing her; assuming she's promiscuous just because she's beautiful.

"So you wouldn't consider someone who's hard to get along with for this project? ... Wouldn't that be more interesting from your point of view?"

"No. I need a woman more complex. Someone with confidence issues, shy! Someone who wants to be liked but never lets the opportunities give her anything. That scenario is definitely more interesting especially when you put that person with someone of an opposite nature."

This has answered my question and her openness has helped me decide, this feels right!

The last part of that sentence does, however, repeat in my head as though I didn't read it properly the first time and have to go back over it to fully understand the meaning. My fears are kick-started again. Who is this man she has paired me with? Someone opposite to me, perhaps really confident and gregarious, a rebel rouser maybe or ...

Her voice brings me back into this room.

"Anyway back to the mundane. This may seem stark and clinical but it's just a formality. I'll tell you what's in the contract then you can sign it if you're in agreement, and we can then go out somewhere, if you'd like? I think I explained the outline of my research and the basic guidelines but I have formally bulleted the rules which are:

THE CONTRACT

Dissertation: Psychology Research

PROJECT MANAGER/STUDENT: Anna Paisley

SUBJECT: Rachel Fleetwood

- The Subject & Project Manager will not divulge any personal information to the other anonymous subject, i.e. name, address, place of work – anything that can identify them. Failure to comply with this will result in immediate termination of the subject's role in the research and non-payment of agreed fees.
- The Subject will be available, within reason and proper circumstance, given enough notice, to take part in other sessions at a later date if necessary.
- Physical contact is encouraged but not a necessity. Sexual contact is strictly prohibited.
- The Subject will be fully clothed at every session but not wearing any perfumes, body sprays or deodorant. Shampoo is permitted and of course ordinary soap for washing in the interests of hygiene.
- The Subject is not required to do anything he/she is uncomfortable with, and the signal to end the session at any time before the allotted hour is completed is to state loudly and clearly "end", where the Subject will be escorted from the room.
- The Subject will be given instructions for the first session to help easing into the programme.
- 1st session – talking only, with a guide to subject matter which may be disregarded.
- 2nd session – male subject to touch female, again with guidance and non-sexual contact
- 3rd session – female to male contact
- 4$^{th\ to}$ 10th session – hopefully some rapport or common ground will enable the natural process of relationship building .
- There will be total silence from the Project Manager. The sign that the session has ended will be a digital alarm which will go off at the end of the allotted hour when the audio recording will also end.

- Payment at the end of the project will be £20 per completed session plus £50 bonus if all sessions were attended. Totalling a possible £250
- The room will be in darkness except for one small night light at the back of the room for health and safety purposes. The Subject should not be able to read the facial expressions or see the eyes of the other subject. The Subject will be led into the room blindfolded and when the door is closed the Subjects will both remove and hang the blindfolds on their chairs. When the timer goes at the end of the allotted time the Subjects will have one minute to replace the blindfold.
- If after each week there are any issues which need to be addressed there will be a ten minute debrief session. As this experiment has never been conducted before there may be some unforeseen problems which can then be discussed and resolved along with how the session went in general.
- Anna Paisley will not divulge any information to either subject or a fourth party. All data and information gathered is confidential and for dissertation publication only with no names or personal details given apart from gender, age and a synopsis of personality traits.

Signature...
Anna Paisley

Signature...
Rachel Fleetwood

After reading all of that I am feeling disconcerted and overwhelmed – It's all real now. The blood starts throbbing in my feet and my extremities are contracting into my body telescopically like a tortoise's head going back into its shell.

Silence.

I'm getting quite used to Anna's mind-reading talent and reluctance to verbalise her thoughts. She's looking at me expectantly, so I'll indulge her

"Before I sign can I ask one question?"

"Of course." She speaks deeply and knowingly like she has an inkling of what I'm going to ask.

I hesitate …

"This might sound flippant but I'm going to ask anyway, are you living out a sort of fantasy by doing this?" Have I been too direct, crossed a boundary?

"I'm really glad you asked me that. It's quite perceptive of you and I'm liking the way you're thinking."

That's it? Nothing to add!

"And …?" I'm surprised by my school ma'am expression.

"I'm not telling!" she replies with a childlike air of stubbornness. "But now it all seems to be going ahead, I envy you! It is the stuff that fantasies are made of!"

I am reading so much into this. Does she have feelings for the male subject? Does she like observing people in compromising situations? Is she actually repressed and not confident at all or has she issues of her own that she's trying to address?

Must stop, she's doing research and that's all! I need to look at my own reasons for doing this, it's not me doing the research!

"I respect that but, I have to say from my stand point, if I were the onlooker envy wouldn't be the first emotion I would attribute to my situation; sympathy and compassion springs to mind!"

"You will be fine. I think this will be a life changing experience for you … in a good way."

She puts a reassuring hand on top of mine.

I snatch the pen from the table and sign as quick as I can before I change my mind. She does the same then we look at each other and laugh.

"Ok let's go!" she orders and once again I follow obediently.

We go to her local bar 'The Wing Tavern' just around the corner, the sort I really like; old and dingy needing renovation or severe redecoration, dim and cosy with beautiful dirt engrained stained glass windows.

There's the low hum of earthy and friendly clientele patter rumbling along the low ceiling, then wafting down to embrace you as you enter; a back draught of camaraderie.

A cold stone floor and a warm landlord welcome you into another world free of materialistic trappings, my kind of place. It's almost a shame the smoke induced fog you would associate with this sort of spit and sawdust place is now absent. Maybe landlords should employ a dry ice machine to evoke those smoky bygone days of real thriving community pubs. I could almost put up with sore throats and smelly clothes for a waft of that lost socially charged period of affability and friendly disagreement.

Not that I think the smoking ban is killing the pub trade, it's coincidental that the new no smoking rules came in at about the same time as cheap alcohol became more available in supermarkets and unscrupulous pub companies upped the anti and started fleecing their managers and employees.

Joy of all joys! They have proper, real beer, not that horrible chemical keg stuff, pulled from huge brass pumps bolted to a heavily painted ornate chunky antique wooden bar.

A Miracle; they're having a mini beer festival, another one of my favourite pastimes. The beloved real ale is an incentive to travel the country taking in the real essence of differing perspectives, local accents and cultures. In recent years beer has dispelled the north-south divide for me, largely from the uprising of micro-breweries nipping at the heels of the ruthless conglomerates. No matter where you come from if you drink too much ale you get silly, it's just the terminology that changes – squiffy or bladdered, all beer drinkers are the same, it's the beer itself that has the regional differences!

Why didn't I know about this place?

We settle down comfortably.

"So Rachel, I forgot to ask what you do for a living."

"Desk job, but it's not my first choice. It happened by accident and it pays the bills whilst allowing me to be independent until I decide what to do next."

"And what is that?" she puckers her lips and sucks up her Bacardi Breezer through a straw while looking up at me. That's not a drink I would have chosen for her, although it does go with her look of young partying sophistication with a bit of naughtiness and trashiness thrown in to unbalance your view of her. Perhaps an expensive glass of wine – 'Châteauneuf-Du-Pape' or a cool 'Chardonnay' would be more in keeping with her air of being 'above it all'!

I feel a bit like the poor relation supping my pint of beer but I can accept that with her, it's what I am and she likes me for it.

"Well, I gave up on Art College but ultimately the arts and culture are my passions. I'm an artist at heart and waiting for inspiration, if the opportunity arises or something appropriate crops up I will go for it, I hope!" I think I put too much emphasis on the 'will', sounding like I don't really mean it.

"I can see that about you but it sounds like you're getting too comfortable where you are now."

"Don't know … you're probably right but I need to pull myself together before I embark on some major change in my life."

"I don't know you that well or what you really mean by that but I would say don't leave it too long. Try not to get wrapped up in the trappings of the day."

"With my life style I don't envisage falling head over heels in love within the next couple of years or having babies so there's no danger of that. I don't have any credit cards so I won't get into debt. I admit I'm not actively looking for something as I'm happy with my flat and my little hobbies so we'll just see!"

"I get what you're saying. You're in quite a good place at the moment despite your own self-deprecation. Actually

Rachel, I'm beginning to think you're one of the most well-adjusted people I know!"

I am so surprised by this. She doesn't seem the type to be frivolous with her compliments, why should she be? I just don't see myself in that way!

We spend hours chatting about our current situations then before we know it it's really late and if I don't leave to get the last bus I'll have about six miles to walk.

"I hope we're going to stay friends for a long time. I think this is the start of a creative friendship."

Anna is a little tipsy but I get honesty coming through the slurred speech and over the top lovey dovey stuff.

"I hope so too but you might feel differently at the end of our escapades."

"Nope! Your wrong there, I will appreciate you for the rest of my life."

She has obviously come to the end of her alcoholic capacity.

"Let's go shall we, I'm drained."

I use this excuse to get her away. I don't think she'd leave if I told her she'd had enough.

She takes my hand and slurs, "Ring me tomorrow about arrangements."

We part ways once I'm sure she can walk unaided.

Trundling along on my merry way home I am content.

*

As I wake the next morning I am totally unaware of the time and fuzzy about what day it is; why hasn't my alarm gone off, why do I feel like crap and what did I talk about to Anna last night? If she feels anything like I do this morning she won't remember either, I just know I had a good time and I've gained an interesting friend – a warm melting sensation spreads through me.

My eyes open slightly while I gladly realise it's Sunday and the tab on the ceiling, which is the same as the last time I looked, is getting closer. I have that gravity pulling and pushing sensation of a rollercoaster ride and I am moving faster than before, right through the floor of the loft and hovering nose to roof joists right at the top of the building. If I try to look down will I fall or turn? I can't actually feel the rest of my body but I know it's there, like I'm wearing an invisible wet suit – constricting, cutting off the circulation without feeling uncomfortable!

I can turn over to look at the floor but I can't make myself move forwards or backwards, facing down seems to stop the motion but doesn't take me back. My hair doesn't flop down at the side of my face but is fanning out as though floating in water.

As I look around the loft I feel I am a part of the building. I am rooted at the foundations, threaded through the bricks and supporting the roof therefore protecting the house. They are part of me and I'm connected to my surroundings, complete and stable. It's a peaceful and fulfilled state of mind and I don't want it to stop. I feel more a part of anything here than I have ever been with anyone or in any place.

As I am still aware of what is normal yet unaware of time, I must bring myself back down manually, but I wonder how far I could still go, maybe out into the atmosphere. Perhaps I will advance a little more each time like being able to jog that bit further without 'hitting the wall' so soon or feeling sick each time I try.

This is the first time I have had to phase myself back to reality without any aid; so what do I do?

Starting to feel a little scared now… oh, here I am back in bed. It would seem thinking about something negative or feeling insecure will do it, but I don't experience any sensation or see anything, I just arrive back in bed suddenly!

I spend most of the day in a trance. I'm trying to do all those Sunday jobs but it's all a bit half-hearted. Washing, cleaning and organising seems trivial in light of the new direction my life seems to be taking.

It's quite late in the day when I remember to check my messages, my mobile must have run out of charge last night.

There are three messages from Roxanne all completely manic wondering where I am and would I like to meet her in town that night. Oh dear, she will be mad with me tomorrow. There's one from Sarah asking how things went and then my mum wondering how I am and to tell me about her latest disaster; she's not so much accident prone as creating the environment for accidents to thrive.

I ring my mum for a little chat then do text messages for the rest. I will hold Sarah off until I know more after my first session. I'll see Roxanne tomorrow and placate her. For now I need to just chill out.

It's a sultry autumn evening!

I have an old, large wooden Ottoman, with a tapestry lid, picked up for next to nothing from a junk shop.

I used a varnish to renew and enhance the rich walnut body then reupholstered the top with a heavy curtain material, cream with lilac irises – garish if used for drapes but sort of stylish when used in a minimalist way, i.e. for bottom-pampering luxury.

Numerous petite silk cushions adorn the edges, lying against the walls and are scattered all over it like hundreds and thousands on top of an iced bun, creating a cosy indulgent place to snuggle up with a book and relax. The whole oozing gateau is strategically placed in a perfectly fitting nook under a window where I can look out directly over Butterfield.

Brailsford's industrial town blatantly shouts out in the distance through a well-positioned gap in the trees just to the right of my view which looks down over the park and river; this sudden opening in the foliage, where a giant has stepped on and flattened the greenery, has the effect of magnifying the size of the industrial estate to make it seem a lot closer than it really is, like peering through a tube, blinkered to the surrounding image.

As I sit back and take it all in, the romantic and haunting 'Wait for Me' from the *Bladerunner* soundtrack by Vangelis is seeping into the picture and merging with the manufactured clouds of smoke and pollution. The undulating industrial Bar

Chart sky line with intermittent slow-motion flames reaching high and burning holes into the atmosphere emphasises the mood from that film and I'm absorbed into it quickly and smoothly like water into cotton wool.

The hardcore spectacular of concrete and steel is aesthetically pleasing, sculptural; a symbol of the work ethic, tangible evidence of human endeavour and intelligence. Manufacture; man creating things and living side by side with nature's own innate and exquisite, botanic expertise.

I really don't understand people's general opposition to industrial sites, particularly the giant wind turbines with their interactive usefulness. They are a welcome addition to some of the flat wilds of this country. Surely we can't deny the ingenuity and simplicity of harnessing and utilising nature to create power?

After a while my focus pulls back and I notice my own ghostly reflection transposed over the top of the industrial works of art, backed by a blood red and bruised purple sky. I have always felt detached from my surroundings but when I look out at this acrylic composition with myself fused onto it I'm riveted and fixed – a transparent covering.

The music stops and so do my daydreams. I remember then that I need to ring Anna to arrange my first 'session'; the pulse in my head pounds at the thought of it.

I still seem to be focused on my reflection and there's now a change to my demeanour, it's tense, anxious, no longer subjugated, the lenses in my eyes harden and the connection is lost.

I arrange with Anna to be at the college for 7.45 p.m. on Friday to begin the session at 8 p.m. which will run till 9 p.m., in time for me to catch the last bus home at 9.45 p.m.

We chat a little about last night and I'm relieved she doesn't apologise for overdoing it on the alcohol. No awkwardness.

After hanging up I get ready for bed, I'm shattered and it's going to be an arduous week!

When I awake next morning I'm a little dazed and jet lagged, I can't remember what day it is. The last thing I remember is reading.

I can feel something weighty teetering on my abdomen, it must be the book. If I fell asleep reading how did it not fall off the bed in the night? I must have slept so soundly I didn't move all night, that's unusual!

I'm currently reading Daphne Du Maurier – *Rebecca*, I toyed with the idea of including it in the construction of my nightstand, having already read it four or five times but decided in the end that I was bound to want to indulge and lose myself in the identifiable main character again soon,

'She smiled, and pinched my arm, and I thought about being placid, how quiet and comfortable it sounded, someone with knitting on her lap, with calm unruffled brow. Someone who was never anxious, never tortured by doubt and indecision, someone who never stood as I did, hopeful, eager, frightened, tearing at bitten nails, uncertain which way to go, what star to follow.'

Having the character see herself that way yet ultimately becoming the love of Maxim's life as a result of her quiet intuition and mild nature is reassuring to me – a little self-indulgence goes a long way when I'm in a particularly self-deprecating mood and at the moment it's a pill that takes away the pain; it inevitably fails to cure but maybe my low self-esteem is terminal. Any source of relief is welcome.

Whenever I read it I see myself as that nameless woman telling the story, playing second fiddle to Rebecca de Winter; shy and meek, full of self doubt and totally disbelieving that a man like Maxim could be remotely interested in her but hanging in there regardless.

Believing there is an ulterior motive when a man with any charm and charisma shows interest in me is the only way I can accept the attention and allow him in. The other option is unthinkable – that I actually have attributes they admire or that I am desirable; that would mean the eventual possibility of being a disappointment, not living up to some ideal. If I believe a man shows interest in me because there is no one else available then I can organise myself and prepare for the inevitable end.

The final cut has only happened to me like that once in my life and although I knew I would never achieve equality with him, I didn't care, it just felt perfect being with him and knowing he was mine even for a short time. I relished Alan's attention whether it caused reluctant euphoria or insurmountable pain. The end that he dictated caused me agony and I'm still scarred but I have hope and a positive outlook partly due to Du Mauriers' insightful writing.

That last thought 'jaunts' me, precariously, straight to the roof and I'm pushing, short of breath, through to the crisp outside air.

The resistance is heavier through the roof than the floor but the sensation is the same, a strange hypnotic state like falling into sleep but with full brain awareness. The pulley system pushing from beneath and pulling from above forces me through and integrates me into the great outdoors, levitating in wonderment.

I am not cold but very aware of the conditions. I seem to have a built in thermometer that tells me the temperature without me having to experience it. The reading is low but the sun is radiating cleanly and at its best for this time of year, fresh, uncontaminated and resilient with no clouds to obscure or dull its effects.

Just as I start to ponder my current situation the alarm clock brings me back to bed and all my questioning will have to be indulged another time.

I went so much further this time because I 'jaunted' quicker than before. A growing confidence and acceptance of my ability must be a factor here or maybe it's due to a more frequent and prolonged peace of mind.

The more I do this the more accelerated the process becomes. I hope eventually I can slow it down if I want to or vary the rate and distance. If I want to see just how far I can go with this; it will have to be when there are no time constraints.

There's no music to wake me this morning, another of many firsts, falling asleep with book in hand is not one of my routines. Usually the book is put away, securely in place, then music chosen and light off.

*

I arrive at work at the usual time and Roxanne grabs my arm violently as I walk past the opening to one of the store rooms. She pulls me in with quite a yank, it must appear comical to any onlooker further down the office, 'now you see me now you don't!'

"And where have you been for the last two days?" she spouts with some vehemence.

"I wasn't feeling well so I stayed in and 'reclused' all weekend," I blab.

"Oh sorry." She lets go of me. She is now really concerned and I feel rotten for the deception.

As we converse in the doorway the odd person walks in and out awkwardly pushing through so we step back away from each other with our heads down conspicuously refraining from speaking further. We then come back together and carry on the conversation as though we hadn't paused at all.

"What was it sickness, bad stomach?" she continues with a motherly tone.

"Women's problems, you know." I reply with a spontaneous whispering lie whilst patting my abdomen sympathetically. I really hadn't given much thought as to how I was going to pull the wool over Roxanne's 'hard to pull wool over' eyes!

"But your last one was only a couple of weeks ago, you're not usually that irregular!"

She pronounces that last word with too much volume and I pull her away from the door,

"Shhhhh! For goodness' sake ... Roxanne!" I whisper heavily.

I look at her in disbelief. How can she remember such fine details? I find it hard enough keeping track myself.

She sees the horror on my face

"Don't look at me like that, I only remember because you had a particularly bad time of it last month."

"I know I struggle sometimes but I refuse to go on the Pill for it, I think I manage it quite well really."

I think I'm getting a little too defensive here about something that shouldn't really be an issue at the moment.

"I suppose you do if you can call, crying in the toilets doubled-up over the sink whilst having me rub your back for twenty minutes, good management!"

"You're over dramatising it, that was a one off!" I'm starting to spit a little now and want to get off the subject.

"Anyway, this one has come along quickly hasn't it?" she retorts with a level of disbelief.

I'm getting really fed up with this conversation now, my guilty conscience is diminishing and turning into antagonism.

"Irregularity happens when you leave things to nature, don't you remember?" I retort.

Touché!

She knows what I'm getting at and decides she doesn't want to go there – her previous promiscuity and blasé use of contraception is one of the few things we don't talk about anymore, it's been done to death and now she's wiser and more discerning about her sexual partners as well as giving herself little sex breaks every now and then or 'celibation holidays' as she calls them.

I completely agree with being sensible and have used condoms or the Pill myself when necessary but not to the extreme of carrying boxes of them in my bag, the odd ones down the side of my shoe or down the front of my pants; she did get a little carried away with not being caught unawares!

She would also take the Pill without breaks on a regular basis so she could continue her sex life without any interruptions.

Roxanne was verging on nymphomania but only because she was getting all this attention and didn't know what to do with it; she wasn't mature enough to deal with it correctly. I don't think her mum was very open with her about love and sex so her naivety left her open to predators.

She is better now but unfortunately she's learned a lot along the way and likes variation too much to be totally monogamous but she is definitely the one in control now in all her relationships and doesn't leap in head first.

At least I have managed to divert her attention away from me and not divulge anything. She allows me to go and sort myself out in peace and quiet.

Back at my desk Jason seeks me out. He will be light relief compared to Roxanne, which I need this morning.

"Hi Rach." There's a little sigh at the end of that.

"Morning Jason, good weekend?"

I look up into those sultry green eyes with my fists under my chin as he leans across the desk and I think to myself 'Oh you're lovely you are' whilst trying not to show my admiration.

"It was ok," he replies with disappointment.

"Why was it just ok?"

"I'd rather not go into it, suffice to say ... 'unrequited love' does not suit me, I don't wear it well. I am simply not used to it Rachel!" he replies with a wistful air of disbelief.

If I didn't know him better that statement would sound so superficial and egotistical.

So, he's fallen for some bloke and the feeling wasn't mutual, welcome to my world!

"Don't feel too bad, see it as redemption for all the young men's hearts you've broken."

He likes that, his face brightens a little; he is so fickle sometimes!

"Are we still on for Sunday?" he enquires with renewed vigour.

I'd forgotten about our monthly 'get togethers' with everything that's happened in the last few days.

We have our own little two man film club. We meet on the last Sunday of each month where we spend the whole day vegging out watching six films back to back from 9 a.m. in the morning to approximately 11 p.m. at night or whenever.

We take it in turns to choose and provide the films along with snacks, nibbles, refreshments and wine.

The only rules are that the person not choosing has never seen any of the films chosen by the other person and that if we don't have the DVD already, or can't borrow it from someone, that it should cost no more than £3 from eBay or Amazon or by whatever means.

I also stipulated when we first thought of the idea that there should be no horror films but that was ok with Jason because he didn't like them either. A good thriller or gratuitous sex and violence was acceptable every now and again!

It's my turn this month at my flat. I had an idea at the end of our last meeting of some of my next choices and after confirming with Jason that they were new to him just finally need to organise a short list and get the order right.

I relish the opportunity to share my likes and loves with a willing participant. I can get a little over-excited by the prospect and sometimes make myself shake with the anticipation of Jason's reactions to even the smallest scene or dialogue or an insignificant facial expression by an actor or by an apt piece of music played at just the right moment. I suppose I'm looking for someone to share my fine tuning!

Even though I've seen some of the films a million times it's like seeing them for the first time when Jason is watching with me all excited and eager. Sometimes he's disappointed but not often.

His choices have been interesting if not a little predictable at times, I have been exposed to genres I probably would never have considered but have embraced, in the main, with enthusiasm.

His penchant for foreign – subtitled film, British cult classics, westerns (surprisingly), musicals and little known gay erotica verging on porn have been an eye opener; he said he didn't want to leave them out because he believes they have 'artistic merit'… any excuse!

I love our decadent days together, I'm totally at ease and feel so relaxed with Jason. We get on incredibly well and I can lay back with my legs across him or rest my head on his shoulder with calm and conviction without having to talk if we don't feel like it.

I like that I can flirt with him a little if I'm in the mood. He likes me and understands me enough to play along to keep me happy. He says 'he's giving me practice, to keep my hand in.'

"Oh yes, I'm really looking forward to that." I reply with honesty I'm only too happy to express after my altercation with Roxanne. Film club is a welcome distraction, a treat to keep in the cupboard and save for later. I can keep thinking about it and savour the anticipation.

Knowing the first week of torture will be over by the time 'Movie Sunday' comes along is also comforting.

Jason taps me on the shoulder as confirmation of our date and walks back to his desk.

The week goes without much incident, my jaunting carries on in much the same way as Monday and before I know it Friday evening is here and I'm on the bus to College.

Chapter 4

Week 1

Cruel or Insecure

On arrival at the College, scarecrow woman indicates the direction I should go without saying anything yet again ... charming!

I knock on the same door as usual and enter when beckoned.

Anna is most welcoming and almost runs over to give me a totally heartfelt hug that would intimidate a bear, which is really nice but not at all expected.

"Thank goodness! I wondered whether you might have second thoughts!"

Her relief explains the overzealous embrace.

"Sorry, bus was late. You don't need to worry, I'm totally resolved about it now and besides, I wouldn't let you down Anna."

She nods in agreement and gives me a thankful stare, she then sits back at her desk.

"Oh Rachel, I forgot to get your personal details, home address, phone number, etc."

I give her all the appropriate info and then we get down to the nitty gritty,

"I'll take you through to the room in a minute, it's all set up and ready. The other subject is already waiting for you." My stomach flips at this statement.

She gets up to collect a bundle of equipment from a cupboard and brings it over to me.

"Just stand up a minute, I'll need to strap this around your middle and attach these pads. They're not uncomfortable, they're so small you won't even notice them once they're on."

She carries on attaching things to my midriff while talking,

"I've got some ideas; subject matter you might want to use, just straight forward stuff it's up to you;

Politics and Current affairs – elections
Music, Film and TV – gossip
Sport – The Olympics
Art
Sex and Relationships
Fashion
Industry
World affairs
History and modern life"

That's given me no help at all, some specific questions to ask would have been better as I'm sure my mind will go blank once I'm in there.

"Right. You're ready. Follow me and then I'll blindfold you when we're outside the room." She says this as though it's a normal everyday occurrence while looking me up and down admiring her handy work.

My heart rate steadily increases as we walk further away from the only room I know in this cold concrete jungle, being led away from familiarity to 'God knows what!' – must pull myself together!

I realise then this is my last chance to refrain from starting something I may later wish I hadn't, it's crunch time and I'm going for it.

I'm sure the little machine taking readings from this waist band must be registering my excitement and straining into overload. I can picture a little cartoon explosion spluttering out puffs of smoke with springs and cogs poking out by the time Anna gets to it.

At the other end of this long, high perspective corridor there are some double fire doors but we don't go through, just to the left before them is an insignificant plain door, at first glance it could just be a store cupboard. Anna stops outside. She turns to me,

"Here we are, I'll put this blindfold on then lead you to your seat, ok? Are you ready?"

"Yes." I say when really I should shout 'NO' and run!

I look at the closed aperture, while Anna gets the scarf ready to tie round my eyes, and it starts to enlarge. I'm reminded of Alice in Wonderland and feel as though I'm shrinking.

This gateway to the unknown is now claustrophobically towering above me, the doors in *The Lion the Witch and the Wardrobe* – what magical world is waiting for me in there, what mythical creature waits to be discovered?

Blackness is forced upon me and then I experience those spirograph shapes you get when applying pressure to your eyes – ironically soothing given the constricted situation I'm in.

She opens the door then cups my right elbow in her left hand. I am led to a chair.

I can hear, smell and see absolutely nothing – a non-world without atmosphere, it's more than disconcerting to have no control at all, it's completely debilitating.

Just as Anna tells me we're at the chair my toe catches one of the legs making an uncomfortably high-pitched scratching noise along the floor, causing me to loudly blurt "Oops!"

I feel immediately stupid, not the best way to start.

Anna tries to reduce my embarrassment by blaming the 'stupid chair' but the damage is done and the nerves I've tried so hard to control get the better of me. The shakes take over.

She pushes me downward gently by the shoulders telling me to sit. She then announces to both of us,

"When you hear the door close you can remove your blindfolds and hang them on your chairs. The alarm will go in an hour and you should then put the blindfolds back on, if you have problems just hold them in place and tell me when I come in, I'll sort it for you."

She leaves and peace descends.

There's an awkward silence but I get the impression the feeling isn't mutual, it's as though there's no-one else in the room.

I tentatively remove my blindfold but can't detect him doing the same, as my eyes try to focus there is then some movement which I guess is him now untying his.

"It's good to get that off." I say in a voice that's just too loud, I will have to re-evaluate and turn my volume down. I hope my sentiment will be reciprocated, but … nothing.

Eventually, in reply, I hear a low and quiet,

"Mmmm".

I hope he doesn't think I'm a crass loud mouth, based on the happenings so far I wouldn't blame him if he did.

As my eyes adjust to the dimness I can make out a vague outline. He appears to be quite tall, hard to tell though when a person is sat down – I have to lift my head to see the top of his shape, his head appears to be bent forward.

There's not a lot of distance between us, our knees must be almost touching.

There's a small insignificant night light plugged in at the other end of a very large room, no windows, it's probably used for functions and conferences but there's no other furniture that I can make out, our chairs are all there is – bareness, bleakness, aloneness!

I have left perpetual sensory overdosing completely behind that door. All the surrounding myself with acrylically vivid colours, keeping visually rich textures close by and holding on to tightly voluptuous shapes and rolling contours is forsaken. I have abandoned engrossing and losing myself in the wealth of history that is my overgrown, friendly neighbourhood for a grey blank cell.

I had complete immersion in a vat of musical spirits and over indulgence of mass media on demand, all of this has been taken away from me and replaced with this withdrawal into darkness and silence – the hallowed depths of a sensory deprived space.

Self-will and a bared soul are all I have now – this sudden nakedness leaves me shaky and paranoid.

This is my alternate empty universe for the next nine weeks and the man in front of me is the satellite with the potential to either break the void or consolidate it!

"What do you do for a living?" my voice quivers, it sounds like someone else or a recording which I refuse to believe is me.

What a stupid question, we're not supposed to reveal our occupations, it's in the contract. I metaphorically smack my temple with the palm of my hand.

He slowly replies with a dismissive tone, his first words to me …

"Breaking the rules already?"

His voice is pitched low, quite rich but is light, nearly a whisper almost breaking! The dryness is dehydrating!

I gulp trying to wet my mouth.

"I know, sorry … No, I'm not a rule breaker, just nervous."

I'm hoping for a bit of sympathy but all I get is a throaty sigh. Not a big demonstrative sound, more of a slightly impatient letting out of air; not quite a tut! He must be holding back on being completely patronising!

I'm not making a good first impression and I'm getting the distinct vibe that he doesn't really want to be here.

More silence.

I decide to be brave and talk.

"Shall I tell you something about me, my history, I'm sure that's allowed, it has no bearing on my life now?"

I sound like I'm on a talk show, I feel sick!

"… Ok."

There's hesitance then slight expectancy, an afterthought? That's promising. It's amazing what you can read into one tiny little word when you're blinded!

"I went to Art College … in another town, straight after my A levels but the travelling was mind numbing and the whole further education student life wasn't what I expected – too many people, too regimented and I wasn't learning how to express myself in the way I'd hoped. I wanted something more intimate and reflective but I found it a bit juvenile and too chaotic, dumbed down. I was disappointed at the mass marketing and to say I became disillusioned is an understatement."

I stop for breath, and then become very aware of the silence, like getting used to a pneumatic drill or a car alarm going off in the distance; only really noticing it when it finally, suddenly stops.

No interruptions? I'll just carry on then,

"I wanted to find depth, passion and inspiration but I found flatness and mediocrity. I left without planning my next step or knowing what my options were, a bit stupid really. I was back at home and very low. Then a friend suggested a casual job available in his office, this would do nicely until I decided what was next for me ... and ... er ... I have been there ever since but at least it's well paid flatness and mediocrity. I don't want to sound patronising but it's not really for me. I'm looking for inspiration to get me moving on."

I stop for breath again.

"Anyway I then left home and got the flat I have now."

Now fed up of the sound of my own voice I ask,

"Can I ask why you wanted to do this?"

It's surprisingly easy to talk to someone when their eyes aren't on you even when there is some hostility there.

"I don't want to talk about me, I'd like you to just carry on as you are."

His lethargy and sarcasm bugs me and apart from that, the ridicule I'm detecting is completely unfounded!

"Is that derision in your tone? Why don't you just answer me?"

Can't believe how brave I'm being.

"No." He lowers his voice and elongates the 'o' showing continued frustration, I'm the naughty little puppy and next he's going to order me to sitttt!

I don't really want to speak anymore and if that's the way he wants it I can give him agitation by the bucket load. Am I being too trivial, am I annoying – I just don't know.

I shuffle in my seat ready for a fight ... which is unexpectedly exhilarating!

Suddenly he carries on unprompted,

"Don't force me to talk before I'm ready, I don't like being backed into a corner or cajoled. Don't try to manipulate or interview me, it won't work, you'll be wasting your time. Any 'niceties' will be totally lost and wasted on me."

His voice is strong and smooth without being loud or obnoxious, pity his words are! A lot of threatening 'don'ts' in there! Why this splurge of vitriolic waste?

I can't work out whether he's trying to intimidate or provoke me. Maybe he's reserved and doesn't suffer fools, either way he could try and compromise until we find some common ground.

"I don't really care, it's not like we have to get on so answer the bloody question."

I don't think I have ever been so infuriated by someone for doing so little. I'm doing all the work and getting nothing; also I swore and I never do that!

No answer, why on earth is he here if he isn't going to talk to me.

"Do you have a problem with women or is it just me that makes you so rude?"

Still nothing, although I can hear him breathing and it's quite deep and laboured, right down into his diaphragm.

I'll have to change tack because we'll end up going round in circles.

Why do I feel I have to take charge anyway, we could sit in silence for the next ten weeks, what would that tell Anna? Perversely I do sort of like his reluctance to speak, it tells me what he 'isn't' – pretentious, unfortunately it doesn't tell me what he is! If I'm going to survive another nine weeks I think I'll just have to be totally honest, be myself. I'll try to not let aggression get the better of me again.

Peering into the darkness I can just make out his outline, his head is hanging which I read as dismay. Body language is an unattainable luxury so I will have to retrain my focus to decipher and interpret shapes and sounds as a way of reading this man.

For now I will attempt to tackle each of his 'don'ts' in turn.

"I'm probably the least forward person on the planet; this situation is definitely stranger for me than most, but you are something else I think It's probably not a stretch for you to deal with all this. I didn't mean to 'interview you' but you have to give me something. I think I'm more uncomfortable with the silence than actually having to speak and that's really saying something considering how shy and introverted I am. I promise I have no ulterior motives and I certainly don't want to con or trick you. I'm struggling here, please don't let me form an incorrect impression of you."

I take a deep breath with some pride at being able to articulate my point fairly well.

Then out it comes in a deep slow expressive husky truth and I'm captivated, like switching on a light in a pitch black room, illuminating everything you didn't know was right there in front of you!

"At first I was intrigued by the ad, probably like you. I became really serious about doing this when I found out what it entailed, it's a means to an end for me – my own research if you like, an opportunity not to be missed. The thing is ..." he has a deep intake of breath, "I am so worn and tired by 'the chase'. Women ruthlessly pursue me then once I relent, they assume they can change me. I know I'm over simplifying but I want to get the point across as simply as possible without embroiling you in all the sordid details. I want to try something where I can have a little more control or operate as an equal and not be seen and judged on my appearance. I want to just talk without ulterior motives. I acknowledge I haven't gone about it very well so far, I'm not as open or friendly as I thought I would be!"

My first reaction to this is that it sounds credible. He wants the same experience as me but for completely opposite reasons, but when I take the time to analyse what he's just said and pick out the subtext I come to some disturbing conclusions.

Either he has a monstrous ego or he is actually very attractive, maybe even irresistible to women. I remember Anna's words about him being amazing and think it must be the latter in which case he's probably quite experienced in relationships. I'm missing the point though, surely there must be more to him than that or Anna wouldn't have chosen him for this. Maybe it's his character and his looks combined that make him such a delicious subject.

There's a strangeness to his voice, an authoritative candour and suddenly I do feel a bit intimidated; not by his words but by my own perception of him. If what he's saying is not ego then he must be a man of substance. I mustn't judge him if he's trying to be honest.

When I put everything together, in one split second he's gone from cantankerous recluse to intelligent sex god, get a grip Rachel ... my mind's wandering again.

I have to come back on this revelation of his.

"Be honest though, aren't you the slightest bit lecherous ... deep down at heart, you know ... using your appeal to achieve self-gratification?" It's the only word I can think of that gets the point across. "I know that sounds flippant and not very intelligent but I'm intrigued by your derogatory opinion of all those women who obviously can't help themselves, you must enjoy some of the admiration you get?"

My derision and sarcasm are a little shocking to me but honest! Maybe this is a side of me I need to explore to greater depths along with allowing myself to freely express anger and hurt.

"No, it's the complete opposite, the 'ladies' 'letch' after me! ... that's not to say I'm not a passionate man which is completely different."

That was not the answer I expected. I thought he would be defensive and guarded, instead there's an unexpected attractive softness.

I have the inclination to be antagonistic towards him which is quite uncharacteristic of me. I have an uncontrollable urge to push his buttons and get a reaction despite my new found fascination.

"But don't you take advantage if they're 'lying at your feet'?"

"To an extent, I suppose it's inevitable – I am human – but I have never connected with anyone physically or spiritually, after trying on numerous occasions and I'm beginning to think my looks or the way I'm perceived will forever dictate my 'come and go' love life. I don't see myself as particularly handsome but I have been told on numerous occasions that I have, and I quote, 'magnetism and charisma'. I really don't know what that means but whatever it is it doesn't give me the ability to respond romantically to anyone. Magnetism implies mutual attraction but it's always one sided; I draw women in … reluctantly before you say anything!"

There's definitely a smile in that sentence. Good, the glimmer of a sense of humour.

"I think you've got that all wrong!" I say that as if I know what I'm on about, but it just flowed out of me spontaneously without the slightest contemplation.

He now seems to be resting back into his chair with arms crossed, I can just make out his elbows sticking out either side of him and his shoulders have raised ever so slightly. He has stretched out his long legs and crossed them at the ankles between my feet and under my chair – daring me to surprise him!

He replies with intrigue.

"Go on."

"Surely it's two sided, you know the saying 'love and hate being two sides of the same coin'. Magnetism also involves repulsion and it sounds as though you're the negative attracting the positive whether you like it or not. You're then repulsed by what attaches to you but then it's too late, they're attached well and good. I would say magnetism sums you up quite well but not in the way other people have meant it. Anyway nothing is ever black and white is it?"

I enjoyed that run of metaphors and clichés, don't often get the chance to do that without sounding pretentious.

"Maybe you're right."

He leans forward, lightly brushing his legs against mine as he brings them back to a normal sitting position, and I'm sure he's rubbing his chin – I can hear the faintest friction of finger lengths scraping eleven o'clock shadow!

He leans back again and continues with his original train of thought.

"Anyway this seemed the ideal opportunity to see if I could get to know someone and be truly honest without appearances, judgements and sex getting in the way, to confirm whether this influence I seem to have is purely on a visual level. I want to interact with a woman as an equal, no powers or charisma, just a man."

The integrity and vulnerability running together in that sentence is inspiring and has me totally enthralled with him. Oh dear, just the effect he wants to avoid. Maybe there's no getting away from it as far as he's concerned. I must give him the chance to achieve his goal though and try to remain impartial and not too easily swayed by him. It's definitely going to be a challenge for me not to be switched on by 'him'.

He continues with that pliable but strong rich gritty voice like a mouthful of warm 'Green & Black' – 'honeycomb bits', dark chocolate; melting but chewy in parts. This image seems to define him so well,

"I don't draw the line at chemistry though, to me that is mutual, and highly desirable – a must!" he projects.

He is sitting upright now and his posture is majestic. I can just see the outline of his broad straight shoulders.

I find I'm really moved by this revelation and the warmth I now have towards him must be escaping from me and radiating around him. If he could read my body language he would now deduce, as I'm leaning forward, heels elevated by the increased pressure to the balls of my feet, elbows on raised knees and fists supporting my chin with a transfixed look on my face, that I'm totally absorbed in him and his rhetoric. I hope he doesn't think I'm charmed by him, which I probably am! I quickly adjust myself and sit up straight again.

He was obtuse and defiant when we started out which is weird because he obviously wants to learn something about himself from this. Maybe he's not what he thinks he is. He seemed to be arrogant at first, I can't put my finger on whether there is some egotism there or whether he's over-compensating for a lack of confidence. Maybe it's neither and he is just different to everyone else.

We seem to be getting somewhere so I'll carry on with this same theme although what I really want to do is explore his sensitive side by showing him mine.

"Well my first impression was not to like you."

Think I put too much emphasis on the 'can take it or leave it' attitude.

"I don't know for sure if I would have felt any different if I were introduced to you in the 'normal' way. Being a shy person I may be intimidated by you, I am by most men."

At this point I think he brings his right foot up and rests it across onto his left knee. He seems to be resting his right elbow on his knee and balancing his chin on his right hand palm.

I continue with my analysis.

"Maybe you wouldn't come across as so egotistical, or on the other hand perhaps you wouldn't be so open, even though the details about yourself did seem to take some coaxing out. If I'm honest though I'm intrigued by you, you're a bit of a paradox and for what it's worth I do like to listen to your voice. You sound like you should read the news on the radio or maybe the chap that calls out the numbers on the lottery."

He lets out a small appreciative guffaw but says nothing.

It then suddenly occurs to me that he must have got to know Anna just as I have and given the ease with which he seems to get into relationships with women I would be surprised if she hadn't been seduced by him even if he wasn't trying to as she puts it 'get into her pants'.

Despite her ideas about her own inability to be attracted to men she surely would have been tempted.

So changing direction slightly, "Weren't you attracted to Anna at all?"

I wonder what she will make of this on the tape but I try to put that out of my head. Surprisingly this is the first time I've actually thought about being listened to!

"She is beautiful – simple fact!" He offers this *fait accompli* with no equivocation – bother.

He continues,

"But it's of no importance to me. I had already decided I'm doing this to find out who I am, not to exacerbate my current failings or triumphs, depending on your point of view; besides she's not my type and I know she's not interested in me, I could tell by her body language. I have taken advantage of women, whether they're attractive/plain, interesting/shy, intelligent/shallow, whatever combination, that side of things is of no consequence and has never been the issue. I have let flattery consume me and therefore taken advantage of these women's unnerving boundless attraction to me, and used it for self-gratification. And there have been many women. But I always end up hating myself for it and suffered the sometimes embarrassing and awkward outcome – 'bunny boiler' is a horrible term but very apt in my case and sums up some of the unfortunate women I have regretted letting into my life. I don't go looking to sleep around and compared to most men I think I'm quite restrained given the level of interest I get. I suppose I've become so self-absorbed that I've lost my sense of self-worth and how I affect other people. I know I have cheated every one of those women, although as an aside to this soliloquy, and in my defence, I have always told them the score right from the start. Not one of those potential partners has been able to dig into my core or get anywhere near to understanding me!"

He talks about these women and their effect on him, never the other way around, which is a little grotesque yet sad, but the biggest irony of all is that I want to tell him he's over-analysing everything, which is exactly what I do, it's like hearing my own thoughts out loud although his predicament is the complete opposite to mine.

"It sounds to me as though you haven't tried very hard to understand them and besides I think they may feel they got something out of the deal; if you were 'any good' I mean!"

I want to challenge him without it sounding like sour grapes.

He laughs and it is a lovely warm sound that makes me feel relaxed and at ease. I like him on a new level now but I don't want to!

Will my growing acceptance of him increase each time he reacts positively to something negative I say, maybe, but what does that mean, is this how relationships, friendships are supposed to happen? – I question his motives and mock his failings while he dishes up his emotions on a platter.

It's easy to see how it works when you analyse in this way. In the darkness I can visualise the different levels of intimacy like climbing a very high and steep staircase. I'm very much more aware of where we are on the social scale. At the moment were going three steps up two down, four up three down. It's going to be a slow, deliberate climb!

It's all honesty and we're getting to know each other without chit chat. I think neither of us has encountered that before and this situation in its uniqueness is the reason for it. Maybe blind dates should be literal and arranged like this. This is not a date, must get that idea out of my mind. I don't want to be inclined towards him, I want to stay upright and focused.

"Does all that's happened to you make you cruel? Do you think you have developed a dark side?"

"Hurtful, selfish, difficult, a cad and a bounder and that whole collection of 'bad boy' adjectives … maybe … possibly, but cruel – never"

There's no hesitation but I sense that's not everything!

"And?"

"Look. I'm blunt and I don't lie although I have kept some truths to myself longer than I should have. The word 'cruel' means to intentionally inflict pain on others and I wouldn't do that. I'm suspicious of most people and I keep my dearest friends close to me. I can't say anymore, you'll have to make your own mind up about me!"

I believe him and I'm sure all will be revealed in time. I decide to change the subject, dramatically,

"Do you have any distinguishing features?"

I seriously want to know but my tongue is pushed firmly in my cheek and I hope he picks up on it.

He's probably pleased to get off the previous line of questioning and rises to the challenge,

"Well … my hunchback is very noticeable and sometimes my wooden leg falls off."

We laugh slightly and together, not loudly, not forced and it's spontaneous, sparkly, nice!

"I have a tattoo." He announces with some apprehension.

He didn't need to tell me so perhaps he's starting to trust me.

"Where is it?"

"Low down on my back, on my hip!"

"Left or right?"

"Just at the top of my left buttock."

He's leaning forward, almost whispering but still able to converse with a dynamic gravitas. His now silken voice is still heavy and clear as though he's plugged his vocal cords directly into my inner ear, for a split second the combination of his soft murmur and well defined words in close proximity, filling my head, rouses a sensation I haven't felt since my mid-teens, limbs turning to mush and butterflies in the tummy. It gives me an uneasy buzz.

His head is not far from mine now and I'm tensing up, he's utilising my space and doesn't seem aware or bothered, or is it intentional?

Am I reacting like this because I'm starting to like him and reluctant to acknowledge this so early in the relationship or is it because his familiarity is so sudden and can't therefore be genuine?

It certainly isn't due just to his close proximity which I'm enjoying as a guilty pleasure – the same way I make sure no one is looking, when I'm alone watching lightweight 1990's blockbuster films like *Under Siege*, every time they're repeated on the TV – without fail – can't help myself!

He carries on whispering while I wonder if he's looking up towards me.

"It's only about an inch in diameter but it's quite dynamic, not easily forgotten."

What on earth is he talking about now? … Oh yes, the tattoo!

He's still whispering for some reason but I maintain the subterfuge,

"Well, put me out of my misery."

"I don't want to tell you. Maybe I'll be in the position of showing it to you one day and I don't want to spoil the surprise!"

He's almost gloating. What is he doing? Is he playing games, testing me again? Maybe he's pushing me as I did earlier.

"You'll have to give me a clue, I don't want to build it up only to be disappointed ... no, no wait a minute, I'll guess. Is it a fox?"

Something predatory and cunning but cute I'm thinking.

"No." he says with a wry acknowledgement of the reason for me choosing that image.

Too obvious!

Yes that was a ridiculous guess, he wouldn't be so predictable. I'll try again,

"The male symbol, 'Mars'?"

A permanent reminder of his effect on women.

"Ha Ha!" he whispers patronisingly, *"that's not exactly dynamic is it?"*

"No, hang on,"

It must be something strange and energetic maybe with a sense of humour, something that fits all the criteria,

"Alright, how... about ... err... Speedy Gonzales... oh even better, Road Runner – taunting and unobtainable? – definitely dynamic!"

His laugh is rich, infectious, and brings our volume back to a normal level.

"No but wish I'd thought of that."

"Erm, what about something modern but full of nostalgia ... the Star Ship Enterprise?"

It's probably something strange or off the wall ... unguessable. I like this game though, with him anyway. I know I'm never going to get it but I like the banter.

"No, but good try. Do you like Sci-Fi?"

"Yes, amongst other things."

His tone lightens a little,

"Going back to something you said earlier, who was the friend who suggested you work at his office?"

Where did that come from all of a sudden, I mentioned that ages ago. Another good quality – attentive, but in this case regrettable, I can see where this is going and I'm not sure about it.

"What made you think of that?" I snap.

"When you said 'Enterprise' it made me think of work and then I remembered you said after Art College a friend suggested you work at his place and I wondered then who that was. I forgot to ask. Does that explain?" Impatience returns but I like the way his mind works so I'll forgive the tone and tell him what he wants to know.

"His name is Gary, the best friend of Alan, a boyfriend I had at school. We stayed in contact after Alan and I split up and have stayed friends ever since."

"Who was the boyfriend, what was he like?"

"Are you really interested?"

"Actually, yes. I'm curious about you, I want to know more about the kind of people you have as friends and what your relationships have been like. It's a good way of sizing you up!"

Sounds like I'm a donor brain in his wicked laboratory. Should I be flattered by his interest? Be positive – yes I should be, but this is a period of my life I have already gone over in my head this week and I'm not keen to revisit it. I don't want him to pick up on my vulnerability or the fact that I was infatuated with Alan, still am to a degree or at least with the thought of him and the feelings I had then, I'm infatuated with the feelings of infatuation!

"Ok, so you indulged me, I suppose I can humour you. I was just fourteen or fifteen, Alan was a few years older than me, about eighteen in the Sixth Form, the age gap seems bigger at that tender age. Anyway, we had a summer romance then … 'The End'."

I zoom through the scenario announcing 'The End' with a certain *joie de vivre* as though I didn't have a care in the world in those days and hope that's the end of it.

"What happened?" he enquires with genuine interest.

"Not much." The pleading in my voice says 'please don't make me relive that episode of my life.'

I think he knows not to push it further. Sympathy! That's unexpected, but I have a feeling the subject will come up again.

"What about post-Alan, did you manage to transfer your obsession onto someone else? Did you rebound and relinquish your ardour onto another man?"

He's leaning forward now and I can feel his intensity handling me and squeezing for the answer.

How does he do that? How can he interpret my relationship with Alan from just one sentence? His observation is expressed in such a brutal forthright way but with such insight. I'm hypnotised into answering him and don't deny the infatuation.

"No. I settled eventually for an amenable, intelligent caring boy nearer my own age that I liked a lot. I adored him but unfortunately I didn't need or crave him, the pride I felt from him wanting me as a girlfriend out of all the girls that liked him was enough for a while. He was always around, quite popular, part of my extended circle of friends. We were together quite a long time but it ultimately fizzled out when he went to university."

"Were you a virgin when you started out with him?" His voice is low and keen and I feel compelled to answer all, be it with some reservation.

"Of course, I was only seventeen!"

Depending on who I impart this information to I'm usually either really proud of the fact or completely defensive; with him I'm divulging a simple fact to a sympathetic therapist.

"Why 'of course'? Many girls that age would have had some sexual activity or experience."

"I'm not 'many girls'!"

I'm sounding pompous but what I'm really trying to say without having to say it is I wanted to save myself for that perfect moment, not necessarily marriage but an absolute, unconflicting desire to be taken, knowing I have plenty to give someone!

"Did you have sex with Alan?"

"Why would I answer yes to being a virgin when I started to see Simon if I had already had it off with Alan?" my irritation on this subject is making me sound crass.

"I thought maybe you were lying about that and I could trip you up."

"Why would I lie? Surely if I'm going to fabricate anything it would be the opposite way around, not admitting I was completely immature and sexually unaware!"

"That would normally be the case. You're interesting to me, something new to me, a wisp of fresh air! I just wanted to test my instinct, it isn't meant to patronise or belittle you!"

"Look, I may not be a butterfly like Anna; delicate gorgeousness oozing sensuality and mystique. I think of myself more of a 'tiny unobtrusive midgey in a huge vat of ointment' – swishing around on my own and making a few distinguishable permanent waves which could possibly be noticed one day by someone who's looking!"

His silent speech bubble is this time filled with knowing and understanding and as its solid outer casing bumps around the walls without bursting, remaining intact, I somehow sense he's starting to get me, there's a permanence about this revelation.

On digesting this I remember our conversation and return to it,

"Going back to your original question, I can try and enlighten you as to why Alan and I didn't 'do it'. I sometimes regret not making myself more available, I wanted to know how he would have approached a physical relationship with me, being quite a bit younger than his previous girlfriends, but if he'd taken advantage and someone had found out he would probably have been prosecuted."

"Oh, of course, a minor?"

The way he says that almost sounds like he's accusing me of being immature and naïve.

"Yes, but I did have strong feelings for him, I may have been immature in some ways but I wanted him as much then and as passionately as any urges I have had in my adult life, probably more so. Maybe I would have been willing if he'd pushed hard enough."

"So what were your experiences with the boy after that, what was his name?"

"Simon."

"Did you want Simon in the same way?

"No, it was completely different. I was comfortable with him from the start, the first time we did it, and it was a first time for both of us, turned out to be incredibly awkward, not what I expected. It got better though and eventually we devised a method we were both happy with, not very passionate ... eh! We weren't very experimental. I'm pretty sure he wanted me but I simply didn't do it for him just as he didn't rock my world!"

"Didn't you connect with him on a higher level at all when you were intimate with each other?"

"I suppose not, I didn't let go completely. There was something holding me back so I couldn't surrender and let myself go wild, it was all a bit contrived if that makes sense. We did the deed and were satisfied with each other but there was something missing. At the time I didn't really understand."

He has listened and heard me!

"Mmmm."

I seem to be confirming something he recognises. He's rubbing his chin again and nodding in agreement.

"There have been a couple of reasonable physical relationships since then but the friendship, interest and understanding hasn't been there so none of them have lasted. It seems 'never the twain shall meet' for me."

I'm really into this by now and could carry on but I don't want to end up boring him to death.

He breaks the silence and the mood

"Sounds like you have a lot of catching up to do."

"I resent that, are you implying I have had no successful sexual relationships?"

"Yes!"

That deep authorative voice makes me feel like a little girl but I still have my common sense, there's no point lying. I almost want to laugh at his bluntness.

"Well you'd be right ... but I deplore the assumption."

He laughs and leans back.

"I think you will be a formidable lover for the right man."

My face must be glowing, someone is shining a high voltage light through it from the back like pressing your finger over a torch.

He stands up right in front of me.

"Where are you going?"

"Just stretching."

He towers above me and stretches his arms out to the sides. The resulting shape is that of an animal spreading itself out to intimidate the enemy.

He must be wearing a long coat, it's undone. When he lifts his arms high like that it brings the front panels out to each side and the image is powerful from my position. I am cowering in his eagle shadow.

"Would you mind not doing that, I'm finding it ... claustrophobic."

I sound sheepish but I can say what I want when there are no consequences. This small but significant freedom is liberating and addictive!

He apologises without sounding humiliated,

"Oh, I'm sorry!"

There is something powerful about a man who can reel back and apologise.

He immediately sits down and I can feel him trying to pick out my features. A slightly ominous silence follows while he gathers his coat onto his lap.

There's a tangible thickness to the air, a sweet syrupy heat, is this chemistry building between us – attraction – or some sort of awkwardness? – surely not, we barely know each other.

I hear him draw in a deep breath as though he's about to say something profound and then the sudden sound of the alarm makes me jump.

After composing myself I'm drawn back into the reality of my situation but don't feel uncomfortable anymore. I wanted to ask him about music and art, likes and dislikes but it's too late now.

"See you next time then, or not!" I announce with a grin.

He replies with a skip in his voice,

"Yes, can't wait to not see you next week."

I laugh.

"Better get your blindfold on, you don't want the Paisley wrath descending upon you."

I can hear the twist in his throat as he's moving round to complete the instruction he gave to me.

I come back questioning that statement with some confusion

"Well she said there was no problem with that... didn't she?"

"You really shouldn't believe everything she says, not only does Anna hide a lot behind that gorgeous façade but she has a short fuse too; a temper that makes the Incredible Hulk look like a child having a tantrum!"

He says this with some authority as though he knows her better than he should and my doubts about him come flooding back. He didn't need to use a measly excuse like the blindfold to reveal this opinion of her!

I had actually forgotten about the blindfold. I quickly grab around the top of the chair for the piece of cloth and tie it uneasily around my head.

"How do you know that, did you rub her up the wrong way or something?"

"You could say that, the first thing I asked her when we met was whether she was gay! Didn't go down too well. I think she overreacted."

That's a bit of a relief for me to hear but at the same time very disconcerting, it's a queer thing to say to someone on your first meeting. There's definitely more to him than meets the eye or 'lobe' in our case!

He could be incredibly insensitive and moronic or really good at reading people with a penchant for frankness. I prefer to think the latter, it goes with my understanding of him so far.

I'm still going to dismiss his opinion until I have evidence to the contrary.

"You didn't mention that the first time we talked about her, earlier when you said she was beautiful. Why do you assume she's a lesbian anyway?"

He is just about to answer when the door opens and I instinctively turn my head towards the faint brightness penetrating my mask, but before she enters I hear that smooth dark chocolate flow of whispering syllables,

"I'll tell you next time ..."

I instantly swing back around to him with a need to stay.

My voice breaks slightly as I reciprocate.

"Bye." Clearing my throat doesn't remove the obstruction at the back of my tongue. I haven't swallowed for a while and my mouth is dry, I need fresh air and a drink but I don't want to leave.

The next thing I know Anna is touching my shoulder, I shudder in surprise,

"Are you ok?" She sounds concerned.

"Fine." I lie.

I'm led out of the room and the door is closed behind me, closed to my newly discovered comfort zone. Quickly fumbling to remove the blindfold I am dazed by the light and feel ripped from safety and seclusion. I would never have believed I could respond to someone in this way. Is it him or the situation that's captured my imagination? I went into that room as though it were a coffin but now it feels more like a warm secure womb.

"Is that an hour gone already?"

"Yes," she replies enthused. "Did you lose sense of time?"

"I really did. I can't believe how quick that seemed." Those silent moments must have been longer than I thought!

"Come back to the office with me and we'll chat."

I stumble along behind Anna, slightly dumbfounded, and after sitting down she leaves me alone in the room to readjust in solitude for a few minutes.

I am really taken with this man, and I have no credible reason why.

At first I didn't like him but his honesty and mood swings became quite compelling along with his sultry hypnotic voice. I think there's more to his standoffish demeanour than his battle with women and the search for love. There seems to be more to his pain than that and I find this hidden depth attractive. And there's the matter of that extremely brief but very definite induced shudder – I can't ignore that. I mustn't get carried away; the circumstances we're in play a big part in our emotional reactions. Just get a grip and be pragmatic about it.

Anna returns and is pleased with how things went.

"That was excellent. You responded really well to each other; not totally at ease, arguing a little and confiding in each other as well as other things. I couldn't have hoped for a more varied range of emotions ... brilliant!"

Hearing our private conversation, responses and reactions dissected and trivialised like that feels demeaning but I have to remember this is the point of me being here.

"Yes, it's really strange don't you think?"

"No, I had the instinct you were going to be an interesting match and I wasn't wrong."

"Oh yes, this tormented, bitter damaged man is definitely a head turner, his mystery and bewitching supernature will charm me into oblivion if I'm not careful!"

I'm paradoxing myself here! I want to say he's entranced me in some magical/supernatural way and that I want to be affected by him but at the same time I'm sarcastically admitting he's put a spell on me, something unnatural and unwanted.

"Very enigmatic isn't he?" she admits reluctantly.

I don't want her opinion of him anymore, I don't want to think they know each other better than I do so I change the subject.

"So the first session was a success as far your concerned?"

"Well, I got lots of fluctuating readings. Obviously I can't discuss 'his' charts with you but I can tell you yours were off the scale to start with, especially when you weren't getting any reaction from him. Your perspiration levels went sky high towards the end, it will take me some time to tie up all the conversation with the highs and lows of all the readings."

She alternates her gaze between me and the reams of paper containing data and notes.

"Are your notes responses to our conversations or just facts and figures?"

"Both. Your whole conversation and silences are dissected and laid out like a script with asides and notes."

This makes me tense and I immediately lose my confidence, I hadn't thought of all this in quite such a clinical way, I wonder whether he's aware of the scrutiny.

"I am really happy with today although there was a point when I could tell there was some conversation going on but I couldn't hear the specifics, it was when you asked about his tattoo. What did he actually say, his voice was too low."

"Well really that's between him and me and if you couldn't hear well surely that's all part and parcel of the research." I blurt surprisingly with some defiance and glee.

She leans back in her chair with her hands pushed into her hair and sternly announces,

"That's your prerogative, I understand your reluctance to divulge a confidence but can I ask that you try and keep speech at a normal level so I don't miss anything, it's all confidential and I won't be discussing the content of your conversations with him or anyone else for that matter. A transcript of your conversations goes into my dissertation but you, the subjects will be anonymous. What you talk about is quite important to my research. I hope this isn't going to be a problem, after all, everything you say has to be linked with the readings etc., that's a given, do you get it?"

The sharp patronising inflection in her little voice has induced the first strong negative reaction I have had towards

Anna. I'm not happy with her tone but she is the one with ultimate power and I have to respect that.

"Sorry. Yes." I feel suitably reprimanded.

She changes the subject.

"Were there any problems, did it go how you expected?"

She gets up and comes over towards me then goes down on her haunches while putting her hands either side of me on the chair. 'His' opinion of Anna's sexual preference springs to mind but I mustn't start being uncomfortable around her so the idea is nudged out of my head just as quickly.

"It was actually enjoyable. I don't think nerves will be such a huge factor next time, surprisingly I feel quite relaxed about it now."

"Good."

She has already started to remove the strap and sensors without asking permission. Am I her property now? It occurs to me she will be doing the same with 'him' and I experience just the slightest fleeting pang of jealousy and fantasy.

"Although having said that, I will probably build up the nerves again over the coming week."

"I'd be worried if you didn't."

She stands up and demands, "Same time next week!"

"Yes."

That must be my cue to leave.

Anna escorts me from the premises and then goes back, I assume to debrief 'him'.

I so wish I was a fly on that wall, not just to see what this charismatic man looks like but to hear any thoughts on me.

When I get home I can't stop thinking about 'him'. The dark baritone voice with a whispering halo, his slow, definite movements; self-assured and powerful, but with grace and elegance. All this locked in with a searching and yearning.

His voice and mannerisms reminds me of Michael Fassbender but more imposing; sizing things up in a deliberate way, his voice very masculine but breaking occasionally in a light cool softness.

He's urgently looking for something in life and probably questioning everything around him but he's not desperate. I want to know more; how he thinks, what he likes. I realise I have only just started to scrape the surface.

As I sit on one of my fragmented pieces of furniture and look across this huge living room space *The Angel of the North* papier-mâché replica, merged on to a wall, the body between two windows and the wings reaching out either side over the top of each curtain pole, looms over me just as he did; powerful and provocative.

I put the CD player on not really caring what's on it at the moment – Zero 7 – 'Give it away' entrancing and moody, (which always makes me think of the wonderful but ill-fated Mark Speight from the kids TV art programme 'SMART' with his smiley faced brilliant talent – what a waste; I miss him!) followed by David Sylvian's dreamy 'Ink in the Well' and I am transported back to that sensory deprived but vivid moment when he stood up and I felt defenceless. I found that experience unnerving but so intoxicating.

I shiver with the memory and want to relive it. I go through the scene over and over and wonder what next week will bring. I'm enthralled and consumed by the anticipation.

Chapter 5

'he' touches Rachel

Saturday was a daze.

As I wake I thank goodness it's Sunday and I can look forward to having Jason round today to take my mind off things. Lots of escapism is exactly what I need to steer my thoughts away from 'him'.

My jaunt takes me higher than ever and today I make a new discovery, if I move my arms from the shoulders and keep them behind me, like rudders on a plane, I can become vertical and see above and below with no barriers or restrictions, the drawback is I stay static and rise no further.

My hair is still floating out to the sides, it's all around me, fluid. The fact that I'm now vertical seems to make no difference to the way gravity is affecting me.

I want to test whether my 'Jaunting' experiences are definitely real so I need to find a point of reference and observe anything out of the ordinary. I can then find out later if an event, no matter how insignificant, really happened the way I witnessed it.

It's Sunday and there's no one around so nothing of any note occurs. I'll have to try again next Saturday or choose a weekday to do this when there's more going on at this time of the morning. Choosing an evening or some other time to do this is pointless because I will never be as relaxed as I am in those waking moments when I jaunt naturally. I'm sure spontaneity has also got something to do with it – I just can't recreate serenity at will.

I can focus on getting higher today but just as I proceed by moving my arms back to my sides, I'm abruptly returned to my resting place. I forgot I'd set the alarm, I don't want to oversleep because its film club with Jason and he'll be here soon.

After changing into the soft comfort of my black velvet track suit and piling my hair loosely up into a band, all I'm really doing is trading in one pair of pyjamas for a fresher set, I double check the munchies and drinks, then go through my short-list of movies just to verify the order and make sure they all coordinate and complement each other.

I don't pretend to be a critic, I just know what I like and enjoy performances as much as storylines and cinematography.

I have a passion for popular culture, pop art and some mainstream stuff just as much as the brain nourishing, so called 'highbrow'! – one does not preclude the other. It's like diet – food and drink, 'everything in moderation' as they say, but letting yourself indulge every now and again is good for the soul.

In retrospect I probably over indulge on a regular basis but this sort of decadence doesn't have health issues. A psychiatrist may argue that point but I think despite my reliance on visual and audio crutches I'm on the brink of being normal – aren't I? I'm not a thief, I haven't turned to prostitution or drug use. I suppose thinking about what I haven't resorted to doesn't actually reveal any positives – a sobering thought! Anyway I like thinking about film, music and books, it gives me security.

I probably do immerse myself too much in fictional life, it may be a reflection of my state of mind – totally closed in – it probably only magnifies my bemused and fuddled version of survival, but surviving I am so that's a good thing!

As well as having appropriate food to go with each movie I decide which cocktail, hot beverage, wine or soft drink is appropriate. I like each film to have its own foodie associations!

Jason says I'm a bit anal about it all but what's the point of doing it half-heartedly, half the fun for me is the research and organisation. He goes to the same if not more elaborate lengths as me to organise his film club turns, but would never admit the outcome is deliberate. He insists it's all thrown together and just happens to have 'style and flow' – I let him continue with this dreamy version of himself. Whenever it's his turn he not only has his films 'coincidently' running in order of the year they were released or in order of sexiest male lead, I know exactly what sort of man gets his juices flowing, but also bakes a different, exotic and alcohol steeped gateau or creates gorgeous elaborate trifles with such pungent fumes that I get lightheaded just peering over them.

He also provides a different type of sparkling wine with each film course, sometimes champagne, along with hand-made chocolates and an assortment of tropical fruits. Jason always manages to come up with some new gourmet delight, I love having him as a friend!!!!!!!!

He indulges himself in every possible way in life and, as long as he includes me, how can I criticise him?

There is one thing that gets on my nerves though and that's his constant pausing in films to catch a freeze frame of an actor's facial expression when they're being particularly expressive, he thinks it's highly hilarious. It was funny the first couple of times but it does get wearing when it's almost every film we watch!

*

The list

1. *Inherit the Wind*
2. *The Goodbye Girl*
3. *It Happened One Night*
4. *Control*
5. *Lord of the Rings – Return of the King*
6. *The Odd Couple*

Inherit the Wind (the original 1960 version adapted from the play by Jerome Lawrence and Robert Edwin Lee) is a superb reflection of this period of movie making – intelligent, engrossing, thought provoking and highly entertaining as well as being a historical parody of the 1920's cultural reaction to McCarthyism and Creationism – it never gets tired and is still as fresh today as the day it was made in 1960 with all the same, relevant issues of today; a 'Court Room Drama' is always a good meaty way of losing yourself in someone else's life. It was a toss up between this, another good 'ole' black and white with Marlene Deitrich *Witness for the Prosecution* or the classic *12 Angry Men*.

The Goodbye Girl is a favourite because it always reminds me of my mum; she introduced me to Neil Simon in my early teens and I have loved everything by him since then. This for me is the best though and I can't wait to see Jason's reaction to what's got to be one of the best and funniest 'straight guy trying to be overtly gay' in filming history. Next time I may choose *Biloxi Blues* or *The Producers*.

'*It Happened One Night*' is a witty romantic comedy, fulfilling the brief of light and classic. The two main characters are played so deliciously that I salivate when watching them; yum can't wait to watch that again! I may choose *What's Up, Doc* next time also with a textured plot and rich performances, but it's a very different era, more in line with another juicy romantic comedy *Barefoot in the Park*. My choices one month invariably dictate the next month's selection. I should have chosen something more modern like *One Day* but when I remembered *It Happened* ... I just had to put it in.

Control – a gritty biographical drama, is one of those few films that makes me not cry but bawl my eyes out; I cry at quite a lot of films but this is different, not because it's sad but because it's so believable. The actors include one of my all-time favourite female British actors, Samantha Morton, who gives yet again another incredibly honest and beautifully soulful but simple performance. I could watch her continuously. I need say no more. Next time I will possibly choose another weepy bio., with no positive outcome, but again honest, having that 'stay with you for a while' factor – *Sid and Nancy* or *Prick up your Ears* about the much loved and tragic Joe Orton or perhaps something more uplifting and recent *Walk the Line*.

Lord of the Rings – Return of the King. It's not just the majesty, adventure and story that's good about this but the music that entrances me. Jason has never wanted to watch the really big block busters – 'I refuse to succumb to hype and money grabbing' – I will change his mind about that, there are a lot of well-crafted big budget films with substance and I will force him to watch them ALL! I may choose *Cyrano* with the intensely charismatic Gerard Depardieu next month, it amazes me that he hasn't seen it yet, or *Prometheus*, or *House of Flying Daggers* which is haunting and artistic as well as having the action and general big film appeal.

I know what he means though, we all have guilty pleasures and big 'Hollywood' style 'over the top' action movies are mine. Some of them are worth the hype but a lot are just big budgeted vehicles for actors, producers and directors.

The only films I've known him make an exception for and actually go and see at the cinema with relish that weren't advertised as 'Art House' or 'Indie' films were *Sex and the City* and *Slum Dog Millionaire*. He had to agree they were good, although strictly speaking 'Slum Dog' doesn't fall into that category but for Jason it did because of the hype – 'feel good factor movie of the year', it put him off but he's glad he 'forced himself'!

He's never seen the likes of *Harry Potter*, *Gladiator*, *Mamma Mia* (the extraordinarily long queue's put him off), or *Indiana Jones* or even older ones now shown on TV like *Star Wars*, *ET*, *Spartacus* or *The Vikings*.

Jason doesn't count musicals in the 'big budget' category and has therefore seen them all, every last one – how convenient!

We have discovered some mutual likes though, such as *Butch Cassidy and the Sundance Kid*, all the Spaghetti Westerns, *True Grit*, old and new versions, and *The*

Magnificent Seven along with *Kiss me Kate, Cabaret* and *On a Clear Day* – they are of course all out of the running for our film club lists.

Lastly *The Odd Couple* – another Neil Simon play which always makes me cry with laughter, it doesn't matter how many times I see it! It was a toss-up between that and *Life of Brian*, *The Wedding Singer* the latest sort of spoof *Star Trek Movie* or *Spinal Tap*; that would go nicely next time with the Martin Scorsese film '*Shine a Light*' which I love for all the bravado and 'old men getting it on' in the most decadent but sophisticated way – highly entertaining.

Considering Jason hasn't seen any of these films, I feel I have the enviable task of opening his eyes and teaching him what I see as necessary film intake for a more rounded movie education.

He has either lived a very sheltered life or a very mature discerning one. I'm not complaining though, I relish the opportunity each month of bringing something to him that he'll love and thank me for. I also enjoy his brutally frank 'what the hell was that…girl?' In a high-pitched cursory tone.

I have a long way to go in his instruction and I'm sure he feels the same about his choices for me. It's a match made in heaven – may the force be with us!

The morning goes to plan starting with a lovely breakfast of *Inherit the Wind* on toast with eggs and juice and continues right through the day until when we cuddle up to engross and gorge on a bottle of Pinot Noir and the rich aromatic *The Two Towers* – I'm completely absorbed in the mesmerizing grandness of it all when everything comes to a sudden holt! – It's 'him'… right in front of me and I feel like someone just threw a cricket ball at me and I didn't know it was heading my way until it hit me in the middle of my forehead.

I must have had a sharp intake of breath because Jason quickly whips his head round to look at me with the roundest eyes.

"Are you ok? You just stiffened like you've seen a ghost or something."

He looks at me closer moving round slightly.

"My God Rachel, your face is bright red!"

I can feel my face burning as I shout at him "FREEZE! Quick, stop, rewind!"

I'm panicking and barking orders like a woman possessed which I'm beginning to think is a distinct possibility!

"Ok, ok."

He fumbles for the remote.

He obliges and gets the disc back to the point I want.

"Stop, I mean pause it there will you?"

I'm calming down slightly and now intent on finding the frame that jolted me, with some modicum of decorum.

"Rach, it's usually me that does this. Well I'm sorry but that's not the funniest face I could find there was one earlier with that Wizard creature, I cou …"

I interrupt

"Shut up a minute Jason … that's not what I'm trying to see!"

I then realise I will have to tell him what it is I'm doing.

How do I explain that the rugged windswept face I'm staring at now with such blatant adoration, the character – Aragorn, not the actor (although of course he may well be that honourable and brave in life), with all his stoic courage and his powerful yet vulnerable handsomeness is the epitome of my engaging mystery shadow man or the idea of him anyway. The beacons have been lit and he sees the flames in the distance, his careworn face fills the screen with windswept hair and a promise of things to come – all mystery, hope, intelligence, majesty and strength is displayed. The back of my neck bristles and admiration overwhelms me. I like the idea of having this secret, something important and personal to me that no one else can attribute to my demeanour.

I'm taking in Jason's voice and understanding what he's saying but I can't physically respond, I'm too enthralled by the sudden immersion into 'him' again.

"Why are you acting so oddly?" Jason enquires with a genuine fascination in his voice that I've never before heard from him. I think it's the first time he's actually been intrigued by me.

I'm still glaring at the 2D visage as though I'm connecting mentally and having some sort of spiritual revelation, the face on the screen is a portal to my memories of 'him'.

"Rachel, where are you?"

Jason's voice spears my imaginary world like stabbing a knife into the seal of a jar of coffee, all the air is let in and my aromatic thoughts of 'him' seep out into his space.

I slowly turn to face him, shoulders slumped and what I suppose to Jason would appear to be completely glazed eyes.

"Hmmmm?" is my blank response.

He grabs my shoulders and shakes me.

"Snap out of it woman!"

'He's such a drama queen' I think as my mind comes back to reality, I can imagine his next step will be to slap me a bit and throw a glass of water in my face.

"Oh ... nowhere. Press 'play' again will you?"

I want to watch more and lose myself again. I don't want to talk or eat or drink, just melt into the screen and enjoy watching.

"No way girlie. What just happened?"

"He reminded me of someone, that's all, now give me the remote."

He hides it behind his back like a child hanging onto his beloved toy for dear life.

"Oh no, it was more than that, you turned to stone, well hot stone actually, well sort of lava encrusted rock really only ..."

I interrupt his insane rantings, he's as bad as me sometimes,

"Honestly Jason that's all it is, someone I knew years ago." Now I'm lying to him which is not good.

"You must have seen this film a thousand times, why react in such a powerful way now? Is there someone new in your life that you're not telling me about?"

Oh no, his face has lit up with that bright eyed and bushy tailed, 'I knew it' and 'Tell me all' look he is so good at camping up. He now knows I have a secret and I can't cover it up anymore. I could kick myself for the reveal. I can't bluff him like I can Roxanne.

"I can't tell you Jason, but as soon as the time comes you will be the second person in line to scoop up what's left of my spilled guts."

"Only the second, who's first?"

"Trust you to be more concerned by your social standing than by uncovering the only juicy secret I have ever had!" – serves him right for being shallow.

"Ok, I won't push you but you owe me one. I always tell you my juicy gossip before anyone else!"

I turn and look at him wide eyed,

"Yeah … but only because no one else is interested."

"Oh ye of little faith. I tell you first because you're a good listener. I could go to Roxanne you know." He retorts in a huff.

I burst into uncontrollable laughter and he joins in at the absurd notion of an outpouring to 'the shrew' and her actually being sympathetic. She's a good enough friend to not be insulted my opinion of her, she knows only too well what her failings are, anyway she likes our honesty. It works for us.

I hug him and we get back to the film but from then on I can think only of 'him'. I disguise it well, ooing and ahhing in all the right places.

*

The following week gets harder and harder to get through. Jason keeps giving me the evil eye and Roxanne questions every ounce of emotion I don't exude, I know she suspects something but for once is being tactful and leaving well alone.

Sarah keeps ringing and trying to wheedle info out of me but I am determined – she's flogging a 'Cheval Mort' *(a very delicious dark mild beer, made by a local female micro brewer, which I savour whenever available)*. I relish having this pinch of power over Sarah, her desperation to find out more about my escapade is a new concept for me and I'll make the most of it for a bit. I think she's enjoying the mystery as much as I am in providing her with it. I'll drink in as much of this glass of 'Cheval Mort' while I have the chance, breath in the aromas, swill it around my mouth for a bit and let it's treacle consistency trickle down the back of my throat, sticking slightly to the sides, until it gradually reaches its destination and then sits waiting to be absorbed! – I love having this secret that people want to know about, I have total control – not over the situation I'm in but over whom I decide to tell and what I want to reveal.

*

So after a week of secrecy, 'jaunting' and complete sensory overload my brain is at a heightened awareness and I'm finally at the point of satisfaction and manageable excitement I've been longing for. I hope I haven't built 'him' up too much only to be severely disappointed or maybe even disgusted with myself or 'him' for being so familiar last time. Why am I even thinking like that? This is clinical, meticulous research not a date!

I arrive at the college as before but as I walk into reception the anticipation and adrenalin drain away as the surge of nerves suddenly hit, the shock is like walking into glass doors; you think you're walking into open air but a force field abruptly stops you dead in your tracks and that split second of not knowing what just happened is disorientating, startling and highly embarrassing even if there's no one else around to witness it.

I don't even bother checking in with scarecrow girl and go straight to Anna's room.

We exchange our normal pleasantries and as she straps me up she reveals the plan for this session.

"This week your partner will be touching you but you mustn't reciprocate. This is an opportunity for me to analyse the readings when you are both in new territory, completely out of your comfort zone. Is that ok?" she sprightly requests as though she has just asked me to pass the salt!

Ironically she doesn't realise, that bland nondescript room and anonymous man are now my comfort zone.

My heart is pounding again and I can't tell whether it's from anticipation or the possibility of disappointment!

Sitting tentatively down in our vacuous chamber I remove the blindfold just like before, my bat sonar bounces around the room in the silence, trying to locate something to train my eyes on to.

As I sit wondering whether I will have to go through some elaborate ruse to get him to open up again, a deep thick grainy voice unpredictably kicks things off and requests my participation, he speaks,

"Hello, was it a good week for you?"

"Strange but ok, how about you?"

"Well, seeing how uncompromising truth seems to work for us, I have to say ... I couldn't stop thinking about you."

There's a tenderness there, a deep-rooted emotion rather than a throw away compliment.

My face starts a chain reaction through my body – the kind of instant burning heat you get from a hot plate. The thought that he has gone through seven days of his harem world but had a secret hideaway to consider me is both reassuring and annoying at the same time along with hearing him referring to our regulated unions as 'us'. I don't want to be just another notch on his score board – just because he considers me different from all the other women doesn't necessarily mean I am special. I must keep some decorum, be calm and normal. I don't want him to think I'm stupid, naïve and embarrassed like I'm sure Alan did.

I must try not to show too much emotion, but the harder I try, the more intense the attraction seems to get.

"I admit I went over our last meeting a few times and I saw a film where one of the actors made me think of you and has sort of put an image in my head now."

He leans towards me.

"Who?"

I lean toward him.

"I don't want to say." I murmur.

He leans in even closer now.

"Why not?" he whispers.

"I'm embarrassed and besides I don't want you to get big headed." I whisper breathlessly while moving in even more.

We must be almost nose to nose now and I have the strongest urge to lay my palms on his jaw line and split my fingers over his ears, just so I can feel the texture of his skin and the vibrations of his voice through the muscles and tendons.

I throw my voice into his ear, *"Are you aware that Anna can't hear what we say if we whisper?"*

"Yes, I think we'll have some secrets."

He pulls back and sits right back into his chair again, I'm bent so far forward that the sudden force of his movement creates a vacuum for a second and I almost fall forward.

He continues at normal volume

"He must be good-looking then, assuming you mean a male actor."

I laugh while straining myself back into position and blow out some air to try and aid the 'pull myself together' instruction.

He continues, "But you don't know, I may be more attractive than him."

"You're barking up the wrong tree, he's actually not all that handsome, it's the character he plays and you know costume and all the acting paraphernalia. It's his on screen presence that made me think of you."

"Oh." he says with some disquiet.

He doesn't push any more but I want him to. I would be more than happy to tell him who it is now if he really wants to know but I want to prolong the conversation a bit more and see if he can guess.

There is an uncomfortable silence and I'm not sure whether I have upset or annoyed him or whether he's just bored.

"Don't you want to know more?"

"No, I don't want to ruin your idea of me, let's just see how things go today shall we?"

I am more than surprised at his agitation and a little confused by his sudden withdrawal. Every time I think I have a handle on 'him' he gets irritated then says something that gives him a vulnerability, another dimension or sensitivity that jolts me. I think I like this mixture of vulnerability beneath a surface of strength, virility and composure, it's attractive and intriguing.

He then dryly announces, "I'm going to start the next part of the programme now, Anna wants me to 'feel about a bit' so hang onto your boots!" that makes me laugh … nervously. It was funny but also makes me feel awkward.

He takes time to compose himself, then remaining seated he leans across to me with his right arm outstretched. I can just make out his folded form, his head is now bent down.

He's not straining to see me and I suppose averting his head in order to cut out the natural need to visually attach his touch to his perception. Maybe this will help him focus better and concentrate his mind on my skin or material beneath his fingers.

It must be difficult to emotionally connect to someone from touch alone, the natural reaction is to look at the person your touching even if it's just purely into the eyes. Presuming I will have to do the same next week is a frightening but exciting revelation. Maybe I'll feel differently by the end of this session, I'm already so conflicted by him.

He doesn't speak.

His outstretched hand finds the side of my face and as the large palm, which is incredibly soft and cold, lands lightly and strokes down and forward, pushing under my hair, to the soft part of my neck, just under my jaw, my skin heats up.

It's absurd to feel this level of intensity from such a light touch especially from someone I hardly know.

I naturally and without hesitation lift my head slightly with a need for him to continue to the 'v' at my throat but instead he lifts his palm away. I jump a little as his fingertips continue a second later landing somewhere completely different.

He deliberately grazes the length of my nose with a finger light pinching motion from the bridge sliding under my nose to the philtrum, lingering a solitary probing digit above my top lip – I would never have thought of that part of my body as erogenous but I do now!

His finger then disappears again with a soft ghostly action that leaves an ectoplasmic sensation still connecting his fingertip to the top of my lip. Breaking the fragile viscous link with a quiet drop of vocal precipitation he asks, "Do you wear glasses at all?"

Eventually, after gulping down a frozen suspension of avidity, I answer him.

"Yes, how do you know that?"

"I could feel those little ridges, you know, indentations on the sides of your nose."

"How could you feel that, how can anyone have such a sensitive touch as that?" I say incredulously.

"Trust me! My training ensures that my finger tips are like a pair of eyes."

He says that with a smile in his voice and I imagine his eyes widening and an eyebrow lifting in that 'evil master' kind of way in an old horror film.

A clue to his profession, that's really interesting but I don't want to pursue or question that at the moment, I have more pressing things to concentrate on, his ability to hypnotise me through his fingers for example. I am now officially once again intrigued and affected by him.

This whole situation feels completely normal and not in the least bit awkward. Surely that's abnormal in itself?

He then hotches his chair forward, that high pitched scraping again – a metaphor for our constant scratching, chipping away at each other's personality making small inroads but big impressions.

As I sit there absorbing his presence just inches away, I'm sensing trepidation as he pauses. I'm sure he's wondering how to find me without touching me inappropriately. Now he's so close to me it will be harder to be careful, I let out a small suppressed laugh.

"Do I amuse you?" he mutters under his breath.

"Not at all!" I reply defensively, "it's just this situation suddenly seems so bizarre. I'm actually becoming quite consumed by all this but when I heard your chair move I became aware of the room again. I think ..."

He interrupts. "When you say 'all this' do you mean me?" he says lifting his head and towering closely over me while still seated.

I feel my face redden as I blush and wondering whether he can tell, I blurt out, "No! I mean everything, you know ... me, you, the room, Anna."

The lady doth protest, I can imagine him thinking.

There's quiet again while he decides what to do next and I just wait.

He bends forward again whilst regaining his composure and the air becomes sweet and thick, if treacle had fumes they would be pungent and heady like this.

There's a strong static current pulling between us as his fingertips instinctively reach and touch my bare elbow, I get a shock – at the very same moment I'm looking down to where I think his hand is and I'm sure I see a flash, he pulls away quickly then tries again. It happens once more so he carries on doing it like a child discovering all the different buttons on a new toy. I'm his personal 'Van der Graaf Generator' and he seems entranced, transfixed!

My agitation gets the better of me and I pull my arm away then he grabs my bare forearm with a firm grip to keep it there which takes me by surprise.

"Wait." He quietly demands.

Just as his voice breaks the silence, Joe Satriani's – 'Flying in a Blue Dream' starts to echo in my mind and infuse the thickness of the air. The volume increases in tune with the rising tension.

I gulp loudly as I freeze, he gradually slackens his grip and releases me slowly to then cup my elbow joint in his large hand. He continues by moving his now rigid straightened palm, so gently it hurts, grazing, almost not touching me along the length of my upper arm to my shoulder. His fingers land lightly and push deliberately under my capped sleeve where he stops and inquisitively feels around my shoulder in one well defined stroke. I'm light headed and absorbed in this act. That single deliberate movement of defiance then intimate curiosity is heart stopping and I inadvertently forget to breath.

He is in close proximity to me and I can hear his breathing just above my forehead getting shallower. I desperately want to reach up and feel the texture of the skin on the back of his hand – hands and wrists fascinate me; if a man interests me I always look at the wrists, hands and neck first – but then he removes it quickly as though he has read my thoughts and maybe in his own head he thinks he has gone too far.

"Why have you removed your hand?" I enquire softly with some disappointment in my voice.

He leans right back in his chair as though weighing me up and as he does so our knees touch. He pulls his left foot back towards him which makes his knee push further into mine, he keeps it there, a pang of coldness travels along my thigh. The sensuality in the small contact point is disconcerting and makes me feel nervous but at the same time the continued pressure on my knee cap feels comforting like applying pressure to an injury for relief,

"I was having thoughts I shouldn't."

His knee still touching mine starts to bounce up and down nervously, only a little but enough to be obvious and I'm not sure what to do.

I wouldn't have expected this from him. His self-assured confident demeanour has dominated but now his vulnerabilities are surfacing more and more, his deliberate self-control is failing him.

He leans forward again and the trembling stops. He puts a hand on each of my thighs, leans some of his weight on me and inclines his head round to the right side of mine so the barely protruding bristles at the bottom of his cheek are brushing the slight tiny unobtrusive hairs on me; I'm lightly velcroed to him and couldn't move even if I wanted to without there being an obvious friction.

Each large hand wraps securely but not tightly around the muscle just above my knee.

As he leans in close his lips are almost touching the top of my ear and he whispers, *"I dreamed about you last night... you were taking care of me, I wasn't ill, you were just a presence, moving around me doing everything for me that I would normally do for myself. You tied my shoelaces and meticulously combed my hair. You buckled my belt and strapped on my watch for me. You slowly and gently but firmly wet shaved me then carefully wiped my face with a warm soft flannel. It was vivid and strange especially when you asked me to let you take care of me until I was able to care for you."*

Goosebumps piggy back the electrolytes jostling and surfing the torrents of blood spreading from my legs upwards throughout my entire body, reaching every extremity, then to my shoulders and the top of my head, finally bouncing around in the gap between my brain and my cranium like I've plunged feet first into freezing cold water.

I immediately turn my head upward too quickly to the sound of his voice so the right side of my nose rests against his, he doesn't move.

His breath skims my ear, cutting through the torrent of music still piping out, spreads along my hair and dissolves through the roots; absorbing into my blood stream through my pores.

His silken words continue to pour into my ear, *"A stirring of care for you began last week the moment you started to explain your feelings of insignificance and how you were waiting for someone to notice you. You have made waves in my static conception of life. At this moment my next move would be to make time stand still and cling on to you for all I'm worth but that would be unethical and not the kind of touching Anna really means ... is it ...?"* his voice trails off, searching for a name, an identity to pour his feelings into – for some sort of reassurance.

I love that he can be humorous and show integrity when it would be easy to lose control; it makes him all the more appealing.

The possibility of a relationship is out of the question. We have to move on from this but for the moment I'm going to revel in the adulation, in response I'm going to let him know something small but vital!

"Rachel." I steal into his ear.

I've broken the rules but, just this once can't hurt.

He playfully tells me off.

"Of course you shouldn't have told me that."

This statement should ease the tension but curiously it only fuels the intensity.

We're static, frozen. He is leaning forward with his mouth hovering over my ear while I'm sat upright, arms at my side, my neck twisting my face towards his.

"I'm compelled to be intimate with you Rachel ... I need to stop myself ..."

There's something incredibly attractive about a powerful man with some detachment expressing a fundamental need like that and when he says my name like that I feel more real and acknowledged than at any time in my life.

The electricity between us is at heart-stopping strength and I feel like I'll combust if I don't touch him, but I have to restrain myself, I've already broken one rule.

My arms are still by my side, gripping the chair seat. If I just think about Anna and the most important thing to her I can resist. If I remember the reason why I'm able to feel like I do now and all the other positive things that have happened to me because of her I can see this through. It's like praying to God for help and promising something in return – I have to stay true to Anna!

I must know what he's thinking though, what his intentions are.

Without moving I try to control things with words, the only form of expression we can use with ease and to full advantage.

His jaw is still lightly brushing my cheek, the minutest distance between us, you would need a micrometre to measure it and even though we are completely still our breathing in and out is causing the slightest pulsating friction. It's taking every ounce of self-control to not relax and lean against him.

"I've already compromised Anna's research by giving you my name but, you can tell me ... tell me how you feel now, use that bold, and beautiful solid language you seem to have mastered to help me understand what you want in life, who you are."

He lays his cheek against mine softly with a fervent but restrained pressure and with a regulated, suppressing push moves his hands along my thighs to my hips.

"There's a burning inside me; intense heat – a chemical reaction changing my insides, it's painful, and frightening."

He then commands me, *"If you respond to me, reciprocate, you'll be responsible for my organs fusing, melting into an unusable mass."*

The fact he feels the same as me is overwhelmingly satisfying. The unrequited need for mutual attraction is frustrating and withers the soul!

We stay in this position for what seems only a moment in time, but I fear it's a huge chunk of our hour gone already.

His breath condenses on my cheek while I detect a burning sensation to my right temple. I deduce this to be his eyes desperately trying to locate some sort of image, searchlights trying to focus on a none existent point.

I feel hot and cold at the same time, needing his warmth and a coldness together to pacify me. His power wraps around me like a thermal cloak while he blows coolness on my forehead, fulfilling all requirements.

I can't stand the need for him to change his posture – the contact point, to shift his hands along my torso from where they are now, movement, 'anything' I'm screaming in my head.

Just as I think I will do something I'll regret, or more worryingly not regret, he speaks softly into my ear,

"I don't want to freak you out but... It's getting harder to control myself." The tension in his arms is causing slight shaking in his hands.

"I feel the same."

I want to just put my arms around him and soothe away the intensity of our situation. Despite my eagerness to have some sort of physical 'event' I now want to subdue and make him feel safe, in control again.

I seem to have dropped into the role of the strong counterpart, a totally alien concept but in this case it is the most natural solution to our predicament. I must tell him this,

"I…" the alarm goes.

He leans across me and I can smell just him, nothing artificial – earth. The coldness runs through me again.

He picks up the blindfold off the back of my chair, kneels down on the ground pushing his body into my knees and ties it around my head. His hands are so big but his long fingers articulate so delicately. Chills pass through me and I shiver uncontrollably; flu doesn't cause this amount of changes in body temperature!

He speaks with determination as he moves back into his seat.

"I'll be here, waiting for you next week!"

I'm deliberating about whether to take his face in my hands when Anna comes in. I'd completely lost all sense of time in the few seconds between the alarm going off and the door opening.

Anna leads me back to normality, portal to 'him' now closed, but I'm detached from reality, what I wouldn't give to Jaunt at this moment. As I'm thinking this the urge to fuse with my surroundings becomes almost uncontrollable and I'm having to fight the sensation.

My chest feels heavy as though something with immense strength is pulling me upward, my back is starting to arch in response and my focus is fading, a reflex is taking over making my head move back and eyes look up. I mustn't panic, I still don't know whether there's a physical change to my body when this happens.

I have to talk to Anna, feel negative, and focus on something worldly.

My voice sounds like someone else's, light and throaty but the pitch is low and robotic, as though I'm talking in slow motion, the urgency is obvious.

"Anna, those chairs in there are not at all comfortable, is there a chance of something more armchair like for next week?" Desperate but fast thinking!

I can see her face, focus on her eyes but still feel as though my head is tilting backwards.

She replies with visible concern. "Are you ok, you sound really weird."

"I feel a bit disorientated but I'm fine … really!"

My body's inner core, the emotion artery that links my organs to my soul is shrinking and returning to normal, I'm starting to feel anxious again and my limbs are becoming individual; no longer sublimely linked to each other or the environment, no longer working in sync. My spirit, the essence of me, is disconnecting from the earth – unbalanced, empty and alone again, an empty plastic cup teetering precariously and knocking against others on a bent metal tray.

I didn't realise how tense and disjointed I felt all the time until I started Jaunting and meeting with 'him', and there it is … my eureka moment!

I need to get home and think about everything, consider my life – 'him', Jaunting. What just happened to me and my standing on this planet, my purpose of being. There has to be a connection.

Anna's voice completes my transformation back to reality.

"I wondered whether you would wait around for a bit, after our debrief, and then go for a drink with me at the Wing again."

"I'd like that but I don't have enough time before my bus." My reply is flat and monotone

She's looking at me knowing there's no way around it but trying to think of a way to keep me here, her face is contorted and divided into sections of disappointment, coercion and submission

I can see she really needs to speak to me.

"What is it?"

Resigned, she sighs in dismay.

"It can wait. How about meeting me tomorrow like we did a couple of weeks ago. I really need to speak to you about something important."

"Ok I'll meet you in The Wing say 4 p.m.?"

Placated, she sighs in relief, "Great!"

I get home and on realising I am starving and haven't eaten all day. I fulfil the life preserving need to masticate and fill my stomach, then precariously press the play button on the CD player, using the same hand I'm holding my glass of wine, not caring whether I spill it or not.

I lay back and let the music Joe Satriani – 'Flying in a Blue Dream' transport me back to re-run this evening's events with 'him'. I want to analyse exactly what he did to me, how he affected me.

Certain aspects just go round and round like one of those looping *Groundhog Day* dreams.

While staring at the beautiful home-made non-asymmetrical, purely ornamental 'Plaster of Paris' fireplace – blended purples swirling into royal blue, washed over with orange and gold and accented with patches of deep red – Joe's resonating guitar mixes with the red wine in my head and brings to life our conversations and the moment he held onto me with such a firm gentleness.

The sensations that followed upwards to my neck and face were as though everything I had ever known with any man before that moment were no longer meaningful, it was a defining moment.

When I think back I should have been shocked when he grabbed my knees and used the whole length of my thighs to manoeuvre his body into position so that his head was next to mine. I wasn't remotely surprised or anxious by that, it felt right.

I don't even consider he was taking liberties, it was simply the next step, a natural course of action, a firm act to reinforce his words. And those words, his phrasing, it's so unusual. He talks in a poetic way that along with his rich tones makes you want to just listen to him talk all the time.

There must be a reason why he uses language with such authority.

Right now I just want to be back there and relive the moment, when our jaw lines hardly touched and his breath pulsed down my neck. I have never experienced such significant intensity from such a small insignificant act.

I didn't expect that I would actually start to need to be with him. This seems too strong a reaction after such little time together but I think I'm either falling for him or developing an incomprehensible crush. It's like the craving or obsession we get for a celebrity, someone we revere and find extremely attractive but know we can never meet or have – a fantasy.

The difference is I am actually getting a little taster, a piece of him, like the feelings I had with Alan except I'm older and wiser now and can keep check on myself. I'm more mature and in control; not so quick to show my adoration. I have the chance to get to know an idol with the knowledge I will always be a part of his history.

The flip side of that is I have deeper emotions and can interpret them better which makes me think this isn't just a crush or passing phase. Time will tell, we have lots of sessions to go yet.

I think about his profession. What on earth can it be? Large hands with a delicate touch, permanently cold but incredibly soft. His deft and ludicrously sensitive fingers. He said his occupation resulted in this unusual sensitivity. Maybe he's a surgeon or works in a dark room where your fingers are your eyes. Whatever it is it's produced a talent when it comes to women, maybe his mysterious personality reels them in and then this hidden talent secures them.

On a sensory level I wonder whether I would have felt the same if it had been anyone else doing these things to me under those conditions. My instinct tells me not, his personality intrigued me but I wasn't necessarily ready to be moved by him.

The thing I have to ask myself and recap on is 'what is the connection with 'him' and 'jaunting''? – There must be one. The most obvious comparison is the feeling of euphoria I have, a feeling of being where I should be – no limits, no trappings or reservations, but how can he and Jaunting be mutual. I'll have to see how the sessions go and question, analyse whatever transpires, if that is the case why did it start to happen before I met him, was it the impending meeting that connects 'him' with 'Jaunting', pre-ordained the day I read the advert? That would make this a supernatural and spiritual happening.

I may have to discuss my theory with Anna depending on how my relationship and the 'Jaunts' develop.

The other big question of course is should I discuss anything at all regarding my feelings towards 'him' with Anna would it be prudent for me to tell her in order to help with her research or should I keep these deeply personal responses to myself?

Maybe this is the sort of thing she wants to discuss with me anyway. Should I be completely honest or keep some things back. I need to sleep on this and think about my options.

Next Friday will be a test of character for me, subservience or domination?

Chapter 6

Rachel touches 'him'
Lunar revelations

We're together but not in our room of solitary shadows, 'Arlington Way' – Cerys Matthews is echoing around us in and out of hearing. Everything is moving in slow-motion as we casually walk around a large, spacious art gallery soaking up the richness of the colours and abundance of classic, decadent and modern imagery.

A larger than life chef with slow but overzealous, passionate arm movements and wild facial expressions is yelling and demonstrating an Italian cookery master class in one of the offshoot rooms, but he's totally inaudible like he's been muted by remote control. I can smell and taste the aromas wafting around us as we meander.

In the middle of this particularly grand room is a blacksmith forging an elaborate metal shape and the sounds and heat sparking from his hammer create a spectacular show infusing bitter sulphurous smoke with the sweet pungency of sweating onions, tomatoes, basil and olive oil.

We're holdings hands, but I'm not looking at him, I'm just glad to be mutualising all the senses we haven't before been able to experience together.

A giant green and blue translucent Dragonfly ratchets loudly past my ear and comes to rest on *The Kiss* (Gustav Klimt) right in front of us. Stopping to admire the beauty and tenderness of this oil painting allows me to experience a perfect moment in time with 'him'.

We don't speak, it isn't necessary. Sharing the stop motion illuminations around us provides all the communication of contentment and happiness we require – there's nothing that needs saying.

In the distance I hear the faint cry of a baby which breaks my sensory heaven. The urgent crying becomes repetitive and pulsating, more and more monotone and piercing and then I come out of the dream realising it's my alarm. Instead of being disappointed at being dragged from Utopia I hold onto the feeling of perfect serenity and I Jaunt through the building, leaving 'Arlington Way' whispering in the distance. I'm moving up towards the sun then as high into the blue atmosphere as is possible before being totally engulfed and surrounded by silent blackness, and as I look back the hazy stratosphere halos the Earth giving it a surreal iciness.

Next I'm dodging the debris that surrounds Earth … it's shocking! I've heard about Earth's orbit and how bad it is out here but I never imagined it was this cluttered. – It looks like a dredged riverbed bereft of water, left pitted with old prams, rusty shopping trolleys and holey boots, but instead up here in this vacuum it's expensive shiny bits of rockets, dysfunctional satellites and what looks like flattened panels and twisted clips.

I adeptly avoid the hazards and once free of all the rotating man-made chaos I'm struck by the intensity of the stars, they don't just sparkle, they pulsate and leave a shadow on my cornea. They're in much greater abundance than they appear from Earth, but have an energy all their own, an energy that seems to link them all together as though they have a spiritual awareness mutualising them. It's an incredibly powerful connection and I feel I belong with them.

I zoom with greater acceleration towards an ever growing spot lit grey ball which I then realise is our Moon and it takes me seconds to travel a distance that has taken the Apollo missions days to complete.

Circumnavigating the dried up tundra at light speed enables me to scrutinise everything on the lunar surface and to wonder at the beauty of the landscape. It reminds me of the barren and dry flat plains of Earth that I consider stunning and provocative in their own way.

The line known as the terminator where the light meets the dark, giving the moon that sliced off effect, disappears and I can see everything clearly for miles until I suddenly reach the dark side.

The baby is crying again but instead of bringing me back, this time I'm able to make the choice and stay, which is another area of control I seem to have developed therefore maintaining the feeling of serenity for longer periods. I decide to stay a little longer and will return the next time it screams for attention.

Whilst whizzing around the seas, valleys, mountains and craters experiencing the gift of flight and total freedom, something takes my eye.

Throwing my arms back to stop I turn over to take a better look – I'm pretty sure it's the American flag!

I turn back and with all my mental capabilities I move slowly down. I will need to practise my manoeuvres using the vastness of space to see whether I can hone these skills, find a better way of navigating and moving around.

Swinging my arms back and turning over in one swift movement I am now within arm's length of the famous Stars and Stripes. I'm expecting my heart rate to rapidly increase but instead the excitement I feel just magnifies my calm euphoria.

The flagpole is stuck into the lunar gravel but lying down just as popular belief would have it. Would I be playing with history, is it sacrilege to prop it back up?

I don't know if I can actually touch, feel or manipulate anything while in this state, it will be interesting to try and find out. Smiling to myself I decide to try and lift it, I reach out with a nervous hand and I'm surprised to see that the object of my desire actually moves towards me. The top of the flag touches my fingers and the pride of a nation and of the whole world hits me like the force and energy of a large crowd at a music festival – unified and synchronised in our adoration of the performance.

I carefully and steadily 'will' the pole solidly downward into the dust with love and determination and leave it standing unaided. Then there it is in all its simple evocative glory. Will anyone ever know? Will I ever tell anyone? I don't know but it doesn't matter, just having experienced this is enough for me – no one would believe me anyway.

The alarm's crying to be pacified again so I reluctantly try to remember why I need to return – getting up to get dressed, eating, washing clothes and shopping – mundane life; that's enough to bring me back to my bed.

I feel shivery and hyper, more insecure and alone than ever. Hopefully this is just the result of my intense journey and will not last. This side effect is probably a magnification of how I really feel all the time, except for when I'm with 'him' of course.

I get out of bed now on automatic pilot and remember that I'm meeting Anna today and need to get my thoughts straightened out.

Soaking up the atmosphere as I walk into 'The Wing Tavern' is a prerequisite in aiding my relaxation and as I walk up to the bar the barmaid says,

"Half a 'Jennings' isn't it?"

I'm impressed that after only one visit she remembers me and which beer I had last time. I was going to ask for the Mild, which you don't see that often but I don't want to disappoint her and want to keep the friendliness going.

Some people don't like being predictable when it comes to their drink but I like that 'treating you like you're one of the family' feel in a pub.

"Yes please. Thanks." I smile in appreciation, she smiles back then goes about her business.

I look around for Anna but she's not here yet so I seat myself comfortably and soak up the 'lost in time' atmosphere.

While I'm happily waiting for her, my worst nightmare pokes his head round the door and I nearly choke on my ale – Alan!

Luckily he doesn't see me. I automatically try to sink into the seat, if my head retracted any lower into my neck my shoulders would be level with my eye brows.

My heart is beating so hard that my body is pulsating against the back of the chair, why do I let him get to me like this, it's so frustrating that I can't control my emotions when I see him. I don't want to have anything to do with him ever again yet when he's there right in front of me my legs go to jelly and I would be putty in his hands.

If he sees me I'll just try to be nonchalant and breezy, something I've never managed to achieve yet with him.

Since the last time we briefly spoke, about four years ago (that's a lot of avoidance control and jumping into shop doorways), I've come a long way recently and hope my new found interests in life will give me the confidence to be dismissive if necessary.

I catch his eye and the grin that grows on his face is surprising; I have had the impression in the past that he was also practising spontaneous avoidance especially considering the way he dealt with me and cast me aside all those years ago, but then I have been clever in hiding and have never given him the opportunity to show how cunning he can be in avoiding me, perhaps I've misjudged him! That's stupid, he could have avoided me successfully and I wouldn't therefore know about it … stop ranting!

I look around just to ensure it's actually me he's smiling at and when I realise I'm all alone over this side of the room, my heart melts and tingling spreads throughout my body.

He walks over and I brace myself. He stands the other side of the table one hand confidently in his jeans pocket.

"God Rachel I haven't seen you in ages, you look amazing. Your twenties certainly agree with you."

He has always been so self-assured and easy with the chat up lines, but why now and why me?

"Hello Alan, is this one of your haunts?"

"Not really but it may be now."

There's relish and assumed mutual expectation in that sentence.

He sidles around the table and plonks himself way too close to me putting his pint on the beer mat as though he's staying a while.

It's a pity that such a womaniser and shallow character should also be intelligent and charismatic, how on earth does that work. He makes me feel nauseas and flattered at the same time.... where's the justice?

He's not all that good looking maybe even a little ugly in his 'pig-like' large features and 'waxwork perfect skin' way, but everything fits well together and oozes manliness and sexuality; he just lures you in.

I'm sure when Anna gets here she won't suffer him for long, she'll be able to see right through him and send him on his way.

"So Alan, what are you doing these days, happily settled down with adorable little Alannettes absorbing all your attention?" my scepticism shows through my lack of interest and my cocked head.

"Oh ... you've learned sarcasm, even more attractive."

Yuk!

I don't think I'm going to win here but I'm up for the challenge.

"I just thought if Miss Wonderful came along with all the right vital statistics and self-sufficient bank account, you'd hang up your spurs eventually, after all you must be a thirty something by now!"

Oooh, good blow. I know he's not quite thirty but I want to make it look like he appears older.

He looks at me and I know immediately what he's thinking, 'Gosh she's still bitter after all this time.' Not such a good blow then!

"Feisty! If I didn't know any better I'd say you still have a thing for me." He says flippantly while looking down and scooping up the condensation on the side of his glass. He then glances up sideways to read my reaction.

Since 'truth telling' seems to be my new order of the day I decide to lay it all out in the open. I lay my left hand securely on the table top to show how serious I am, but speak in a matter of fact soft tone,

"You broke my heart Alan! You were my first love, and of course that will always stick with me, there's nothing I can do to change that, but the way you broke my heart does have a lasting effect. It's not that I have a thing for you anymore, I have moved on, it's just been difficult to get over you, there is a scar but it doesn't affect my decisions anymore."

His expression completely changes, like he's seeing 'me' for the first time.

"I had no idea!"

"Well of course not, you were quite the experienced Romeo spreading yourself about, I was so young and naïve, it was a bad match from the beginning. It was bound to end in disaster and from my point of view it could actually have been a lot worse!"

To eventually get that off my chest is incredibly cathartic. I don't feel pathetic at all.

"Rachel," his head hangs down while he looks up at me with those doe eyes, "you're right!"

He then straightens his powerful, vein bulging neck and looks down at me in resignation,

"I was in the rugby team, learning to drink out of all proportion and full of testosterone, I'm amazed I didn't take advantage of you. You were different from all my other girlfriends. You were sweet, charming and honest, I couldn't resist just trying you, but then I realised it couldn't go on, the age gap, you were only fifteen, so I had to think of a way to 'ditch you' as they say. I was such a coward; I couldn't bear to see your face when I told you so I did what I did."

"Couldn't you have found a more humane way of putting me down? What you did was mortifying for a young innocent like me."

"I know it was cruel. I didn't realise it affected you that badly!"

"That's where your insensitivity and immaturity comes in. I think you thought you were all man at nineteen but you were still a boy really."

The silence while he looks into my eyes says it all. The genuine sorrow pouring from him now is not pitiful or guilt ridden as I had always imagined and hoped it would be in my perfect fantasy. There is a graceful contemplation and grown up acknowledgement.

The suspended moment and eye contact is broken suddenly by Anna's soft:

"Am I interrupting something?"

"Oh … no this is Alan, an old friend. Alan this is Anna, a new friend."

I clear my throat under my breath at calling him a friend as twenty minutes ago I would have called him 'the bastard that broke my heart'!

I notice her eyes widen, as I embarrassingly then recall my recorded and documented conversations with 'him' about Alan.

She leans over to shake his hand.

Unexpectedly he looks away from Anna which is amazing in itself, she's looking more stunning than ever, neat and shiny, right up his street.

"Could we meet again?" he requests with gusto.

I have to think quickly, Anna is stood right in front of me, scrutinising and judging my response. I don't know whether I want to see him again, once bitten twice shy.

"I'll be in here about the same time next week. We may bump into each other then if you're around." I say this nonchalantly – I might turn up, I haven't decided yet.

He gets up to leave and as he towers over Anna she looks up at him and kind of grimaces like she's about to devour him. Was that contempt or something else?

She shuffles up to me.

"He's not how I imagined at all, he's got something about him, a way with him, hasn't he?"

I look at her incredulously as she observes him across the room. He's now stood at the bar with his beer buddies, all quite intimidating huge rugby playing types but he's not looking at her, he's looking over his glass at me.

I look immediately back at Anna.

"Don't tell me you like him after one hand shake?"

"I don't know, it's weird, I know he's a bit of a lad and all that, I can tell just by looking at him with his gang of brutes and from what you've said in your sessions, but he definitely has the 'it' factor, and of course those bedroom eyes!"

Well that dispels the myth of any gay tendencies she may have but unfortunately creates some new ones!

My disbelief is hard to put into words and has completely overshadowed my own feelings of flattery and confusion from him asking to see me again. I change the subject.

"So what did you want to talk to me about?"

"Hang on a minute Rachel, tell me what happened between you two, I'm intrigued."

Now that I have exorcised my demons in regard to Alan I feel I can carry on with my therapy.

"At the end of the school summer holidays and six weeks of hanging from Alan's coat-tails I waited for him to phone. I would cut the hedge around our house every day hoping to see him walking along my street but the call didn't come and the hedge got smaller and smaller.

Eventually I had decided to go to see him at his house but before I got the chance I was in town with some friends when I overheard a group of older boys near us talking about Alan and saying 'He had this girl after him and he couldn't get rid of her. Whenever she went to his house she would stay for ages, it was never meant to be anything special. He was hiding out at all his friends' houses trying to avoid her.' – Then they all laughed.

He must have spread this around everyone he knew hoping it would filter through to me. It was almost too convenient that I overheard it"

"Rachel that's horrible, what did you do?"

"Absolutely nothing. I tried desperately to avoid him. He had already left school that summer anyway so it wasn't difficult. It was what went round my head afterwards that was so debilitating for a while. I hid away and cried every day for weeks at the embarrassment of throwing myself at him."

"Why are you talking to him now then?"

"It was unavoidable, he came over to me, but he seems to be genuinely sorry and it would appear he had ulterior motives for his actions that I was unaware of. Anyway it's the past and today has been good for me, it's sort of ended a chapter."

"Oh, good. How would you feel if I approached him?"

Anna's first failing finally shows itself; strange circumstances and timing!

Although I'm shocked by her request I'm also intrigued to see how things would transpire between them.

"Go ahead, he's nothing to do with me, he's yours if you want him."

"I don't know, I just want to get to know him, see what he's like for myself. I'm intrigued."

"Oh another experiment, be my guest."

She looks at me and we laugh.

I instruct her for a change.

"Make sure you're prepped though, you don't want to record false data and if he hurts you make sure you document it thoroughly for future reference."

She smiles then looks across at him but his gang have gone.

"Right," she says with authority "I want to talk to you about your sessions."

"Mmmm," I mutter while supping my ale pretending I haven't a clue what she wants to discuss.

"It's a delicate situation but I'm not going to beat about the bush."

She has my attention,

"I know there's something going on between you and your counterpart, I'll call him 'B' for arguments sake ..."

I interrupt, "Look Anna, I want you to ..."

She interrupts back, "It's ok, don't panic. I want there to be something going on!"

She pushes up my chin with her index finger in order to close my open mouth!

"The development of your relationship is one of the main reasons for this – my research, you're supposed to be natural together and follow your instincts – don't question what happens between you. What I want to remind you of though is that anonymity must remain between you so I can follow up at a later date. I get the feeling you're a bit 'too' much of a good match and I want to be assured by you that ultimately your reason for doing this is the same as mine and that you believe in the process."

Her words cut off my fuel supply and I hit earth with a speed and force that creates this crater I'm now rolling around in. I'm quivering childlike and alone in the centre, a solitary pitted ball. This ridged cavernous bowl surrounding me is the scar of guilt and embarrassment left over from letting my emotions outside the room take over from the purpose of my being with him inside the room. I'm back to square one with no confidence and all my old insecurities.

She's absolutely right! But how on earth am I supposed to let this relationship continue on its natural course without feeling the need to be with him in the outside world. This conundrum will cause me to combust unless something unforeseen unravels this complex knot.

"Yes, of course it's the same, I'm in this for the duration … please don't doubt me Anna. Your research and faith in me are completely safe. … Err … have you had this same conversation with him?" My coyness is a little too obvious, but then so is her reply,

"… Yes!"

She's obviously not going to divulge anything so I'm not going to pursue it further, although I'd love to know what his reaction was. I wonder whether they sat here in these same seats. The thought of him in a public place with other people around, courting this room, looking out at the same scene I'm taking in now is comforting.

*

I'm calmer at work the week following my chat with Anna; sort of numb and flatlined. It's not a horrible feeling just a 'slumped' resignation.

My friends leave me alone and for once we all get on with our work without any histrionics. At one point my team manager stands up and shouts over our heads:

"What's up with you lot, I can't stand the quiet and diligence, you're unnerving me. Shouldn't you be winding each other up or discussing your love lives or something!"

We all snigger then get back to work. It would seem my 'zombiandering' is having an effect on the demeanour of the whole floor!

'Jaunting' takes on a whole new dimension and after using 'time' to master my comings and goings without the use of an alarm, I've learned how to efficiently manoeuvre with grace and precision.

I can now stop and go quickly and monitor and control my speed. I can hover succinctly and have discovered an inner clock which I can use, accurate to the second, when needed.

I have jaunted through space, keeping within Earth's range, experiencing its beauty and vastness which is not at all intimidating and now that I feel I'm in reasonable control of flight, have made plans in my head to take a long journey around and eventually out of our galaxy to see what is out there. As a second thought I could also visit the amazing unexplored sectors of my own planet including the bottom of the sea. I need to mentally prepare myself for this though so will make the attempt in a couple of weeks when I have got to know 'him' better.

Now that I'm sure there is a link I will need to build up my power by absorbing 'him'! I know I'm meant to do this, it feels right, so I don't consider this action to be selfish. He says he's fed up of the leeches, but there's a difference between having the humanity sucked out of you and letting someone depend on you.

*

When I arrive at the college I am reminded it's my turn to do 'the touching' and assume the position for the now ritualistic placement of pads and wires.

I hope Anna doesn't notice the pounding from my heart while she's doing this. Trying to suppress the excitement is making me feel sick, if only I could feel two dimensional like I did at work this week.

I'm now sitting opposite him quietly.

"Hello," I say demurely and innocently … Silence.

"I saw Alan last week." I blurt out with an unintentional provocative sneer.

He replies, "Which doorway did you hide in? Nowhere embarrassing, I hope."

I can sense ridicule lurking beneath a wry smile – only what I deserve.

"I didn't do that, there was nowhere to go."

He shuffles forward, "What did you do?"

"I faced him, I was honest, he apologised and wants to see me again!"

The thick unfolding darkness acts as a conveyor and drops a dollop of vomit – directly into my lap.

"I hope you put him in his place or are you still as gullible and naïve as you were all those years ago?" – I put this down to his just acting out the stand off which now seems to be the norm at the beginning of our sessions, but If I didn't know any better I'd surmise a possessive undercurrent beneath this criticism.

Why did I start by telling him that anyway, maybe subconsciously I wanted to make him jealous? My intention was just to tell him something of interest, a situation I found myself in, which we had discussed before and that he could therefore relate to, something I was able to deal with in confidence, something attributable to him. It looks as though I've hit a nerve when really I wanted to flatter!

I won't go into the whole subject now maybe it'll come up again later and then I can tell him about his totally off the mark impression of Anna.

I dismiss his comment and change the subject.

"What did you do this week, see any films, listen to any good music?"

"I saw Lisa Hannigan play live at the beginning of the week then I played live, out of town, in my own band last night. I haven't been back long actually and I'm quite tired."

My immediate thought is that he has an artistic sensitive side I had never considered, for him to like Lisa Hannigan with her bohemian, poetic disposition is surprising, but it would go some way in accounting for his love of language.

"I had you down as more of a 'Metallica man."

"I like them and Led Zeppelin, etc. but I also like classical and folk stuff, obscure and indie – a bit of everything."

"I'm beginning to understand that. I know some of Lisa Hannigan's stuff, it's beautiful!"

I know I sound incredulous but why shouldn't he know he can fascinate me.

"What instrument do you play or are you vocals in your band?"

"I can't sing but I'm a competent saxophonist."

"You don't play guitar then?"

"No. I learned sax at an early age, played in the school band and continued it as a hobby, I couldn't leave it alone for some reason and now it's very important to me."

I am again surprised as this doesn't go with all the other strands of his personality, he's a paradox; he likes metal and folk music but plays a saxophone. Maybe he plays jazz then?

At this moment in time I am excited and desperate to know what he looks like.

As my eyes strain awkwardly into his darkness, Cerys Matthews' cleansing voice swishes around the room renewing my calm; the same song in my recent most vivid dream. I won't warn him of my next move, it can just happen.

Carefully and tentatively through the forced gloom I offer out my quivering hand trying to tempt a wary animal toward me. By the time I finally reach something it's as though he is the one who has been moving toward me. The length of time taken by the painfully slow advance of my reach is like the stealth of an electric train starting off and pulling away from the station without anyone realising it's moving.

The warm silicon skin covering his cheek bone holds no imperfections but then just below this mannequin feature is the beginning of a gradual real life bristling roughness. I like this show of a man; the reluctance to change flaws or the acceptance of not fighting nature tells you more about a person. He's a balanced mix of a statuesque Adonis and an unshaven Hercules! An elegant peaceful earthiness – it's all part of the charm.

It could just be he likes that brusque unkempt look but I prefer to think he just didn't have time to shave today – not vain. I may have the courage to ask him about that later. It then occurs to me that if ordinarily I'd seen this on a man I wouldn't have even noticed it, let alone question it. Exploring someone in this intricate way makes me query every little thing – lifestyle, choices and motivations.

I push my fingers beneath his heavy hair, which drapes velvety on the back of my hand, and along his mature side burns, he grabs my wrist – my spine loses its cord and is swiftly replaced with a gelatinous substance.

"This is really hard, you know, controlling the urge to touch you; don't torture me any more Rachel?" He pleads with some humour but with a strong meaningful inflection on 'torture'.

How does he expect the torturer to comply with this request? – This is torturous enough for me to have to do without any supposed acknowledgment.

I whisper back, *"An indication of how I felt last week. I'm sorry I can't make this any easier for you. I have a truth to tell you though, no pretences."* I brace myself … *"I've been thinking about this moment, about you a lot. I've been excited by the prospect of forming a picture of you in my mind; your face and hair, to help me project some sort of mental image of referral. I can't lie, it's been a powerful motivation for me all week. "*

I said it and it feels good to let him know. I don't want to be sly or deceptive about my feelings. I really don't think I have anything to fear with 'him'. I know it's all going to end and I know exactly when, so for once I can be in control if I want to.

His voice is thick and gritty.

"But Rachel, this is the crux of the matter. The way you just brushed your fingers along my face … that wasn't just a

field trip, it was more like digging for buried treasure! You're enjoying it too much! What does all this mean to you, I mean what do you think is going to happen?"

"Nothing! I don't think anything is going to happen. I'm following instructions as requested, but if I say or do something that affects you then you'll just have to 'deal' and get on with it. ..."

My voice inflects upward at the end then trails off like I really don't believe that last statement.

I instantly regret the defensive tone but it's too late.

He now takes the tone of the detached man he told me about before.

"I've told you about the effect you're having on me but I hope you don't think I'm trying to seduce you. All this ... it's not like me at all. Last week I admit I lost control a bit, you know... got carried away but that's all. I don't want you to think ..."

My interruption is harsh and I feel so angry with him now; it's difficult to whisper and demonstrate my contempt at the same time.

"Don't worry, you know you're reading far too much into this. If you don't want to hear about my feelings then simply don't pose those questions, besides I can't control how you perceive the way I touch you. I'm not trying to be sensual I'm trying to be detached. Maybe you should be questioning yourself, not me!"

My snideness has got the better of me because I'm hurt. He's cut me already and we're only just into the third session. I feel stupid! This all too confusing and difficult.

He breaks his silence, *"Sorry!"* – Emphatic!

He's been holding my wrist tightly this entire time but instead of now letting go he relaxes his grip and brings my fist up to his mouth and kisses the knuckle briskly but with intent. As he lets go tears form uncomfortably in my eyes but I don't let on that I'm withering inside from the futility of the tenderness.

So, back to square one and I now have the huge unbearable task of 'the laying on of hands' again. This man who, in the space of one minute, has managed to draw every kind of emotion from me but expects none.

I can sense that he has now tightened up as though bracing himself for impact.

Reaching out with both hands I grace his temples with faltering palms. Despite my reservations I'm going to continue with my initial plan of scanning his hair, which I feel is a fairly innocuous thing to do.

Anything I do now could be deemed by him as a potential seduction. I regret telling him my thoughts and won't make that mistake again. I'll try to keep it clinical and without emotion but I won't lie as I have already promised myself.

As I push my palms towards the back of his head fanning my fingers out through the depth of his hair, it's thick, soft and just above shoulder length, he shudders. I push right through to the back of his head so that my fingers entwine at the top of his neck. I've never before had the opportunity to run my fingers through longer hair on a man, I like the feel, gathering up the weight and plunging my fingers into the thick of it. It's wavy – a sort of messy, bouncy confusion of fibres – but I must be imagining it; surely you can't feel waves!

I surprise myself by this act. Even though I'm now irritated by him I'm still fascinated.

He's obviously taken aback by his own reaction to me doing this. He shakes his head and admits under his breath,

"Ok, everything I just said is bullshit!"

I stay in the same position which isn't easy, my arms are tiring but I don't want to start again, I'm frozen, not wanting to change the plan but I've been stopped in my tracks.

"Will you make up your mind – what do you want me to do, what do you want from me ... whoever you are?"

"'J'... call me 'J'."

"Well 'J', we can do this the hard way or make it easy on ourselves," I lean toward him keeping my hands clasped to his neck and take my whisper up a notch, *"What say you?"*

My ultimatum is clearly a turning point, I think he knows from now on it has to be honesty all the way or things are just going to get too difficult between us.

"Rachel, listen and listen well." He says keeping the gritty medieval theme going.

I can't deny my eagerness.

"You have my undivided attention."

My grip on his hair tightens but he keeps his hands wherever they are, securely by his side I think. I can't wait to hear this.

He speaks loudly, without concern.

"I suppose I just didn't want to admit to you or myself but I have also done nothing but think of you, and our time together, all week. I have actually not slept or eaten properly and to top it all I haven't been able to concentrate on my work. My career is everything to me and for the first time ever, I have made mistakes which in my profession can cost thousands. You could have cost someone a lot of money this week."

"What? Little old me! What on earth could I have possibly done to warrant such ludicrously wild behaviour from a cynic like you!"

I cannot believe I said that, it's as though some audacious side of me I didn't know I had has bubbled to the surface and my subconscious has taken over to try and lighten things. I'm torn between accepting he has feelings for me and not wanting to dig myself in too deep.

He lays his head into my shoulder nestling it perfectly into the round crevice between my neck and shoulder. As he breathes harder stemming the chuckling now gurgling in his throat, my bones act as a tuning fork against his vibrating throat and my compassion and passion for him bounce and resonate through me.

He's shaking his head slightly and I can read the submission; he's thinking we can't fight the obvious and must give in to the inevitable.

His breath billows down through my shirt past my chest and as the effect of that hits me he lifts his head.

I let go immediately resisting the temptation to now stretch my elastic fingers further up along the back of his head.

"Don't let go!" his breathy demand is almost too powerful to ignore but I must maintain control.

I flippantly bring our volume back to the correct level, to give Anna something to work on.

"Shall we start again?" Which doesn't seem such a bad idea to me.

"No," there's definitely the hint of frustration in his voice now, "but what made you want to start like that, it was pretty provocative for a shy woman like you." Anna will like that!

"I don't know, it just seemed the natural thing to do." He completely disregards all protocol and takes my hand by the wrist again but this time puts my finger tips to his mouth – he has bunched them up to form a posy and as he skims them across his closed mouth I can feel that wry smile again under the soft finger pads. I realise he has now totally relaxed and obviously wants me to know that.

He lets go and my hand just drops, all control has left me. I don't want to lose command of the situation so I decide to take matters into my own hands again.

I lift my right hand again to his face, whilst hutching my chair a little closer, our knees just brush against each other.

My index finger barely traces along his strong powerful jaw line down to the square chin. I guide my finger sideways gliding down under his very slightly stubbly chin to his Adam's apple. He lifts his head a little and I stop for a second to press all my fingers to the rise and feel him slowly gulp. The lump moves up and down just once, it's a very strong slow deliberate movement and my goose bumps spread faster and raise higher than ever. How can such a natural bodily function create such an intense response in me?

I continue down to his collar bone.

"Breathe," I order with a slightly patronising smile. He grunts and I can feel the embarrassment radiating out of him; the heat extracts defiantly through the pores in his neck. I sense this is an alien emotion for him.

Should I continue or give him a breather, the power is addictive especially with such a strong enigmatic man. I will push on, keep the momentum going.

I touch the neckline of his shirt. I can feel the gap between the collar and his neck, which is almost as sensual as the electricity I feel directly from touching his skin. There are just a couple of buttons open revealing the soft inverted 'v' at his throat, I keep a solitary fingertip in that well for a while.

Sliding the other hand along the left shoulder of his coat I decide to ask him to stand up. I now move with him keeping everything in place whilst standing up at the same time so I can judge the movement in his height. As he gradually raises himself to full potential, he is very tall – about six feet, my nose becomes level with my finger in the 'v' and the other hand resting on his shoulder is raised to my eyebrows.

My natural reflex is to move my left hand along the shoulder towards his throat then up his neck to the back of his head. I struggle to fight the urge realising it could be too much to handle at the moment, too near the knuckle. Instead I decide to explore his clothing to get more of a mental picture of his general appearance.

We are standing very close and again I'm super conscious of the oxygen between us and the attracting force; it's a magnetic field.

I slide my hand down his arm and can sense his discomfort at this action but my curiosity has got the better of me and I'm inquisitive as to the material and cut of his coat.

I find the cuff and then move my hand to the front of the coat where the buttons are and bring the other hand down to the same level. I bend my knees slightly while moving both hands down the front line of his coat right down to the hem, finding it is very long and soft, like wool or some natural fibre. Does he have 'Gothic' tendencies or the business man ethic? Could be either at the moment. Maybe he doesn't fall into any stereotype; he's been quite individual so far. Perhaps he just simply has style. I need to explore more to make a judgement on that.

I stand up straight again and I'm so close to his face that I can feel his warm breath on my fore head, I didn't realise I was quite this close, I must have swayed forward a little when I stood up again.

His breathing has become a little louder and more erratic.

"Just performing a simple act, feeling my clothes or just standing still right in front of me, it's like you've starved and gagged me then wafted my favourite food under my nose, cruel!"

This statement stops me abruptly. I seem to be getting under his skin which is an interesting thought but I don't want to speak, I just want to carry on and do things to him, see how far I can take it while satisfying my own curiosity.

I pinch the neckline of his shirt, pushing my elbows outward, with my fingers on the inside of the material – my thumbs downward. I follow the crease down to the first button accidentally touching his chest with my little finger. The skin is soft and makes the baby hairs bristle on the back of my neck.

Even though my touch is slight he makes a sudden move like 'jumping in your sleep' or shivering as though 'someone is walking over your grave' but he says nothing this time.

I continue, gently tracking with my finger, tracing the contour of his chest through to the smooth tight skin just underneath his shirt. My casualness is quite shocking. I don't know how long I have been doing this but on realising I'm now absent-mindedly 'caressing' him I quickly move my hand away.

He grabs my shoulders then quickly follows the length of my arms to the wrists and holds them both still down by my sides; our arms are in parallel and locked,

"Why did you do that?" His voice is quiet not angry like before but with genuine interest and an urgency for the answer.

"I wanted to see if I could."

Silence.

I continue, "It seemed like the right thing to do at the time, I really don't know, I was just trying to create a mental picture of you and strayed off course a little."

"If you hadn't stopped when you had I may have attempted something I've been trying desperately not to do for the last five minutes."

"What?" I really, really want to know, I want to hear him say something sensual to me, something provocative.

He replies softly, "Kiss you."

I try to hide my disappointment that he didn't follow through, and my preoccupation with the idea of him kissing me, by shrieking with a louder than intended contrived gasp of surprise and incredulation

"Oh!", so not very successfully I fear.

He continues, "So, anyway, what's your conclusion?"

"Uh!"

"Your residing overall picture of me." He says that with an underlying 'I know what you're thinking about'. He must know I'm imagining him attempting to kiss me; how embarrassing.

He lets go of my wrists and the image I'm trying so hard to conjure fizzles away. I feel like I've been detached from security, the umbilical has been severed and I'm suddenly deprived of oxygen.

Back to reality, if you can call this bizarre situation real,

"Ok. Well, you're obviously very tall with wavy hair and you're wearing a well-fitted shirt and long luxurious coat, don't know about your trousers … 'yet', but your clothes so far seem to be good quality and tailored; loose fitting coat for comfort maybe or are you making a particular statement? I don't know enough yet to work that out. You're unshaven either deliberately, or just didn't have time or you did shave this morning and it just grows really quickly. I seem to be affecting you in some way but still confused about that, I'm not sure enough of myself let alone try to work anyone else out."

"If I were a shy person I could understand my reaction to you, but as I'm not, *Rachel,* I am totally perplexed by the speechless idiot you seem to be turning me into … I just don't recognise myself."

My impertinent response to his self-clarification comes a little too easily.

"You say that like it's a bad thing!"

I know I'm looking straight up into his eyes, I'm sure his are staring straight into mine. I'm getting the strongest feeling of someone looking at me, that sinister uncomfortable feeling of being watched when you think you're alone, except in 'his' case it's warm and mellow. I can just make out the outline of his head, the lenses in my eyes must be straining at full capacity to try and look at him, to see him.

'Flying in a blue dream' starts to echo through my ears then surges around the room, it's so clear I wonder whether he can hear it, it continues …

The combination of his moody slow voice and attractive strange presence sends all my senses above the max – '11'! I have read about fictional swooning women but didn't think it actually happened.

Am I just another casualty or does he genuinely feel something for me? I'm going to show surrender too easily and must calm down.

I look down but feel his eyes still in the same place, a laser fixing the spot. The heat is pinpointed onto the side of my skull.

While the music swirls around us I return focus to his face. The back light is silhouetting his head and highlighting some of the long wayward hairs floating, effervescing in the gloom. The slow-motion effect is surreal and hypnotic, giving him a fantastical aura; a kinetic energy drawing me in.

I lift my hands to the top of his face to scrutinise his hairline. His rich locks sweep either side of his visage, clean, bold and complimentary. The thick waves cascade either side of him. There's no fringe but somehow his hair doesn't droop in front of his face, it's soft but messy.

I can't help smiling to myself, he reminds me of Colin Farrell. I saw him on some award ceremony on TV once and thought then how sexy that look was on someone like him. It can be very attractive on the right man.

"Are you smiling?" he dryly enquires as he straightens his head back to its centre of gravity.

My hands are still either side of his face while he asks and I can feel his strong jaw move while he speaks.

There's an unexpected intimacy in cradling the bones and muscle that produce vibration and communication, it makes me quickly move my hands away and I try to completely detach myself from him for a moment.

I ball my hands into fists and place them, with defiant pretension on my hips.

"You can't possibly tell!"

"I could feel it through your abnormally cold, deft fingers."

"How on earth do you do that?"

"I don't know, I just sensed it, if you had been slightly more heavy handed I wouldn't have read it, your touch is incredibly light and graceful." He pauses, "It's you, you're projecting yourself onto me. Hmm!"

He thinks for a while and I let him continue, I want to know what's coming next.

"I have to say though, it felt like you were mocking me."

"Complete opposite, I was just thinking how your hair reminded me of someone else I quite admire."

"Oh, another idol! Who?" now who's patronising?

"I'm not saying, but he's not an idol!"

"Well if I told you I was thinking of having my head shaved would you still smile?"

"Who's mocking now?"

"I don't mean to sound irritated. I was actually trying to infer that you might prefer men with longer hair. Besides that I'm just finding it difficult to accept compliments from you, if it was a compliment that is?"

"Sort of ..." my thoughts suddenly swerve and double take, "Why ... don't you want me to tell the truth? Don't you take kindly to criticism ... or compliments for that matter?"

"Of course I like compliments, and yes, I do admire good criticism – gives me something meaty to discuss. I'm desperately trying to not get carried away here though. *I accept there is something happening between us but I don't want to end up in the middle of something messy and irreversible.*"

"Look … I made a promise to Anna and I don't lie. This is the experiment! If it gets too much for you then use the code word and end it."

If I could see into his eyes I'm sure there would be a happy confusion.

"Are you scared of me for some reason?" I say with bravado.

"Yes I'm petrified of you; I don't want you to steal my innocence!" he replies with friendly sarcasm, "Of course I'm not scared of you. *It's not what you think, I just have a fear that something amazing is happening and that would be so sick knowing I will never be able to have a relationship with you.*"

I gently put my hands back to the same spot, before all the questions began, knowing he says what he needs to for Anna's benefit, and I adjust his hair so I can revolve my fingertips around his eyes and over his eyebrows.

His brow is furrowed as though permanently frowning, a tortured soul which would fit with the whole brooding, sceptical, questioning personality I have experienced so far. His puzzled expression is probably apt after his last statement which I now choose to ignore, if I take him too seriously I'll fall even deeper and I just can't have that!

The music comes to the foreground, snaking around us, bringing another presence to the room, a romantic ambience.

Mirroring my stretching digits on either side of his eyebrows I push against the grain to eventually meet my fingers in the middle at the bridge of his nose, I move them down the length of his ruler straight nose and come to rest, after sliding off the end, onto his top lip. Taking one hand away I explore his top lip with the length of my little finger. There's a ridge along the top giving it an extra well defined volume and as I brush along it, his lips part very slightly, the warm moist air heats my palm.

The tension in the gap between our bodies is clingy tight, heat sealed and vacuum packed and I have to fight the urge to press myself against him.

It's my turn to pull away and he lets out a sigh like the relief valve on an air bed when forcing out every last gasp of air.

His agonised relief is tangible. By the time his exhaled breath reaches me my racing pulse is beginning to slow, leaving me also deflated. I don't know how much more of this I can take!

He walks backward slightly knocking his chair a few inches, then leaning forward and putting his hands on his knees to support himself, in his dizziness, he declares, "My God, I thought I was a gonna' there."

I laugh almost hysterically and he starts sniggering as though we have just averted a major disaster and are now languishing in our survival skills whilst at the same time realising how near to the end we came.

"In light of your frailty is it wise to continue?" my sarcastic tone is supposed to lighten the atmosphere.

"Not at all, don't let my delicate condition deter your efforts. All the more reason to carry on breaking me down until I'm a blubbering fool. I'm sure there are more strange and scary tools in the chamber left for you to try."

His sarcasm hits the spot and I find it makes him even more attractive – it's that whole schoolgirl/schoolboy thing of not admitting you really like someone; the embarrassment makes you horrible to them instead in order to receive that much craved attention. Do we never grow out of juvenile antics or is there something inherently fundamental and primitive at work here.

He then gradually stands erect and statuesque above me, and with one determined step forward, stoops and whispers, *"I suspect this is only the tip of our ever growing and looming, picturesque but doom ridden iceberg. I can't wait to find what lies beneath it. That's what I'm good at!"*

His humour and reveal is diluted with an expectation and excitement that grabs my heart and squeezes it so that the pressure in the bulging bits press against my rib cage.

Is he trying to tell me something?

My retort surprises me.

"But I don't want to end up developing some sort of stereotypical passion fest, don't you think there's a lot more to us than that? This is something strange and unique. I want a closeness that's about how we are together not a 'make the most of it' scenario."

"But Rachel, humour aside, that's exactly what I'm trying to say. This is new for me and I can't deny it anymore... apart from one small chapter in my life a long time ago, this is an epic land mark. The strong mental and physical connection I already have with you is significantly more than I thought credible all those years ago."

Hearing his words so eloquently explain his feelings like that has created a fuzziness in me and I have to sit down. He pulls his seat right back up to mine and sits. He curls both my hands into a ball and completely surrounds them with his own.

Before he speaks again, which I can tell he's getting ready to do – I'm sure my senses are beginning to link with his. A psychic connection is forming, I ask him.

"Who was this woman?"

"She was a student and I fell for her as soon as I met her."

"Love at first sight?"

"Not exactly, no. I suppose it was your basic physical attraction to start with, but there was also an immediate familiarity like you have with a brother or sister – nothing mind blowing but the more we spoke the more I liked her and my consideration changed and matured; the attraction was no longer the need to be around her, it was her personality, a feeling of contentment. I began needing her opinions her thoughts and ideas or even just a look – it was like a drug. Before we had chance to get to know each other really well, intimately, she was whisked away from me. I will never know what could have happened and like you I don't want to talk about that particular episode in my life, suffice to say those feelings have never been experienced again until now and they were nothing compared to what is happening to me with you – the emotion and need that now packs my brain and my heart – if this is only the tip, as I suspect, who knows what lies beneath it all and where things could end up, what a thought."

His grip tightens on my hands and they now feel as though they're merging with his. I feel as though my whole body is going to gradually melt into him like the wax of a candle melting down the sides of itself to eventually blend and fix to the structure that supports it.

I push my fingers through the gap at the top of his balled hands; petals opening from the budded shape pushing the outer husks of green to the sides while it blooms. While pushing my fingers out I then grasp and hold his wrists and start to feel my way along his left arm.

I come upon an obstacle, a large chunky watch with a wide leather strap. Winding my long fingers around his strong wrist I so slowly move my palm over his thick warm leather watch strap and cool watch face. I can feel the ticking syncing with my pulse. One solitary finger apprehensively points up gliding along the pronounced vein on the underside of his forearm towards the soft virgin skin inside his elbow. I can sense his lungs filling with air but then he doesn't exhale for a while and I stay softly where I am until he relaxes again.

He is aesthetically pleasing to touch, a beautiful sculpture you just have to caress in some way, and while I'm doing this his breathing and movement react in tune with me; perfectly choreographed poignant moments in time. The ebb and flow between us is memorising.

I follow the line of soft tissue and then gradually twist up over his firm biceps and onto his hard, sturdy shoulder, the coat and shirt sleeve have concertinaed up with my hand to the top of his arm, the cuffs were undone, free and loose like the rest of his clothing. As my forearm slides along his upper arm the sleeve drops down over both our elbows' and I am now inside his clothing.

The smoothness of his shoulder keeps my fingers there wheeling around the muscular joint for a while. He moves his arm slightly, carrying mine with it. The rolling bones under his skin create little pockets and bulges of sinew. The power is gently harnessed reinforcing his subtlety and restraint like a tamed wild animal.

I spread my fingers as far as they will go trying to cover as much of the area as possible and lay my palm over his shoulder. I push along the expanse of skin that covers his shoulder blade but the limitation and constraint of his sleeve stops me.

I quickly glide my hand back down the full length of his arm, hastily bumping over his forearm and finally stumbling over his watch. I slow down and my finger tips are the last to leave via his.

We then sit in silence facing each other but with no contact. The sweetness of the air, which I have experienced before, is again thickening and surrounding us. This would be the moment in any normal relationship when the anticipation of a kiss would be the next natural emotion. It's getting harder to breathe through and I'm starting to feel sick, if he doesn't do something I think I'll collapse.

He pushes his chair back with such force that the excruciating sound clears the treacly fog and I can breathe again.

"I need some air." He gasps into the middle of the room but my emotions are tying up my vocal cords so I can't respond.

Finally after what seems an eternity I offer some instruction to guide us.

"Why don't you stay over there for a bit."

"Ok!"

We need a diversion, something else to talk about. The blankness in my brain makes me notice the rest of my organs and I'm suddenly hungry.

"What sort of food do you like?"

A subject that's quite close to my heart, and will hopefully take the edge off our current appetite for each other.

He gathers himself together and stands upright.

After a long pause he answers, "Well … I like most food really but I suppose my favourite sort of thing if I'm cooking at home is a roast, a good quality joint of meat, with roast vegetables in olive oil and washed down with a good wine."

My voice is low and sultry, languishing in his procured images. I can smell the caramelised roasted potatoes bubbling in the juices from the joint

"I'm salivating for it…" I pause then quickly realise what I've said. "I mean for your meat and veg…" oh no, "I mean dinner!"

I know deep down I really did mean how it sounded in the first place!

He gusts out a short relieved laugh under his breath and then crouches on his haunches.

Even talking about food is sensual with him, I continue.

"What about afters?" The short silence infers innuendo, yet again. I can almost see a raised eyebrow "… I mean pudding, what sort of pudding do you like?"

"It's ok, I know what you meant. I'm not a big pudding person but if it was offered I'd go for something chocolaty I suppose."

The beeper goes and my heart sinks, there's so much more to do yet and to talk about!

He swiftly moves back over to his chair but seems to be searching about on the floor.

"Have you lost something?" I enquire while trying to find my blindfold.

"Yes, the cloth has fallen off my chair and I was hoping to speak to you again before you leave."

I can infer from the frustration in his voice that he means he wants to whisper something so I swiftly complete tying mine and carefully crawl over towards him on all fours then kneel next to him.

I enquire urgently, *"What did you want to say to me?"*

After quickly tying his own blindfold he goes down on one knee, resting his left arm across the other knee and pushes my hair away from my shoulders; he wraps his now hot right hand around the side of my neck to hold me gently but securely in place whilst clearly and brightly whispering in my left ear,

"This isn't going to sound too eloquent or elegant in the time I have, but to put it succinctly … I sincerely believe that I

belong with you, I'm yours Rachel, do whatever you think is right with that information."

He lets go and from the way he abruptly moves back, I'm able to continue his statement, with that flippant passing on of information, in my head. 'There it is, I've said my piece and now I'm off, see ya!' leaving me to deal with this startling revelation on my own.

I stand and stumble backwards to my chair just in time for Anna to open the door and shed unwanted light on my wonderfully elated confusion.

He knows by now that I'm devoted to keeping our confidence with Anna and he's not going to ruin that for me. He's leaving me to make the decision whether to carry on being Anna's subject or finish it and possibly have a life with him.

It's too soon to make that decision but I sort of admire his respect for my loyalty to Anna. I can't believe how strong I'm being about that principal considering this could be the man of my dreams, perhaps the man I'm supposed to be with!

*

That night in the bath whilst absorbing 'Be Here Now' – Ray LaMontagne along with the dry white wine lapping a tall champagne flute, I lay back and become subservient to the reassuring lukewarm, almost cold water. I don't like a hot bath – it dissipates the calm and makes the whole experience for me more of an intense cleansing sprint than a cause for relaxation.

The water laps over my emotions and disperses them around me, down to the depths of a spectacular sky-blue moulded bath with bulky, clumsy, oversized silver taps – part of the twenties chic bathroom suite with art deco patterns, still going strong in this time warp house. The glamorous exciting vogue of the 1920s.

Ordinarily this combination of strong colours in a bathroom would be garish but the authenticity of the original mouldings, desperately in need of a touch up, creates a beautiful memoir of a bygone age.

All the tiles are lilac with Rennie Mackintosh patterned inlays, completely embracing the bathroom in a gliding sweep of luxury. The large round mirror over the wide oyster shell sink is surrounded with a robust multi-coloured metallic mosaic frame and reflects the oversized tiered ceiling lamp all around the room. The lamp isn't switched on but the luminescence of the mother of pearl layers gives off its own energy, a misty soft white aura.

I sometimes lay in here with the lights off and only a couple of lavender candles, smells of a time lost, flickering light around the reflective surfaces.

The silvery mosaic pieces on the mirror send a white light bouncing around the room while the rippling of the bath water reflects from the mirror onto the ceiling. The whole room becomes a shimmer of silver purple and blue.

I love to relax in here surrounded by another age, and copious amounts of bubbles, reading Nancy Mitford's 'The Pursuit of Love';

We gazed and gazed, hoping thus, in some magical way, to make ourselves feel less peculiar. Presently we did a little work with damp handkerchiefs, and toned our faces down a bit. We then sallied forth into the street, looking at ourselves in every shop window that we passed. (I have often noticed that when women look at themselves in every refection, and take furtive peeps into their hand looking-glasses, it is hardly ever, as is generally supposed, from vanity, but much more often from feeling that all is not quite as it should be.)

I love this passage. I wish I had read this as a girl to use as ammunition when a particularly matronly and bullish English teacher once asked for examples of situations of feeling insecure; I drew on all my courage, stuck my hand in the air and offered my – 'continuously looking in shop windows at my reflection when in town' – synopsis.

She immediately retorted, 'No, Rachel, that is vanity and quite the opposite', and moved onto someone else. I was left shell-shocked trying to think of some way to tell her she'd got it all wrong and to not leave my peers thinking I was shallow and full of myself. That moment has never left me but reading this passage always makes me smile about it rather than agonise over something that should be long forgotten.

At this moment I have the need to put myself in a faraway place – to relive my day in a dreamlike state.

I want to know everything about 'him', get inside his head but at the same time I want him to remain 'the unknown' – a mystical creature in a fairy-tale.

I have never wanted to root around inside a man's brain, normally it's more exciting to retain the mystery but in 'his' case I'm compelled to delve. I want to know his opinion on things, to question his outlook on life and discover his past. It's frightening and exhilarating, the thought of discovering something questionable or heroic about him. What is it in his life that has made him the man he is now – this virile and slightly intimidating, thoughtful, troubled man?

I'm inquisitive and hungry for knowledge. I want to read him like a book and learn, to be taken on an emotional journey of highs and lows with an interesting and surprising conclusion.

I may be fooling myself but who knows what the future holds? I know we have rules, a lot more than most couples but no one's future can be set, even with our debilitating constraints.

If Anna is our God, creating an environment suitable for habitation and dictating the conditions, then free will is quite rightly a liberty that's ours to immerse ourselves in and enjoy, even under scrutiny. The importance of our own decision making – impulse and spontaneity is imperative whether we're right or wrong in what we say or do. It is only now that I realise that this is the essence of Anna's interest.

While drying my prune-like over-soaked body and dressing in cosy radiator warmed pyjamas I absentmindedly think back to the debrief, only a couple of hours ago.

The strangeness of that encounter enhances the surreal life I seem to have at the moment. Anna sat me down and instead of the usual dismantling procedure she just stared at me. Her piercing eyes burrowed through my eyeballs and the homing device in her brain searched for something in mine.

My head started to pound immediately and I couldn't speak. She probed my mind, seeking to unlock secrets and ideas. I couldn't have that, even though the thought she can read minds is insane, so I tried to physically block the intrusion. I closed my eyes and thought about work. I floated around my office building, mapping the rooms, shelves, cupboards and desks, anything bland and non-descript to frustrate her. She then suddenly stood up and abruptly demanded I leave.

I left the college that night confused and dazed but still heady from the events in that room.

Falling asleep tonight I feel like I'm in a soap opera, drama, comedy, romance – my life could take any turn and the new characters walking on set could be permanent or just passing through.

Three weeks ago I lived a two dimensional life within a multitonal world and now I have so much to think about based on a room with no depth or colour at all.

My life is turning upside down and I have no idea which direction it's going to take … I think I like it!

Chapter 7

Which planet next?
'The Kiss'

I'm dodging heavenly bodies with immeasurable, adrenaline-fuelled speed, they've become annoying obstacles in the road.

I must now be millions if not billions of light years from home.

I'm drugged on the heady euphoria of flying with no end in sight, sometimes a wonderful experience can be marred by its impending end.

I can enjoy this episode 'in the now' and not worry about the next thing I'm supposed to do. There is no end to the universe and I can keep going for eternity if I want to. This inconsequence of time and abandonment of limits is pure and without flaws, it feels like those brief gelatinous moments of expectation before the solid disappointment sets in.

A planet catches my eye, I don't know what it is, I'm in another galaxy and I'm not an astronomer. I doubt whether scientists have actually explored this far!

A fine mist surrounds this stunningly beautiful planet. The atmosphere is warm and moist like a steam room. 'Mistoph' springs to mind immediately and seems an appropriate name for it!

Mistoph is the approximate size of Earth and is completely covered in hills and mountains, no flat terrain at all, with the occasional waterfall whose lake at the bottom seems to go nowhere.

The only sign of life is a fine jade green moss with an aqua and turquoise sheen, depending on the angle of light, that covers everything.

A very distant sun gives the sky a red and purple dusky light effect as though it is on the verge of setting but never does. Tiny puffball spores are highlighted in the air like dust caught in the evening suns indoor haze. I'll have to make many return visits to see if this is a normal everyday occurrence here.

I think this particular planet will become a special place for me, a place for contemplation and to let go of my emotions. There is something engaging and magical about it, as though it can absorb all negative vibes and enhance the good ones. It seems to be doing something to manipulate me so that I feel even more euphoric and transcendent.

The strange beauty of this place reminds me of the mythical lands in fairy tales, if only I could photograph it.

By the time I return home to the landing platform that is my bed, it's later than I would normally wake at the weekend and I feel exhausted. I know I have been gone for what my body clock is telling me is the equivalent of many hours, maybe fifty to sixty but on Earth that equates to a small amount of time, about one hour! I'm no scientist – all I know is hours, minutes and seconds aren't a factor in comparison with Earth, it seems to be the speed with which I'm travelling that gives me the advantage over time.

I feel as though I've just run a marathon, heaviness and tingling in my limbs, then realise how hungry and thirsty I am.

Whilst having a late breakfast and going back over my journey, 'J' pops into my head and my stomach turns while a cold chill passes through my entire body. It takes my breath away like smashing your knuckles on something hard, stubbing your toe or activating your funny bone, but without all the pain and nausea.

For the first time in my life I have a strong passionate want, an 'erotic episode' – it's a need of fulfilment from 'him'!

I can't eat any more. I suddenly have the most steadfast hunger for 'him'. This feeling has hit me so hard, I need to quickly get dressed and get outside, go somewhere, do something to distract myself.

After wandering aimlessly for hours I seem to end up at the Wing Tavern. Unbeknown to me, the last Saturday of every month is open mike afternoon for local bands. Today its Paralex, an indie metal/rock band with mild progressive undertones. How apt – an extension of my current inner conflict.

I'm sitting here completely overcome with every kind of emotion, leaving my home hasn't rid me of tension, and I feel vulnerable!

'What am I doing here?' and just as I am about to leave to try and find a retail diversion in the town centre – *there's nothing erotic about shopping unless you're in an 'Anne Summers' boutique; although the state I'm in now the veg counter in the supermarket could be rather appealing! These thoughts are completely alien to me, more in keeping with Roxane's behaviour; maybe I should also explore this side of me along with anger and even exploit it a little, this notion makes me even more excited – I'm almost out of control –* I notice Alan at the far side of the crowded bar!

This is not good; he could sense the sexual frustration of a self-inflicted celibate sex addict from a mile away! I have to leave before he sees me, he's so good at creating something meaningful from nothing, but … it's too late!

He has seen me and is peering across the room. Had he noticed me already and was waiting for eye contact? He doesn't move, just stares. I know he knows I've seen him, our eyes are locked. If I look away it will be obvious I want to avoid eye contact which could tell him many things. If I continue to hold his stare he'll think I'm interested. What to do?

I want 'him' not him, but I can't control this mass exodus of pheromones from my body and if he even just brushes against me or shows the slightest sign of interest in me … I might not be able to hold back. I really don't know what will happen.

Would it be so wrong to utilise Alan, if seduction is his plan, just for the experience, it's not as though 'J' and I are going anywhere or am I just making excuses, would I really ultimately be betraying 'J'?

He puts his empty glass down and looks toward the barmaid, this is my opportunity to escape but I'm frozen. He picks up a newly poured pint then pushing and excusing his way through the crowd he strides towards me straight faced and determined. It's only now that I think of Anna and her interest in him and that helps to dampen my ardour ... for the time being.

It then occurs to me that Anna has control over my thoughts and actions on both the men in my life!

"All alone? ... Can I join you?"

The band Paralex starts playing 'Lionheart' but they're in another room so the sound just whispers suggestively around us.

"I saw your friend in here during the week and we've arranged a date next week." He says.

"Oh." I'm taken by surprise.

"I think we've clicked. She's unusual isn't she?"

"Yes. She's very intelligent you know and intuitive." That doesn't seem to put him off, he still has his Cheshire cat smile, "and rich and beautiful of course. Did she tell you anything about our relationship?"

"She just mentioned that you hadn't known each other very long but that you got on instantly as soon as you met."

"That's about right." I'm relieved that she didn't divulge anything. The least he knows about my private life the better, less ammunition.

"I have to say that despite being drawn to Anna for reasons other than her looks which is a revelation to me, I have an ulterior motive for getting to know her better."

"And what's that, Alan?" I say with a tone of 'Oh yeah, we all know what your ulterior motives usually are!'

"So I can get closer to you."

His blue eyes look deeply into me, and for a split second my heart just stops beating and moves elsewhere to allow my somersaulting stomach to take over then return to its position.

His confidence is memorising, it grabs hold of all my insecurities and flippantly throws them over his shoulder, that's how he kidnapped me the first time but then I developed Stockholm Syndrome and I've been his ever since.

"Anyway, you don't usually need a reason to get someone into bed. What are you doing?"

"I'm trying to obtain you!" he says in that matter of fact throw away style of his. How does he have the nerve to say things like that to people, I can't help admiring as well as loath his sexual ego.

"Oh, how succinctly put, I suppose you think I'm just going to let you do that?"

"On the contrary. I'm looking forward to the fight, the challenge will be life affirming. You're a worthwhile prize Rachel."

He's the 'Columbo' of seduction. He just puts all this rhetoric out there in black and white then waits for his subject to betray themselves.

His language is so intimidating – there's no answer to that and as I try to keep my lust hidden from him and think of a suitable repost he gets up to leave.

"So round one doesn't start now then!" I say rhetorically.

"The fact that you just asked me that question means I've won that one already, roll on round two. I'll be seeing you."

If my jaw dropped any lower it would be dredging the lunchtime crisps and pork scratchings off the floor.

I'm thankful he has left, a short term reprieve for me, but the long term implications are massive.

Unfortunately now my craving for physical contact is worse. I need some female company to bring me back down to earth – Jason isn't an option this weekend, he's off on one of his manhunts. The previous rejection has made him hungry for revenge, to inflict ecstasy; pity the poor innocent he will dazzle, tease then drop!

Sarah would be my best bet but she's too far away for such short notice, I haven't seen my sister Kathryn for such a long time, now would be the ideal opportunity to get together.

I ring Kathryn on my mobile, mindful of her reserved attitude and ask if she would meet me here. I can tell from her reply she's not happy about coming to a pub but for once I don't back down and I instruct her to be here in the next thirty minutes.

Her introverted arrival makes her conspicuous. Nothing says, 'Here I am – stare at me as though I'm the most wondrous thing you've ever seen', more than a sheepishly slow entrance in a residential public house; it has the opposite effect and gives her a captive audience that watches like she's Gloria Swanson sweeping down the stairs in *Sunset Boulevard*. The speech bubble above her head says, 'I'm ready for my close up Mr DeMille!'

That image makes me smile, the irony is satisfying. This is one of the few places I can feel a little superior for a change, she dominates me to an annoying level which is frustrating for me as the older sister. Despite our differences though, I know I can rely on her to be around if necessary, and vice versa.

"You enjoyed that didn't you," she vehemently spouts while sidling next to me for security. She throws her long blonde hair violently from the front of her shoulders to the back.

"What do you mean?" I enquire understanding perfectly well, but wanting to hear the answer; the winding mechanism is working very well today even though it hasn't been used for a while!

"You know, making me push my way through the sort of people that make me uneasy."

My invisible metaphoric arm is now rotating and winding so fast I fear it may disconnect from my shoulder!

"And what sort of people are they?"

"Lazy and drunk." And there it is laid out for all to see.

"Thanks Kathryn. I am, 'this sort of people'; you're such a snob."

"I don't deny it … yes I am a snob, it's helped my career no end and given me the lifestyle I always dreamed of. It's got me somewhere and I'm not going to make excuses!"

She pontificates this flat explanation but I know deep down she doesn't really believe it, she is, however, using the opportunity to have a dig at me and my 'wasted life'.

"Anyway," she enquires, "why am I here?"

With secret glee that's hard to conceal I answer, "I just wanted some company today and all my friends are busy."

She looks down and sighs then slumps in the seat while looking up at me with that 'you're a hopeless case' expression on her face. She takes her coat off and asks me to get her a drink.

"Well I might as well stay now. I came on the bus so I should have some sort of beverage I suppose, while I wait for the next one to take me back."

We smile at each other then laugh at the stupidity of a wasted five minutes of one-upmanship. I'm always so horrid in that first few minutes of seeing her but I'm sure she would argue the opposite that she is the one doing the winding or at least giving as good as she gets, and I can't argue with that.

We then have a fine evening of catching up and bonding which reminds me of why I love her, we have a reluctant liking for each other and it keeps us sharp.

*

I forget my lusting and get home that night in a good mood.

Whilst talking to Kathryn it became obvious to me that I need to express my feelings at the moment, I need an outlet, some way to 'vent my spleen', so I make a hard, fast decision to start a mural on Monday, inspired by that dream I had about 'him' in the art gallery; by using Klimt's *The Kiss* and *Fulfillment* as inspiration. I will create one big homage, along with my own artistic input, on the wall behind the bed using his colours and some of his patterns: gold, silver, orange, pink and purple in swirls and squares, triangles, birds and little pink flowers. This arrangement will team quite nicely with the carpet instead of fighting it.

I'll mark it out on the wall behind my bed tomorrow then pick up the materials on Monday. It will be a way of expressing my emotions when necessary, along with visits to 'Mistoph', and will help me fine tune myself – self therapy – yes, that's an excellent idea!

I am pleased with my abstract artwork and the following Monday lunchtime I choose acrylics and brushes.

Monday evening starts my emotional journal, a documentation of frustration and appeasement; this spiritual testament will become evidence of growth, passion, chance and living with the unknown.

Whilst meticulously whisping spontaneous strokes of gold around contrived vivid shapes I hear the Foo Fighters – 'Come Alive'. The words and music mix with the thick paint and embed into the composition.

I invite my landlord Paul to view the masterpiece. I didn't ask permission before I started in the hope that he would like it so much that he wouldn't mind; the thought of him saying no would have been devastating to my plans.

"It's really lovely," he says with sincerity, genuine appreciation and a little surprise "I can see you in there, your personality in the contrasts, colours and shades, I'll never let it be painted over. I'm quite proud of you."

He then gives me an unexpected fatherly shoulder hug, whilst still gazing at my visual outpouring, which brings a tear to my eye; that moment will become a savoured memory from my now adopted surrogate parent.

*

Friday arrives quicker than normal; focusing on the mural has given me something creative to immerse myself in.

Anna now leaves me standing alone at 'the door' knowing I can manoeuvre myself without help and so after blindfolding me, she walks away allowing me to independently enter the room. As I blindly open the door a blast of radiating heat takes my breath away. His simmering personality is larger than any room, his exotic defiant spirit is tangible and this along with the concoction of deep emotion and passion is an overwhelming force.

I realise I have been fused to the spot, allowing his convection to surround me – I need to get in the room.

I step forward and close the door behind me, dropping my blindfold to the ground. I then lean back against the door to catch my breath – neither of us speaks.

My mind is racing, how can my puny aura penetrate such an intensely projected persona. I am insignificant compared to him but maybe I am only now starting to experience this from him because he is affected by me.

In the gloom I see him rise and slowly head my way, his shadowy figure getting bigger and bigger until he towers above me.

Be Here Now spreads through the hot porous air, filling it to saturation point.

I'm standing in front of him completely in awe.

Why doesn't he say something? Why can't I open my mouth and utter just one word?

My eyes scan his outline from the loose wayward unbuttoned shirt cuffs dangling over his wrists, along the crisp sleeves to his broad moulded shoulders and as I move my head up to complete this picture of today's man he tilts towards me, hands pushing into the door either side of me and places his closed lips without movement onto mine, carefully as though defining an object with finger tips. There's no other contact, all limbs detached, separate and static.

The point of connection is dry but delicate just like the feeling I had the first time I jaunted, a slight resistant pressure.

He shyly locates my neck with his fingers then recognition exerts the confidence I'm used to from him; clasping his large palm around my throat. Then with a levering thumb under my chin he pushes my face upward, while synchronising his head back slightly, the perfect positional play.

His lips are tantalisingly barely touching mine and I grab the front of his shirt pulling it upwards. With my other hand I skim my fingers along the width of his abdomen just above his waistband.

My eyes are open and absorbing the headiness of the room while my mouth is using osmosis to collect the sparse moisture from his.

Our upper lips brush while we inhale and I shimmy stretched hands upwards over his hard clenched stomach.

His hands corset around my waist and I scale my hands through his shirt to his neck, the response I have needed from him begins and so do flashing colour images from my mural zoetropping in front of my eyes; the stored drifting plates of my mind:

Bulbous Cadmium Red drips – intermittent warm pressure,
Pulpy Purple strokes – gliding tip of subtle tongue,
Crossing ribbons of Ocre – barely contacting with a need,
Blanc washes – co-existing puffs of breath,
Umber noisettes – slow gentle skewed fused mouths,
Flourishing Maroon – tongue smoothing, measuring mouth corners,
Gregarious Orange – pulling closer and deeper,
Rich Gold – wanting!

His delicate tongue briefly brushes the inside of my mouth then disappears. I hold his bottom lip in my mouth while his tongue tastes and traces the ridge of my upper lip. I feel weightless and absorbed.

I thread my fingers through the baby hairs at the back of his neck then bringing my hands round to his throat brushing his Adams apple. I'm guiding his neck in my hands while he holds me close to him with my waist. He murmurs ever so slightly and the vibration resonates through his mouth onto mine.

He opens his mouth as if to speak while resting his lower lip on mine and while tilting his head a fraction to one side I mirror him and a prolonged anticipation of a full rounded open mouthed kiss makes my fast breathing suddenly stop!

Everything continues in slow motion as our mouths gradually fit together. I see him, a surreal outlined image of a gorgeous, sensitive erotic man coinciding with the malleable pressure and warm wetness.

This one kiss never stops, its passions and pressure points change but it is a continuation of one act, our first real personal intimacy. This single moment imprints onto me, the blacksmith branding, battering my copper muscle and tissue, setting off sparks between my brain and skull –indelibly marked for life.

The heat in my chest rushes along the sides of my throat gathering speed and force, it fuses our mouths together while we bond undisturbed in the eye of our own storm.

The empowering emotions within keep us from letting passion overtake and the tenderness and love keeps our lips revolving gently together, warm and secure. Our kiss is powerful in its simplicity and the air that circulates between our now, only slightly, touching lips, resuscitates us without the need to breathe. The perfect kiss and consummate embrace.

My lids finally close and eyes dissolve into the back of my head, my brain is redirecting all its energy and capacity to my heart.

There is something troubled, strange and unique about 'J' as though he is detached from mankind, I am able to channel his need to be part of something, but there is more to it than that, something indefinable – it's incredibly attractive to me and I need to know what is at the root of this perception.

He pulls away and before he has totally detached, his tears trickle down my cheek and I ask.

"Why are you crying?"

In reply he asks me the same thing!

I croak, "I didn't know I was."

In surprise I wipe a knuckle across my wet face and manage to answer

"I'll try to answer but you first!"

His reply is made all the more touching by his own disbelief.

"Such tenderness, emotion and intensity. It was … overwhelming"

"My tears are fear, I think."

He takes my hand.

"What's frightening you?"

"You!"

"Me!… Don't you trust me yet?"

"I don't know … and that could be part of it but it's more about this whole situation, something you can't control. Also you're larger than life, a real man brimming with substance and contradictions, you're dark and enigmatic, you're everything I'm not and I think I'm in love with you; a ghost, a dream, an aura in the dark. There is no way of reconciling this and I feel trapped. On top of all that I hardly know anything about you. How can I be in love with a stranger? How can I fall so deeply for someone I can't ever be with?"

He then speaks or rather lyricizes to me in a way I have never experienced; his words are poetic but spoken in a matter of fact way as though in conversation:

"I walked on solid ground until I met you.

Now I'm crawling over fractured crystalline sheets of ice water,

Thinning all the time from the pressure of constantly wanting you.

A ghostly reflection of my minds image of you appears everywhere;

Tantalising, frustrating and teasing.

You lie beneath my icy pathway while I keep sweeping aside

Desperate to break through without killing us,

To keep you I have to lay still but in time you always float away

Your vague features sliding under another frosted coating.

The things I know about you twist and fuse to me

Increasing my wanting of all of you.

I haven't seen you but I know the fundamentals of you,
I know your hair, bones and demeanour.

You glide around appearing momentarily only to increase
my pointless wide eyed urgency to hold onto you.
My breath fades your face and quickly I wipe away the
condensation so I don't miss a second of you.
I can never reach you!
Why can I only claw at the divide whilst trying not to
shatter it?
I constantly renew my search with vigour,
The harder I try to find you the more dangerous it becomes
And the more I realise how futile this is!"

He continues,

"You think I can switch off and control myself? If you
think it's easy for me to be carefree about you then you are
wrong. I'm more in love with you with every second that
passes and I can't understand why! – it's as though there is an
endless supply of love available. I know why I'm attracted to
you and why your personality is so addictive to me but there is
no logic I can attribute to my needing and wanting you from
only three or four hours of being with you. There must be
something supernatural happening."

He sighs deeply,

"Please don't doubt me *Rachel*! Why can't you believe
that a man like me could need you? Apart from this, a physical
and spiritual change has happened to me. I can't describe it to
you because I'm not sure what is going on but I know it must
have something to do with you!"

The whole poem and speech is wonderful to experience
but that last sentence is a show stopper. The rest of it was
music to my ears and needs in depth discussion, but his
revelation of some kind of supernatural occurrence which is
maybe comparable to mine is important.

Every week our relationship gets more and more
complicated and so many unanswered questions are splattered

and stained around this room like years of dust and life that needs cleaning up.

I'm just about to ask him a burning question about our fate when the alarm goes. We haven't even moved away from the door yet or spoken at length about anything and it's all over.

"What are we supposed to do now?" I enquire desperately.

His broken gravelly voice lands on me with dead weight –

"Nothing!"

I'm dumbfounded and stuck to the door like a smiling magician's assistant – spread eagled with grave reservations, putting on a brave face and awaiting thrown knives to scatter around me.

I stoop to grab the blindfold from the floor and have to move away from the door which is now pushing me forward from Anna's pressure on the other side.

'J' glides perfectly across the room on his bespoke dolly track and retires to his chair gracefully; in the meantime I lurch here and there like a frightened animal in headlights not knowing which way to run! The literal and metaphoric gap between us now seems huge and I wonder whether my loyalty to Anna is worth the ever nearing, ever broadening heartache. What will happen next week? What turn is this brave and doomed relationship going to take next?

The debrief starts cold and clinical. Only after several minutes of Anna's generalisations about the session do I realise that neither 'J' nor I whispered and most of everything that was said – was 'said'.

My embarrassment floods the room and Anna looks right into me.

"You two have something very special … I envy you and pity you all at the same time!" she says with sadness.

I am so taken aback by this that I flop to the ground onto my knees and cry into my hands.

Anna kneels and cradles me telling me everything will be ok and she is going to halt the experiment. It's apparently not too late in the proceedings to start again with a new couple. 'J' is still in the room and I should go to him … or at least that's what I imagine in that split second as I collapse; unfortunately the reality is that Anna just watches me, balancing on a fine line of either contempt or pity and then leaves the room without word.

Right then when the door closes I know that I have to see this through, she isn't giving me an out, in the knowledge of all the anticipated pleasure and ultimate pain. I'm proud of my dedication and loyalty to Anna's project but is it at the expense of finding my soul mate and everlasting happiness?

I pull myself together and as I leave it suddenly occurs to me that I haven't even considered hiding somewhere outside the college in order to get a view of 'him'. Subconsciously I know why – I have made a committed promise to Anna which I am desperate to keep, it would seem like a cheap move to be devious now. Deep down I know I am truly entwined with this wonderful man at a level that goes way beyond deception, I can have no hidden agenda and truth is too important.

As I walk the streets toward the bus stop with the diminishing backdrop of the college behind me I start to feel strong and resolved. The tears stop and I begin to feel exhilarated; Anna's right, she doesn't feel sorry for me and neither should I – I am lucky to have this in my life and I'm going to embrace it.

Chapter 8

Week 5

'Abandonment'

The following Thursday is one of those 'mind elsewhere' days.

Anna left a message on my machine Wednesday night. I deliberately didn't answer the phone (I have caller ID, I like to screen my calls as it gives me a heads up on whether I can handle the onslaught, I'm not particularly a 'phone person') so I knew it was her – I didn't have the strength for either a telling off or outpouring of feelings. She asked me to meet her in the usual place for an 'emergency meeting' and it's therefore no surprise that I couldn't get on with my work that day.

Scanning the pub on entrance was easy, not many people here tonight; it's cold and windy, a cowardly wintry night, so just a handful of local people pepper the warm rooms.

I walk toward Anna with some reservation while unravelling my chunky stripy scarf, my gloves scatter and as I look up while retrieving them from the floor I see a defenceless sad Anna, withdrawn and nervous!

"Hi, I'll just drop my coat here and get a drink."

I turn away and feel her eyes follow me to the bar, they don't leave me and are fixed on me until I'm back within speaking range,

"Rachel, I'm wretched!"

"What are you on about?" I say with a 'get out of here, not you' tone.

"I wasn't mad with you last Friday, I was jealous! But since then I have gone through a lifetime of emotions within a five day period."

"What's going on Anna?"

"I arranged to meet your Alan on Saturday, we got on brilliantly and I like him so much that we ended up doing the one thing I said I'd never do!"

I know what's coming but I need the whole story before I beat her about the head with my 'told you so' stick.

"Go on."

"Without going into too much detail we ended up at his house and we slept together, I can't believe I did that and after one date, it was amazing though. We just seem to fit, in every way; you know spiritually as well as physically."

Yuk.

"Aha, so what's the problem?"

"We spent all of Sunday together and it was incredible, I have fallen for him big time and I think he has for me too but I'm not going to push him, it's just too soon."

She says that as though that's the end of this week's story and we must wait another week for the next episode.

"Ok, is that it, because it all sounds hunky dory to me?" I say with scorn and slight jealousy.

What on earth has she got to be down about, she should be in my shoes? She may have let go her principals but it sounds as though the experience and revelation made it all worthwhile!

"No it isn't, I'm just preparing you for the bombshell!"

"Oh!" – A nauseas double take!

"There's another woman and he has intimated that she will be hard to leave out of his life; he could be head over heels for me if he wasn't deliberating over her!"

"I told you Anna, he plays with people, sometimes it seems like he's messing with them when he's not and other times he seems genuine when he's stringing you along. It's a dangerous ga ..."

She interrupts, "Shut up Rachel! It's you ... he thinks he may be in love with you, he told me!"

"Wh- what?"

"On Monday night I went to see him and we talked, all night, no sex, no intimacy, not even a hug – nothing, just talk and we made a connection. I think he's who I'm supposed to be with, but apart from that a weird thing happened that I can't explain. I'll tell you about it one day but I'm freaked out and I'm sure you are at the centre of it!"

Everyone is going insane and blaming me, what is going on?

"He is not 'in love' with me Anna. I've only spoken with him a couple of times. He may just be scared because he feels the same way about you as you do for him and that must be a first for him. He's trying to keep you at arm's length."

"He told me he wants to get to know me because there is something guiding him towards me but he wants to be honest. He then proceeded to tell me he needed to know whether 'Rachel' was supposed to be his or was just 'unfinished business' as he put it. I don't know what to do. What are your intentions with him? Although I shouldn't need to ask you after that session on Friday."

"Aren't you forgetting something Anna, I can't be with 'him'; the end of our relationship is a foregone conclusion. We even know the scheduled end date." I say that with frustration and anger but at my situation, not her insensitivity, "Anyway what do you want me to do, sleep with him just for your peace of mind?"

…"Well, yes if you don't mind!"

Incredulous pause!

"Are you insane?" I shout, then look around in embarrassment and lower my voice. "I can't just sleep with someone to satisfy curiosity or to prove a point."

"Think about it though Rachel, it would end a chapter for you, decide things for me one way or another and avoid any potential awkwardness between us. I bet you've thought about it and I'm actually giving you the opportunity to find out how you really feel without the guilt. How often does an opportunity like this arise?"

She must be pretty sure of herself, and this short formed bond with Alan, to even consider this course of action. If things don't go the way she predicts then this could create a greater awkwardness and put a stop to the experiment. This could ultimately conclude my sessions with 'J'. There are so many variables and consequences that I'm actually tempted to do it. Just saying the words 'making love to Alan' makes me want him more, I detest this hold he has over me.

I know the idea of any kind of intimate relationship with Alan is wrong in every way imaginable but there is a nagging doubt in my mind that she may be right.

"I'll do it but you mustn't let onto him, he has to want this in his own way and I can't make it easy for him." I'm hoping the only reason he may want sex with me is for the challenge and once 'the games begin' he may decide to give up; well that's the hope anyway.

Another thought then occurs to me –

"You're not asking me to do this as research for your thesis are you, as part of 'the experiment'?"

"Of course not," she says with a truthful stare, "I would not pull the wool over your eyes like that; besides I would have nothing to gain from it."

I suppose she's right, so I let that notion drift into the ether to mix with all the other weird stuff that's been happening recently.

We both sit back into the high backed tatty and worn but comfy velvet seats and look around at each other. Anna's face is a mixture of panic and high expectation, I don't want to know how I must look but I suspect it's mostly fear with a hint of 'bring it on'!

*

Roxanne would love all of this scheming and I'm so tempted to tell her the whole story so I can reflect on the events but it would be suicide. Her influence and opinions would taint my own decision and make it all about the sex. I think she'd miss the point, on the other hand if I spoke to Jason about it he would stop me and that's not an option.

I so want to tell Sarah and discuss all the pros and cons but ultimately I know deep down I have to just go ahead and play this by ear. My instinct tells me there's a reason for all this!

It's only when Friday comes that I realise I have only jaunted once this week and all that really happened was a dilatory meander around my neighbourhood (with the realisation that I am invisible when jaunting). Is something else happening to me, is jaunting linked to my decisions or fate? This local unimportant wander did reveal something very important though, an answer to a burning question; I saw two cars collide right outside my building which was later confirmed by Paul exactly as I witnessed it. This is a significant occurrence – I now know for certain jaunting is very real!

As I ponder this, while sitting on the edge of my bed hearing 'Slow Emotion Replay' by Matt Johnson's all-knowing silken voice whispering and confirming perplexities in my ear, I look back at the mural behind my bed and notice that the art work I completed last week is beautiful and accomplished. I'm incredulous that I managed to create something so spontaneous, skilful and mesmerising, yet the good but mediocre work I've done over this week is flat and with less emotion, as though a completely different person has tried too hard and missed.

What has happened to me this week? My enhanced focus of the last month seems to be slipping away and I'm reverting to the timid, confused and inhibited girl I used to be – Matt Johnson you reflect me so well!

*

I arrive at the college to be met in the foyer by Anna. An overwhelming foreboding sweeps over me and my legs start to wobble.

"I'm sorry but he hasn't turned up and as you know if either of you can't get here for your specified times then you're not supposed to come at all, we can't have you bumping into each other, so there's no point staying. There wasn't time to call you because he didn't let me know. I'm sorry but there it is."

"But why isn't he here?" My little words falter and fall.

"Don't know. I suppose we'll find out next week, if he comes that is. I'll see if I can get hold of him for an explanation, I haven't been able to so far!"

I feel as though my rib cage is just that, an ever diminishing cage restricting my breathing, deliberately tightening and torturing me. My body is rejecting the thought of not seeing him, disbelieving my ears and wanting to punish someone, something.

"So what now? Do I just leave and come back next week?"

"Yes, but don't forget about the little favour I asked you, I will be eternally grateful. I know he'll be in the pub Sunday night if you want to get things moving then. I'm supposed to meet him in there at eight but I'll ring his mobile at the last minute and tell him something has come up."

She continues to plan and plot as though she's working out some kind of charitable strategy to bring starstruck lovers together. I turn off to her chatter and hear only my own pulse throbbing through my neck while in my mind's eye I see 'J's' beautiful aura surrounding me and turning my admiration to passion.

Anna takes me by the shoulders

"Rachel please stop crying. I don't want you to do this if it's going to make you miserable."

"It's ok," I say quickly pulling myself together, "It's not that, ignore me. I'm not unhappy just … oh I don't know ... it doesn't matter." I say with a glance and a smile

Can't she see my disappointment is about 'J'. Is she totally blinded and obsessed now by Alan and her antics?

"So you'll go and see him then on Sunday?"

"Yes, of course but I have no idea what's going to happen. You know he'd see right through any deception from me, which I'm not prepared to do any way. I'll just go with the flow and see what transpires.

"Absolutely." She replies with a grin.

And with a one-sided appreciative hug from Anna I leave in a bit of a daze. Even though she knows from my last meeting that there are strong feelings between 'J' and me, she seems to have completely forgotten all of that and is consumed with her scheming over Alan.

I arrange Saturday night out with Jason. I'll get ready at his place and stay the night. I can then go pubbing, clubbing, whatever he wants to do in the town without having to think about getting home to Butterfield. I can try and forget everything for one night at least.

Iron and Wine – 'The Devil Never Sleeps', plays while we get ready, laughing and dancing round his flat, as though we're teenagers on our first exciting venture into the world of alcohol, sex and showing off.

He wears his most outrageously tight fitting clothes looking more stunning than ever, making my best efforts look insignificant next to his blinding gorgeousness. My hair is even bigger than Cheryl Cole's and I'm wearing a low cut, small Peter Pan collared, long, grey figure hugging dress with front split and a small tight black waistcoat which has the corseted effect of pushing my small bosom up and out. I accessorise this ensemble with an antique pocket watch and several large bangles made with the same metal tones.

Jason puts his hands on his hips and says with backhanded admiration

"How can someone look so cute, chic, glamorous and slutty all at the same time?" while looking me up and down.

I curtsy while thanking him graciously for his sarcastic critique,

"Good, that's just the unique effect I was going for!" And so we venture off on our 'Will and Grace' evening of perfect friendship, humour and understanding.

Snow Patrol – 'Take Back The City' starts as we get our stuff together ready to leave and repeats in my head once we are actually walking the 'people filled' dark streets.

Finally, after what for me has turned out to be a disappointing anti-climax of an evening, we end up in our last haunt of the night 'The Marquee' – a club more conducive to my nature, with its Rock and Indie music and live bands. Jason isn't totally happy about this but he knows there are a hard-core of young gay 'Closetees' that hang out here. It's not a gay club but it's not exclusively heterosexual. (Closetees haven't quite got to the stage of being aware of their true sexual orientation but know they like men for some reason and are about to enter the closet – denial is the next step before admitting they're gay then they can make their grand exit – Jason likes to be the one guiding them in, then helping them along with their realisation by showing them how good the sex can be.)

The closetees seem to stand in a particular corner pretending to watch the girls but secretly eyeing up the men. They're just entering the closet but not yet far enough in to break out, so this club is a safe place to hide and wonder. You can spot them a mile away in regular pubs and clubs whereas here, anything goes, dresswise; the weirder or camper the better.

Black Strobe – 'I'm a Man' is playing – Jason's cue. It makes me laugh to see him standing cross legged leaning back against the old paint chipped column, hands in pockets winking at the dancing boys. After torturing himself he eventually jumps in the middle of the crowd to indulge himself.

I'm not in the mood to dance so Jason goes off to cajole and entice the 'young ones' by dancing provocatively on his own in front of them, all that's missing is the pole and leather thong.

I have my drink and stand with my back to the bar leaning against it in what anyone might think is a 'what am I doing here' attitude when I hear that unmistakeable voice, I can't see 'him' but can hear 'him' nearby.

I'm transfixed, and the music and all the voices become muffled except his – it is definitely him! Only when he stops speaking do I come back to reality hearing U2 – 'Magnificent' and realise I should be looking for him! I'm so used to not looking at him in our room that it didn't occur to me to find his face in the crowd.

I'm sure I can see the top of the back of his head in the distance, I would know that outline in the gloom anywhere – he's heading for the exit.

I push past everyone frantically to follow and get to him, it's like swimming in treacle, and the harder I try to get past people the more my energy is soaked up by the masses.

I'm desperate now but eventually I get to the exit. Running down the entrance steps I see him alone in the distance walking elegantly down the street with his big coat flapping around him in the wind, I run but I'm on a treadmill in slow motion. 'Magnificent' is echoing from the club behind me while I chase after him. I don't want to confuse things by shouting, I wouldn't know what to shout anyway so I just try to catch up but his vast strides are like that of a giant and at times he seems to become invisible.

I suddenly 'transpond' to the corner of the street he has just turned into only to see him appear then disappear just as he reaches the next corner. The same thing happens again and again until finally he has gone!

The rain starts to spit then gets heavier Grace Jones drips all over me with her 'Walking in the Rain' and I become aware of my vulnerability and solitude in the back streets.

What just happened? He swept around the streets like a fluid apparition while I seemed to continuously arrive at the spot my laser vision pinpointed, without effort.

I know I'm not supposed to reveal myself to him but I just wanted to see his face, his eyes, see if he would respond to mine, just pass him in the street as a stranger – would he notice me? Would my face alone spark something in him?

I just followed him instinctively and impetuously, it wasn't premeditated. I'm sort of glad it came to nothing though, it could potentially have ruined everything if we had met – I think I get it now, that room is the key.

Walking back I reflect on what just happened. In the grand scheme of things I don't think I'm supposed to meet him face to face anyway. After all why couldn't I reach him just now, I'm fated not to be with him at this time of my life but I am supposed to be with him eventually, I'm almost sure I am … somehow.

Jason is stood outside on the stone steps of the club looking for me and wraps his coat around me when he sees my drenched shivery body tripping towards him. A chivalrous man tease – my handsome homo hero.

He gets me back to his home and doesn't ask any questions. He just tells me he's going back out to secretly meet his latest recruit and probably won't be back till morning, which is fine for me as I am not in the mood now for our usual recap of the night's shenanigans.

Back home the next day I take time to get ready for my contrived accidental meeting with Alan, and with the way I feel about missing my weekly fix of 'him' I can't predict what will happen.

Dressed in my finest alluring combo of little green A-line velvet dress and same length chunky purple cardigan, knee length high heeled clunky buckled biker boots, belted black knee length trench coat and back combed hair, I brave the elements and make my way to the rendezvous point!

It's just coming up to 8 p.m. when Alan walks through the door and he sees me straight away. He starts to walk straight over but then stops mid-stride as his mobile goes off with its overpowering polyphonic ring tone – 'Wicked Game' plays; surprising but apt. Now I can't get that haunting song by the sumptuous Chris Isaak out of my head which only fuels my already fully charged reluctant longings!

He puts the phone back in his pocket, looks at me without moving and grins with those big smarmy lips. His cheeks rise from the force of his huge mouth thereby pushing his eyes into sinister slits. He changes direction and saunters to the bar.

My direction changes just as quickly as I think to myself. 'Who the hell does this man think he is?' This is going to be a lot easier than I thought; it won't be difficult to play hard to get, I'll just let my current abhorrence dictate every move.

He's chatting up the barmaid which is my cue to leave, what on Earth was I thinking? I grab my coat and bag, knocking the table as I clumsily try to flee but when I eventually manage to fight my way from the edge of the table he's stood there in front of me breathing down into my hair.

I step back into the seat which takes my legs from under me and there I sit sheepishly looking up at him covered in coat, scarf, bag and hair.

He leans over me picks everything up from my lap and folds it all neatly, placing it in an orderly pile on the shelf behind the seat. He then calmly sits beside me and adjusts my hair which has drawn across my face from my falling backwards.

"Thanks," I force out while still trying to hate him but then I look up into those cobalt eyes and I can't help but smile.

He laughs and says, "Round two to me I think".

I try not to laugh and it comes out as a spitting guffaw.

"Ok, but even if you win every round what does that mean exactly, you can't force me to relent … can you?"

"Of course not but every time something like this happens it intensifies your attraction to me so that sooner or later you won't be able to help yourself from resisting me."

And that's the sad truth – I mess up or embarrass myself around him, then his manly gesture in reply makes me weak at the knees. His cockiness and confidence makes me both dislike and adore him! Oh the humanity!

"You know Alan, every single time you make me feel like an idiot you revel in it and that's just not nice."

"But you're so cute. I've never been able to read people very well but you are especially difficult to predict. Everyone else has a steely correctness, a contrived perfection but you are more complicated, you're like an indecisive squirrel hoarding your impressions and experiences; you take it all in and have the stored up intuition, information and ammunition to stop hearts but you just keep it all to yourself, it's all so wonderful. I love trying to wind you up and watching the results – you're captivating."

I don't know whether to be charmed and flattered or totally insulted but then I realise he's playing again so I need to give him some of the same.

I whimper, "Oh Alan, you know me so well and of course being the busy little squirrel that I am, you therefore know that … your nuts are mine!"

He looks at me with surprise but smiling

"Round three to you." Then chinks my glass with his.

We have an 'ok' evening and actually get to know each other properly as adults for the first time.

I leave him that night accepting an invitation to meet again on Tuesday. Anna didn't come up in conversation. I didn't want to put myself on the spot knowing full well this was all her idea and I'm sure he's not going to reveal his intentions towards her if he wants to get me into bed! This whole charade is like being in some engineered rom-com but it's very real and woven. I'm right in the middle of this web all spun from one 'spur of the moment' decision five weeks ago.

Tuesday comes and a strange event prepares me for my meeting with Alan in a way I hadn't expected.

I'm sat with Roxanne at lunch time and she suddenly brings up my date with Alan

"Rachel I know you're meeting Alan Rowsmaine tonight and I want to warn you about him; I have to say I'm surprised you didn't tell me about him."

"How the hell do you know about this and more importantly what do you know about him?"

"Oh my God Rachel are you thick or what?"

I look at her like her head just spun around a whole 360 degrees

"Don't tell me you've slept with him?"

"Oh yes!" is her gleeful reply, and as she says it she licks her finger and notches up a line in her imaginary five bar gate in the air. I feel sick and want to run but she grabs my arm and says, "Look, I know what he's capable of, I have never had such a good time as with him, if you know what I mean, but he's ruthless and you have to go in with your eyes wide open. I think you have a long way to fall when he drops you. I don't think you're up to it."

"First of all Roxanne that's got to be the corniest warning speech I've ever heard, second of all you have no idea of what I'm capable of. It's Alan that needs to look out and thirdly how on God's Earth do you know about this?"

"I just happen to be going out with his brother at the moment and he told me yesterday that Alan has been ranting about this chick 'Rachel Fleetwood', and that he has fallen for her big-time and therefore how funny and ironic it is that he couldn't wait to get rid of her years ago but now he's chomping at the bit to nail her. Well it's all very cruel if you ask me and I thought I should bring it to your attention." How succinctly put. I wonder whether these are all his words or hers!

A couple of weeks ago I would have been so upset by this, but now I just take it in my stride and think to myself 'Well, here we go again.' Nothing has been straightforward since I saw that ad and now I'm learning, not to be hardened, but to let something's go – apart from that I'm kind of using him!

I thank her for the information and decide to play tonight by ear, who knows what weird thing will happen next. My nerves have now gone about meeting him and I'm resigned.

We meet and after a couple of drinks he asks if I want to go back to his house to talk. I accept without hesitation as though playing out a well-rehearsed scene and off we go. I'm actually enjoying myself!

He has a modern three bed roomed semi-detached house. Nicely decorated and furnished all 'new and tidy' with that ready-made IKEA look, just as I would expect. Nothing remotely unique or interesting. It's all very affluent and controlled.

We sit on the sofa and talk for a while then he takes my hands and pulls me closer to him. At this moment I feel like I'm echoing the position on this seat, of many other girls before me and that I'm just a rerun of all his many previous affairs but I don't care because when he then puts his hands either side of my neck and kisses me fully without reservation I kiss him back with every ounce of savoured passion from the last five weeks. It's very different from the gentle, loving kiss with 'J'. There's no emotional connection with Alan just lust, and it feels great, like a really good workout!

He pulls back suddenly and looks straight into my eyes. He then starts to kiss me so passionately again with his tongue probing and massaging mine. He lets go of my neck and puts his huge muscular arms around me. I push my hands through his short hair and grip it as though I'll fall if I don't. He pushes the cardigan off my shoulders and as his kissing gets harder and harder into my neck and his hands start to undo the zip of my dress Roxanne suddenly pops into my head. The thought of her with Alan doing the very same thing disgusts me and makes me jump up and I clasp my hands over my swollen mouth.

He just sits there looking at the space now created by my sudden disappearance but he's not surprised.

He carries on staring into space.

"What's the matter?" he says in a very matter of fact way.

"I can't do this Alan."

"I know, listen I have something I want to say to you."

I sit back down, lift his head up with both my hands and look into those beautiful hypnotic eyes that are now very sad and regretful.

He sighs then utters, "I thought I wanted you but the whole time I was touching and kissing you I was thinking of Anna and before you say anything, I know it sounds awful, I didn't know this was going to happen."

"It's ok Alan, I understand completely, I was enjoying it but it wasn't working for me either. Would you have carried on if I hadn't retreated like that?"

"I don't know, I don't think so, it didn't feel right, I think you've given me a conscience, damn you!" We laugh and sit back relieved.

We sit hands wrapped around coffee cups talking for hours and I realise as a friend he's an ok guy and after years of frustration over him I can finally let go.

Just as I'm about to leave he confides something,

"You know I said something is changing in me, that you're giving me a conscience,"

"Yes."

"Well that's sort of right. I don't know whether it's something to do with you or meeting Anna or whether all of this is coincidental but I have started to see people differently … in colour."

Everyone around me seems to be affected by me or is there a network of minds being created as a result of a chance in a million meeting with 'J'.

I try to be nonchalant and not understand what he's trying to tell me.

"Sorry … was everyone so black and white before?"

"No, I'm not explaining very well. I mean … I was never very good at empathising, you know reading people's emotions or understanding people but a week or so ago I started to notice everyone has a different tint or shade of colour about them and then in the last couple of days it's become more intense and somehow I know what the colour means; it's like an emotion indicator. At the moment you're mostly green with a haze of various hues of purple which means your mostly content, even happy but there's some issue rippling the calm. Most people have a deep purple aura with patches of green fading in and out meaning they have emotional problems, depression or unhappiness constantly in their lives with small pockets of joy – it's so sad!

"I have seen some people completely shrouded in red and I know that means that they are in physical pain, that's hard to look at because most of the time they're putting on a brave face and no one else knows. I have gone from being devoid of any kind of awareness of others to being overwhelmed by the amount of emotions people constantly hide. It's intermittent but becoming more regular."

"That's incredible, amazing! I can't imagine what that must be like, life changing I would think. I'm pleased for you Alan, it's a gift you could put to good use. Maybe you'll be able to hang on to Anna and show her the understanding and honesty she deserves. She really has a passion for understanding – for what makes people tick, you'll have lots to talk about, a match made in heaven!"

He nods.

"At the same time I suppose it's a hard gift to live with, not everyone could cope with that sort of power and insight."

I stand up to leave and he does too. He wraps his big brotherly arms around me and I feel secure. I won't tell him about my supernatural encounters, it will only confuse the issue and things are nice and simple between us now. The dynamic between Alan, Anna and me is now perfect and I have a new fondness for Alan. I just need to channel my passions and intellect towards 'J', the very person who induced them in the first place.

The following day Roxanne pounces on me and drags me off to the Ladies,

"Well!"

"Well what"

"How did it go ... with Alan last night?"

"Why don't you tell me what you think happened and I'll confirm or deny."

"He charmed you back to his place then he sat you on his seduction seat, kissed you passionately for a while, loosened your clothes then toyed with you for an hour or so then carried you to his bed and made the most amazing passionate love to you, the sort you never forget and for two days makes you think you're in love with him before he drops you like a stone and you see him with some other tramp. Am I right?" she shouts with vengeful experience.

Right now I'm thinking I should have let things carry on after all, but no, I made the right decision, I let my instincts take control and I know that was the right thing to do. I missed out on an education there; never mind.

"No, you're so wrong, it didn't get anywhere near that far!"

"Oh Rachel what's wrong with you, didn't you turn him on. No I suppose you're not his type, you're not lusty enough, you're just too nice, that's what it is."

"How insulting Rox, it wasn't that at all."

"Well how far did you get?"

"Why does it always have to be about the sex, aren't you ever interested in someone for other reasons?"

"Well I'd like to but I've never met anyone I feel like that with, I only ever want to go to bed with the men I'm attracted to."

I just laugh and she smiles back at me. She gives me a hug and sighs,

"You need to get laid Rachel, I mean really good sex with someone who knows what they're doing."

"Yes and you need to meet someone who will make you wait for it and in the meantime helps you discover some things about yourself, things to love and be proud of."

She hugs me again and we go back to work in a reasonably happy state.

Chapter 9

Week 6

The 'Serpent' Nebula
'Awkward'/About 'J'

I wake Friday morning and a frantic jaunt takes me thousands of light years away, further than ever before, to experience breath-taking life changing visions of spiritual beauty and raw science.

Columns of gas tear through the blackness in luminous transparent plumes and live haemoglobin syrup oozes out, spreading through the stark deep blue inkiness of space.

I feel as though I'm tangled in 'his' guts as I intricately weave through the towers of light and power; it's a strong image of being inside him like he's the universe around me and I'm journeying through his essence, muscle and tissue, emotions, everything that makes 'him' what he is. It's not easy, seeming to be treacherous, fraught with danger and obstacles but is exhilarating and exciting.

I return and I know he's going to be there tonight.

I rendezvous with Anna and prepare for the session. We talk candidly about everything that has happened this week. She tells me that Alan hasn't revealed anything about me but that he has feelings for her and has resolved the issue with me in his own mind. The old Alan would have gone in all guns blazing and told her everything but he seems to be showing restraint and sensitivity now.

I walk into the room of blackness with a strange feeling of unease.

I sit down and my head is silent, no music, no thoughts just emptiness.

He doesn't speak and the atmosphere from Week One fills the room.

Once my eyes adjust to the gloom I can just make out his head resting on his fists, elbows on knees. We don't speak for what seems an eternity then he lets out a huge sigh sits upright and says, "Rachel, I don't know if I can carry on like this."

"What do you mean and where were you last week?"

"I couldn't face coming, I'm sorry."

"Why?"

"Last time … that kiss, it wasn't just a physical act for me, it was pain, joy, hurt, passion, love, hate, every emotion known to man but all at once. It was too much. I didn't want to face it again. I don't want to scare you and I wanted to pull back from it."

"By 'it' you mean me?"

Silence.

"How do you feel now then?" there's anger in my voice and instead of feeling pity I'm hurt.

"Better thanks!"

"'Better thanks' – what sort of crap answer is that?" … "So what happens now?"

He calmly replies, "We carry on getting to know each other, talk and then go our separate ways. We'll do exactly what is required."

I had toyed with the idea of telling him about the night at the club but now I'm not sure it's a good idea.

The silence ensues and I don't know what to say to him, how do you pretend you didn't fall in love with someone and then go on to produce small talk. I feel bad about my reaction, I know it's a difficult situation and I should be pleased he feels so strongly about me but with only the few weeks we have together I would have thought he would want to be with me as much as possible; is it that deep down I don't believe him – but then why don't I believe him? He has no reason to lie and nothing to gain. I should stop processing the poor man and go with his flow.

Finally he speaks as though we have just met for the first time.

"I want to know more about you, we can start again as though this is the first session."

My heart sinks but not right to the bottom, I know he's right and I would also like to get to know him better. Last week we learned nothing other than we are completely compatible and maybe in love, but what the hell – it's all academic!

We talk with odd silent pauses every now and again for the rest of the session.

I learn about his difficult childhood, that he couldn't identify with anyone even his family. His mother was distant and never understood him. He loved his father, admired him but never really connected. I ask him about brothers or sisters but he just pauses as though he's unsure of the question then says, 'none', emphatically so I leave the subject of his family, although I want to pursue the idea of not seeming to get on with people in general, I ask him about university instead.

I establish that he loves to learn and read but then he breaks a rule by telling me his occupation; it transpires he's a freelance archaeologist. He works all over the country and the world, which is fascinating to me and which now explains his sensitive hands.

"I don't just use my eyes to discover and scrutinise, I use my finger tips and hands in the ground to gently feel edges, ridges, and minute detail and to help tease out delicate artefacts."

"I thought you would have to wear gloves in order to preserve the objects you're finding"

"Once you find something and have cleaned it, yes you would but only if it's something particularly special or delicate, you can't really feel with gloves, I like the earth in my fingers, it makes the whole experience of finding something more organic and real to me."

I like his explanation, it reinforces my image of a raw man of nature.

"Why are your hands so soft then, I would think they would be rougher?"

"It sounds ridiculous but I use hand creams and E45 a lot, I have my hands in dirt or the pages of books and I wash them a lot so my hands can dry out very quickly and that's no good if I want to continue to have the sensitivity I have."

"No, it's not ridiculous. You're a professional and you know what works for you. Do all archaeologists do that?"

"No, a lot use gardening gloves, and I do get constant ribbing over it, but I laugh it off and think it's worth the ridicule. You probably appreciate my efforts don't you?" he whispers as he stretches out and lightly strokes my hand which is resting quite nonchalantly on my lap; a tickle to tantalise me.

The joy of his delicate touch, and softly broken words, is liquidising the very real hard gravity that holds me to this chair.

"Definitely." I breath back with every bit of air from my lungs.

Just before the bell goes he leans across and takes both my hands in his. The cold strength in his fingers slowly threading through mine is a small affirmation of his affection and it's all I need for now.

*

At home that night I sit tired and pensive by my window staring across Butterfield through smeared condensation. Simple Minds – 'Love Song' bubbles past my head, bursting out into the night in front of me. Some people have put their Christmas decorations up early and the smudged fairy lights pop around the park like half sucked boiled sweets lying in a puddle – hazy but intense at the core.

I reflect on this week's events and come to the conclusion that a lot of people think they've found their soulmate but have they really?

We can find someone and fall in love with them but is it always a life changing experience; are we truly fulfilled? The right person isn't meant to change us or make us a better, more intelligent, more sensitive or a more thoughtful human being, they should just fit and enhance our own qualities whether good or bad and only change how we see the world. Happiness and contentment with someone else, to me now, is about experiencing my own self!

I don't think soulmates need necessarily have the same opinions or interests, it's more than that, it's a spiritual interlocking and self-verification As I think this I put two and two together; maybe everything in the universe is connected but has gaps here and there. The earth is detached and needs reconnecting to complete the circuit. Finding every last person's eternal partner in life would fix the planet spiritually and reattach it, put it back in its place, linked to the rest of the heavenly bodies.

I think that must be the feeling I have experienced while out in space. I have found 'J' completely by chance and we're now the catalyst for humanity's reconnection – a life affirming responsibility!

On that revelation I wake up, head pressed into the window and condensated hair fronding into the glass; my deep self-discussion has been a dreamy theological nap.

Chapter 10

Week 7

Black Holes and Apparitions
Cancellation

I slept so well last night and I wake up Saturday morning from a jaunt that has taken me to a black hole. The things I'd like to tell the feuding scientists about the truth behind them would blow their minds. (This is all so big! Yet again I have to decide whether I should tell anyone about my ability and yet again I decide against it for the moment. I have to stay anonymous for now and besides I don't know what's going to happen at the end of the 'experimental' ten weeks – as things stand, anything could happen. Best to wait.)

A black hole is like a dimple in the mass – it's the inward pulling of material in a cushion where the button is sewn on.

As I approach the outer rim of this vast interstellar fastening, it intimidates me and gives me a sudden surge of insecurity and fear, but then as I venture forward and try to fly closer, the phenomenon's centre gets smaller. The closer I get, the more diminished it becomes and no matter how fast I accelerate it seems to get further away but never disappears – very frustrating and puzzling. I must have travelled many light years trying to get to the opening but just never could. There are no sides to it. It just seems to diminish around me as I move so I never enter the pure blackness. Amazing, but sort of disappointing, there must be a way of entering – As I leave the hole gets bigger again; it leads somewhere and nowhere, like my life at the moment, I have everything and nothing!

Later that day I get a phone call from Sarah and I'm not surprised when she tells me "something weird" has happened.

"Guess who I bumped into yesterday?"

"I have no idea."

"Go on, just guess."

"Is it someone from our school days?" I enquire with my 'strange is normal for me now' voice.

Sarah still lives in my home town, even though she works in London, and does bump into archived people every now again (school chums I remember but wish I didn't).

"Yes, Simon!"

My initial reaction is intrigue quickly followed by apprehension. I have such fond memories of him but do I really want to go there?

"How did he look?"

"Much older, his hair is receding already but it sort of goes with you know ... his maturity and stature. He is so nice Rachel, he asked about you."

"What did you tell him?" I dread to think.

"That you're still single and still in the same office in back of beyond Brailsford and sti ... ," she hesitates. ... "Doesn't sound that good does it?"

"It's ok, Sarah, it's the truth. I am 'still' all those things!"

That word is a marker for my working life and I appreciate that only I can zap it back to life.

"Anyway he said he may pay you a visit now he's back in the region for a while."

The thought of seeing him again makes me nervous, thoughts of my old naïve self.

Sure enough on the following Tuesday Roxanne runs from the enquiry office to my desk and smacks the surface to get my attention.

"There's someone here asking for you."

"What do you mean 'someone's here'?"

"There's this chap at reception requesting your presence Rachel." She growls through gritted teeth.

"Who?"

"Simon somebody."

"Oh." I don't think I want to see him, It's been so long and I wouldn't know what to say to him. "How does he look?"

"Normal. What do you mean, who is he?"

"An old boyfriend, I haven't seen him for years."

She laughs.

"Oh, this is good, go on get out there." She pulls me out of my seat with the excitement of a child hearing the ice-cream van.

"Why are you so excited?" I quiz while being dragged by arm.

"I don't know, it's just funny seeing someone you have been romantically involved with, I've never seen you with a man before!"

"God, Rox. You make me sound like an old maid."

"Sorry." She lets go of me.

"Look, if I go out there and arrange to meet him would you come with us? I would feel awkward going out with him cold turkey, I need a bit of moral support."

She glances upward playing out the scene on the white suspended ceiling ...

"Ok, that could be fun."

I walk unsteadily to the door of reception and slowly open it to reveal Simon stood elegantly with a banker's reserved demeanour. He has aged beyond his years but there is something dependable and secure about him.

I walk around the counter and stand to face him, he's not much taller than me, and he throws his arms around me without saying anything. I stand rigidly, arms by my side, completely frozen and surprised by his show of affection after all these years.

"It's really good to see you Rachel. You look lovely."

He grabs my shoulders and pushes me back so he can have a proper look. I'm uneasy and don't feel I can return the compliment so instead just tell him it's nice to see him too.

"Are you available for a drink at lunchtime, I'd like to catch up."

"Yeah sure, but is it ok if my friend Roxanne tags along, only she's a bit down at the moment and I said I'd try to cheer her up today." I lie!

"That's fine, shall I meet you in the Crown across the road at say 1p.m. or would you prefer a cafe?"

"Crown's fine. See you then."

He leaves and I feel awkward about the whole thing.

I prepare Roxanne and tell her to pretend to be depressed, which is a challenge for her, she's the most bouncy self-assured person I know.

We leave work together and meet as arranged.

Simon sits in the high backed snug facing us both as we teeter precariously on old rickety dining chairs, like the boss addressing his team of workers. His pinstriped suit, starched collar and plain perfect tie give him an air of unreachability.

We chat light-heartedly and catch up on work related issues while Roxanne sits quietly taking it all in and then suddenly she butts in,

"Are you married, Simon?"

He looks at her as if noticing her for the first time and just stares.

"No."

"Oh, you just look like the type to be married with kids, a Volvo on the brick drive and a loft conversion."

I look at her aghast, who could insult someone within ten minutes of clapping eyes on them and with the first sentence they utter? Besides this isn't the sort of man you talk to like that; it's just not the done thing!

He leans back and crosses his arms staring right into her.

"I haven't met the right woman who can satisfy me yet, the Volvo is a Porsche and sixteenth century castles don't convert that well."

I spit my drink all over the table and Roxanne is speechless but she composes herself then continues in her own blatant style; she is not one to be phased,

"Money doesn't impress me you know."

"It doesn't impress me either, I didn't tell you to impress you, I told you because you haven't got your facts right and you strike me as the kind of person who needs bringing down a peg or two."

This is better than settling down to my favourite programme for the evening, the anticipation is priceless. This is actually turning out to be an interesting meeting.

"Sorry," she retorts sarcastically. "I suppose I just like to try people, to see what they're made of."

He leans forward, "People like you make me sick. You come along here not saying a word and the only thing you can think of is an insult. I'm disappointed in you Rachel, I thought you had better taste."

I hold my hands up indicating a stop sign.

"Hey, don't bring me into this, anyway I told you she's depressed." I lie to try and diffuse the situation.

Roxanne pushes me aside and scooches her chair so she be brazen right to his face. Arms crossed and resting on the table, she leans in; she's a woman on a mission.

"You pompous arrogant oaf, do you really think you can sit there and judge me on one off–the-cuff, admittedly stupid statement. Do you really think you can live in a passionless world not making waves, not dipping your toe in and not making mistakes like Rachel does? I'm right in the middle of it all, doing it, living, and if that ruffles feathers then so be it. You don't know me at all."

She runs from the pub and I just carry on sipping my drink in a sheepish way trying to pretend I'm not with them. He has certainly somehow touched a nerve with her – I didn't think it was humanly possible to upset her like that.

Suddenly he pushes the table away from him with such a force and runs out too. I'm sat there looking like an idiot with the table lodged right into my chest, drink held aloft. She seems to have rattled his cage too!

The barmaid turns up with the food we had ordered and I just look at her like the kid that broke the expensive ornament.

Back at work Roxanne doesn't turn up and I cover for her by saying she was sick and had to go home. Jason comes over wondering where she is and I tell him the whole story.

"Oh that's delicious, what do you think happened, do you think he went after her? She's met her match, or even someone that can dominate her, can you believe it? Wouldn't it be funny if your old flame becomes the love of her life?"

I just stare at him, incredulous at this statement, then after realising what he's said and the possibility of it, I throw my head on the desk and bang it several times before looking back up at him.

"What is going on at the moment Jason? Everything is upside down ... tits up!"

He laughs and says, "Rachel I've never heard you talk like that, what's going on? What are you talking about?"

"Oh never mind, ignore me." I change the subject. "Anyway, isn't it your turn for 'Movie Sunday' soon?"

"Yes this Sunday actually, maybe then you can tell me what's occuring."

He walks away and I just can't work that afternoon.

I call Roxanne that night but no answer and then she's not at work the next day or Thursday.

Friday comes and if she doesn't turn up today I will have to go and see her at home. Luckily she's there as normal and this time it's me grabbing her for the latest.

"Where have you been? I've covered for you and I've been so worried. What happened after you ran off?"

"You wouldn't believe me!"

"Don't tell me Simon ran after you."

"No he didn't, something really strange happened!"

Referring to recent events I let my imagination go wild and come up with the most outlandish idea I can think of hoping that if I say it, it won't be true

"You try to avoid him thinking he might come after you, he knows where you work, so you go somewhere obscure, the library on the other side of town but he does the same. You see each other and hide. You then leave and end up in another out of town place and see each other again. You confront each other over what's been said and discuss the ridiculousness of your situation and the odds of it happening, fall madly in love and spend the next two days together but no sex involved."

"Yes! ... more or less, my God, how did you know, have you spoken to him?"

I sigh, "No, a lot of strange things have been happening recently and really the love angle was more Jason's notion than mine. Weird is the norm for me at the moment, it's a lucky guess."

"Anyway what really matters is he's unlike anyone I've ever met. I want to be with him more than any man before but I want to savour this feeling. I want to know him before there's anything physical, but do you know what's really odd?"

"What?"

"Tuesday morning before I came into work I had a premonition, I was brushing my teeth and as I looked in the mirror I saw myself quite clearly sat in the pub, the Crown, I was looking across the table, at who I don't know, and I had a confused look on my face. It was surreal, like a painting, I rubbed the condensation away and the image dripped down the mirror like paint, I nearly told you that morning, I wish I had now."

I waft the notion of seeing into the future away and add, "Anyway Rox, you've caught yourself a rich, highly successful music writer and producer so pat yourself on the back." I always knew music would be his ambition but I never suspected the kind of success he has now.

"Don't be sceptical Rachel, it's not like you. Give me the benefit of the doubt, you know I have no reason to deceive you. I might be some things but 'gold digger' is not one of them."

"Sorry I just can't imagine you together or what you might have in common, it's hard for me to picture the two of you together."

"It's a revelation, and no one is more surprised than me. It's not something I can put into words except to say I think he might be the one, you know that whole 'soulmate' thing." She utters with a little embarrassment. She has never believed in that concept.

That word or the insinuation of it is supposed to be a chance in a million occurrence but at the moment it seems to be everywhere; 'the norm' and I'm getting sick of hearing it. It's becoming a thousand times more clichéd than it already is!

Everything is gradually falling into place for everyone connected to me yet it's me who's doomed.

As well as having this to deal with I know deep down that I will not be seeing 'J' tonight; my jaunt this morning was half hearted and jumpy, a stark difference to the dynamic experience of last week.

Sure enough in the afternoon I get a phone call from Anna confirming that tonight's session is cancelled as she is really ill with flu – luckily she has Alan to look after her.

Roxanne sees I'm really deflated and disappointed by something when I come off the phone, and kindly asks me to go out with her and Simon tonight so I can see for myself 'the chemistry' they have. Seems like a good idea so I accept; I don't reveal the reason for my sadness and she doesn't ask.

Our evening around the town is an eye opener. Simon is the perfect gentleman as always but there's a casualness I have never seen in him before. Roxanne is the tamed shrew; he brings out the very best in her. She is still feisty but her eyes are for him all night, she adores him and he seems to be in awe of her rawness and honesty. I wonder if that will change when they have their first physical encounter. I don't think they've even kissed yet which for Roxanne is like a cat not chasing a mouse. Perversely I am looking forward to hearing her description of that event and I know she will want to divulge every bit of detail, she will never feel awkward about our past relationship; I don't think it would occur to her.

*

This week I analyse my life and make some decisions.

While completing the mural Snow Patrol – 'In My Arms' consumes me and I slump onto the edge of the bed looking up at the wall of art; from a growing mist between me and the painting emerges a black haloed figure looming over me, surrounding me with emotions, I need his words in my ear, his strong arms around me and the warmth of his breath on my neck. The colours from the wall swirl around and push this apparition, he is here in the room with me, a fog of colour and blackness splashing the walls around me, he's trying to materialise into the room and get to me.

I turn round and round, arms outstretched, the music battering the walls and blowing through me, it's like trying to catch a butterfly in the wind, I almost get it and then it's out of reach.

I run to the wall then he's gone, I run to the next one and he's on the ceiling, I reach up while my tears flow down; if I don't grab on he'll be lost forever but then he's back in the mural and slowly disappears.

Chapter 11

Week 8

Alien Junkyard
The wind through their hair

By Wednesday I'm in a frenzy. I need to talk to 'him' about his materialisation through my walls. I need to know whether it really was him or whether I'm going completely mad, but then Friday comes and I have quashed any idea of confrontation. If I were to talk to him in a calm manner about something so outlandish I would sound completely berserk; it's too strong and aggressive. If the whole thing turned out to be demented love lust I could scare him. His fragility over me wouldn't stand that.

My 'jaunt' Friday morning is very powerful and takes me further than ever before, to a galaxy full of fast spinning planets, asteroids (which are great fun to dodge), vast dust clouds and something I've never seen before – an immensely large open area. I can't see any planets, stars or naturally occurring debris but there are what can only be described as manmade objects!

At first glance the closest object appears to be a perfectly circular disc, tapering at the edges. The diameter is twice the size of Jupiter while the depth at the thickest part in the centre is about the same as the diameter of the smallest planet in my own solar system, Mercury.

As I approach from a vast distance the shape looks contrived but as I quickly get closer I realise it is made of rock, as though it has been chiselled and sliced from a larger object, but heaven knows what; there's nothing around here that it could belong to!

The way it has been cut away from something else is manmade or humanoid made or alien made, or whatever the noun should be.

This section is breath-taking but just as I'm trying to get my head around what this could be I see something even more disturbing or exciting; a metallic perfectly cylindrical column with grooves spiralling around the outside and within these indentations are millions and millions of what appear to be precious stones, diamonds and rubies, sapphires and emeralds, but the colours change and reflect the light from the stars in such a way as to create brief but constant rainbows around the object. The beauty and idea of the skill that has gone into producing this is breath-taking. The length of the column is similar to the Eiffel tower with a diameter equal to 'the Gherkin'. The ends however are broken and shredded as though it had once been attached to something at either end and there are cracks here and there along the whole length of this rigid but effervescent torso.

I come to realise that this area is some sort of alien junk yard. This confirms two things in my mind; we are not alone in the universe and other beings are as reckless as us. They may be so much more advanced but they're not that different.

I want to explore further and investigate this amazing find but I need to get on with my Earth day.

Roxanne is itching to tell me about her and Simon and I am more than willing to hear about her sexploits … for a change. I had forgotten about the situation with Roxanne. She has been off work all week and I have been too wrapped up in my own life which is a new sensation for me.

We disappear into one of the smaller out of the way storerooms and her tale begins,

"Rachel, how did you ever let this man go?"

"He wasn't a man when we were together, he was a boy. Besides that we just didn't have chemistry."

"We have enough chemistry to supply the world for all eternity."

I'm starting to regret my eagerness to hear her story but it's nice to hear her speak so romantically and without the usual expletives.

"So what have you been doing all week, or need I ask?"

"It's been the most amazing six days of my life. We are so in love. He took me to Malaysia!"

"How did you manage that in six days?"

"He knows all the right people and can do anything he wants, but the beauty of this man is he doesn't do everything he wants. He is down to earth, kind and he makes sense. He's not a pushover though and he says he loves me for my honesty and 'devil may care' attitude. He is amazing in bed though, you wouldn't think it to look at him would you, but he has such a power over me that no other man has come close to. He's perfect."

And there it is, perfection for me is imperfection. Imperfect strangeness and unpredictability is my idea of perfection. For the first time in my life I realise a hard and fast truth, I have been searching for that perfect route in my life and a perfect man to walk it with me, when all along eccentric and inexplicable feeds me and fulfils me more.

"What do you mean exactly by power over you?"

She leans back against the wall and slides down it until she is sitting on the floor with her arms wrapped around her knees and looks up at me in a vulnerable little girl way I never thought I would see from her.

"The first time he kissed me was so gentle and restrained but it had a power behind it I can't explain. I suppose it was the equivalent of that bodily, muscular, flesh and blood surging sensation at that point just before an orgasm happens, when you know it's about to happen, and you're not quite there yet, but it was more spiritual and meaningful than that. The whole sensation was about him and me, something special between us."

"I suppose when it came to the sex then you exploded!"

"We haven't had sex yet. Anyway it won't be sex, it will be 'making love'."

"Roxanne this is incredible, are you telling me you have known this man for nearly two weeks and you haven't jumped him yet?"

"I don't want to ruin it but I have been fantasising about him. I've never done that before. I have always acted on impulse … as you know. I just love how this is making me feel. I truly love him Rachel and I almost feel like I could wait forever if this feeling stays with me."

I kneel down and hug her and as she hugs me I know this is a turning point in her life.

"Please don't change though Roxanne, never forget he loves you for the bitch you are."

We laugh and cry then pull ourselves together and get back to work but not before she reminds me,

"We need to set you up with someone, I wonder if Simon has any filthy rich friends or do I mean rich filthy friends, we could introduce you to?"

"Don't go there Rox. If your story is anything to go by then a life changing event could be just around the corner for me so don't force things."

She smiles because she understands and I smile because she doesn't.

*

I dressed down this morning purposefully so as not to be accessible. 'J' wants to play it safe so I have dressed casual in cargo trousers, tucked into my Doc Martins, with several layered T-shirts and big chunky mohair jumper. My hair is piled up and hanging all over the place but it's comfortable and unpretentious, as though I haven't made any effort – which I haven't!

Anna is happy and whistling a little tune while attaching all the paraphernalia to my dutiful body. You don't often see women whistle but it's just the sort of little quirky thing I've come to expect from her, along with pulling her hair up to a point above her head when she's thinking hard about something (as though lifting her hair off her head will allow her brain some room to think things through). It suits her and makes her all the more adorable. She's a mix of Alice (*Through the Looking Glass*) and Germaine Greer; beautiful and innocent with a look of wonderment of the world around her, along with a womanly wise sincerity and intellect that could ruffle a few feathers when it matters.

I enter 'our' room, closing the door behind me but just as I bend my knees to sit down on my chair he takes my left hand with his left hand; he is just lightly holding my fingers in his.

"Come over here with me."

I do as he says, no questions asked, I'm happy to, and I don't see it as a weakness. I believe how he feels about me and I can let go any thoughts of being glamoured or hypnotised for his own gain. I trust him and will do anything he asks.

We walk across the room carefully away from the chairs then he commands gently in a low sensual voice, almost breaking,

"Kneel down."

I kneel and wait to see what he's going to do, my heart is racing, I'm not scared.

He kneels behind me and his thighs now either side of me push into my hips. His knees are just within my eye line so I put my hands on them. He then pushes his arms through mine and his hands are now out in front and resting on my thighs.

"We're going for a ride, I'm glad you're dressed appropriately. Hold on to me!"

As he says that I can feel a vibration running through my feet and legs as though they're either side of a motorbikes engine.

His right hand is moving as though going through the gears and I can feel the vibration surging through me. At the same time a breeze develops in front of me gradually increasing, now it's blowing through my hair with slightly more force.

I lean back into him and push my head back into the crook of his neck.

"Where would you like to go?"

"Anywhere with you, away from people, buildings, things. Somewhere special for us."

"We could skim the beach, then scratch the country lanes and finish at top speed along the moors. We can do anything we want, but if you want something different there's a little known Nordic forest with routes veining through it just wide enough and clear enough for a motorbike but still overgrown and undisturbed"

"Sounds too good to be true."

"Well it is, I made it up, but we can do anything we want!"

We fly with the wind whistling past our ears and the sun on our faces. I can actually feel the speed beneath us and the energy is tangible. We lean into the corners and its real, we're speeding along tarmac, through the countryside and we're in love.

We arrive at the wide entrance to our forest which gradually narrows as we enter, funnelling us in, and as we reach the narrowest point we speed up and fly under the canopy of ferns and ivy with intermittent spot lights of light heating our faces.

"This reminds me of the Forest Moon of Endor when Princess Leia and Luke are chasing through the trees."

"Yes, except we don't need a green screen to make our fantasy come true, you and I can actually make our dreams a reality. How amazing would that be out there in the real world, away from this room? The possibilities are endless."

Eventually we slow down, but before we stop while the slowing breeze is still swirling I turn to face him. His hair is blowing from his face and I can feel the side burns on their own either side. I can put my hands flat over his features without hair getting in the way or having to move it. He blinks and his eyelashes tickle my fingers. His soft breath pulses against my palms while his cheeks lift slightly. His provocative smile captures the moment and I can almost see his sculpted mouth.

I move my hands away and as we come to rest he puts his hands around my waist.

He whispers in my ear,

"We could do amazing things together, we are a destined partnership. We could create a life envious of everyone around us."

"I'm just happy when I'm here with you. Do you know how you have affected my life? Strange things have started happening to me and it's no coincidence that it all started a few days before our first session."

"What strange things?"

"I am having regular out of body experiences and some of my friends are also starting to act strangely. There are things out there that we, the human race, just aren't aware of that I have seen and felt."

'J' continues the theme, "If I tell you I day dreamed recently that I was in your bedroom and that I knew you were aware of my presence, would that mean anything to you?"

We move away from each other knowing that something magical is happening between us.

"Yes." I reply with urgency.

He takes my head into his large icy cold hands, he wasn't wearing gloves on our ride, and for the first time he feels every contour of my face. Each finger is like its own independent articulated probe collecting data on every pore, hair and feature.

His hands slide down my neck then down my front just gliding past my breasts, then he pulls me to him and says,

"I've missed you so much."

Celine Dion – 'Falling Into You' spontaneously swirls around our heads and tantalisingly seduces us into a romantic embrace.

He starts to kiss my neck as I lift his loose shirt at the back. I brush my hands up along his spine feeling every soft bump and dip. As I drag my fingertips back down either side of the bone right down to belt of his trousers he arches his back and lifts his head back. I kiss his throat and rest my hands on his hips and he begins to kiss me more passionately than he did a couple of weeks ago.

We are both upright now facing each other with our shins along the ground, knees touching and we're leaning into each other. I can feel his erection pressing into my abdomen and that first sexual contact makes me realise how real this is. The whole session has felt surreal and beautiful but this now makes him, me, us – very real and organic.

I lift my hands and push them up through the hair at the nape of his neck but then the alarm goes and it's hard for us to stop, to untangle. I don't want to gasp for air, I want to carry on the euphoric sensation of drowning. Having to suddenly finish something that feels so good and right before its natural completion is like being wrenched naked into the cold night air.

We quickly grasp the blindfolds and put them on as the door opens.

I am in control of myself now, not like the second or third time we met when I almost spontaneously jaunted, I can keep the urge down, buried and trained.

Anna takes off the blindfold and stares at me with a puzzled expression,

"Your hair is such a mess, it's going to take some time to get a comb through that lot."

I turn and look at my reflection in the fire doors to my left, my previously piled up bundle of waves is now a ratty, fused fibrous mass of carnage; it makes me laugh and Anna comments,

"It looks as though you really have been on a bike ride, without a helmet. You know that's illegal right? I can't imagine what he's done to you to create that mullet!"

We both giggle and look at the reflection together. She puts her arm round my shoulder and says,

"It's such a pity you two won't be able to do that for real." She turns and leaves me looking at my reflection, only now it's not funny anymore, I'm not smiling and I look ridiculous!

Chapter 12

'Mystoph' revealed
Intimacy

My mum calls and tells me she's going to visit for a few days. She is in need of a break and wants to -

"See your flat before Christmas is upon us yet again."

It seems ages since I saw her. We speak for hours on the phone but I have never once thought to invite her over and now I feel bad about that. We have such a close relationship and it must be hard for her living alone. She isn't the tidiest person and she wishes she was more organised so she is constantly fighting her own nature. Having no one to bounce off or pull her together is the not the best thing for her. Some people like being alone but she is not one of them.

We arrange for her to arrive the following Saturday for some Christmas shopping, the shops aren't as good here as my home town but there are some great charity and antique shops so we could just meander in those for a day which we both love to do.

*

Work is an unusually happy place at the moment; a mixture of Christmas festivities looming and Roxanne's lack of interest in provoking the older members of staff. She is in seventh heaven and Jason and I are waiting with bated breath for the display of sexual gratification.

Jason has had some quick virgin fixes recently and won adoration from several admirers. This has filled the gap sufficiently but I know deep down he wants something meaningful to gorge on. It will do him for now though.

I have established a regular jaunt routine now which mainly consists of a quick journey around my solar system, and slightly beyond during the week, with a substantial distance or something new every Friday. Saturday and Sunday is similar to the Friday but without the intensity.

This Friday is an arresting and inspirational visit to 'Mystoph'. On this occasion I get a real feel for this serene planet. Not only does it absorb my emotions and experiences, bringing them out like perspiration through my pores so I can physically see them before they drip and disappear in to the earth, but it replaces the lost fluid within me with something else. My skin soaks up the positive atmosphere like we absorb rays from the sun on Earth. I don't lose the memories or feelings; I suppose it's like watering the garden from a hose – the water comes from the reservoir which is then replaced with the same substance when it rains, a continual cycle. I'm feeding this planet and it gives me renewal in return.

Emotions and happenings don't look how I would imagine. If I had been asked to make up this scenario I would have said they'll be wispy and cloud like, but they're not, they are very real, objective and definite –

The moment 'J' and I moved off on our motorbike last week comes out of me like liquid metal, it's a translucent fluid but moves like mercury, seeping from my navel and running down my legs in droplets that join together on the ground to form a puddle which is then gradually absorbed into the soft carpet of moss; the mercurial consistency represents the metal and heat of the engine while the translucent sheen containing fluctuating flecks of neon blue is the electronics – stunningly beautiful. The fluidity and malleable consistency is the movement, and the initial realisation that our combined imagination and need for a joint experience making something real is the joining of the drops to make a mass.

I'm not frightened by this; it's fascinating to watch the perceptions of your life, which to someone else is just a thought or an idea, actually manifested like this.

The following emotion oozing from me is my love for 'J'. The sensation is so strange and challenging in itself, my body is dividing up into pieces and I can scrutinize each part of me. I can still feel each individual limb but they are mini entities defining different things about me. The hands are two parts of my relationships with other people, one hand is the welcoming open side of me and the other is how I hang onto the characteristics of others that I like about them.

My legs are my strength and will power while my feet are the support and stability I create beneath me in every direction I turn.

I know this manifestation is love because whenever I'm in that room with 'him' I feel as though I don't exist as a solitary figure anymore and I have started to feel as though at last I'm realising who I am and what my strengths are; love is challenging and hard but not in a negative way Some people think love is about tying things together, pulling things together – a connection. I never really knew what it was but now I believe the opposite. This planet has revealed to me that it's a freedom – letting go; it's not about becoming one – it's about knowing yourself.

Nothing negative is being extracted which is good, I dread to think how they would be revealed. Mystoph has an intelligence and who in their right mind would want to absorb negativity from another being?

The energy replenishing me is satisfying like the sensation of quenching your thirst or hunger after doing something highly energetic such as swimming or running. It reminds me of the scenes in films when someone who has been deprived of food suddenly gets hold of a chicken leg or a bowl of something and can't get the sustenance down them fast enough; the satisfying moment, the feeling of extreme hunger is obliterated and calm follows.

I try to log everything in my brain so I can write it down when I return but it's hard to do when all I really want is to enjoy the moment.

I need to get back now and enjoy the day on the run up to this evening, which I know is going to be powerful and full of revelations of one kind or another.

I put on my favourite very long and fitted 'Save the Queen' sleeveless dress, biker boots, but no woolly tights – the dress is heavy enough to go without them. The top section of my hair is loosely pulled up and rolled into a knot at the back of my head, my long fringe sweeps my face, the thick waves at the back bounce around my shoulders and cascade down my back. This is a good look for me, it makes me feel confident about meeting 'him' even though he won't see all the beautiful merging colours printed all over the soft but thick material. I bought this dress as more of an investment than a centre piece for my wardrobe. I never thought I would have the nerve to wear it, but it was so beautiful in the window of 'the local designer shop' at a much reduced sale price; it was still expensive but it was so gorgeous and rich in colour that I just thought it was like a piece of art – something radical, mysterious and for me to enjoy in the privacy of my own home; way too outgoing for me but a 'must have' thing.

*

At work Jason comments on how lovely I look which makes me flush a self-conscious red.

"That dress is gorgeous but you bring something out of it, it glows on you. If Roxanne wore it, it would be lost on the sassy self-assurance that blurts out of her all day long."

"That's cruel, she is just true to hers …"

He butts in, "Don't change the subject, I know there's something going on Rachel. I can see how you've changed the last few weeks, you're more confident. You shine my love." His tone changes from authoritative to caring. "You're beautiful … well I thought that anyway but now it's like you know it too and are putting it to good use."

Jason is so perceptive sometimes.

"I love you Jason."

He hugs me and only then do I realise we are stood in the middle of the office and everyone is looking at us and hanging on our every word.

Everyone realises we've noticed them looking and they all cheer and clap at the same time and in true *Officer and a Gentleman* style shout,

"You go girl, way to go, way to go!"

Everyone laughs at their own sarcastic wit while Jason and I look seriously at each other and I know instantly what he's about to do. I know what I'd like him to do, which is to keep the joke going by sweeping me up in his arms and carry me down the aisle just like Richard Gere does with Debra Winger but what is actually going to happen is for Jason's benefit. He is caught up in the moment and is thinking this is the perfect opportunity. I squeeze my eyes tightly together with a cringing apprehension and wait to hear the words he has longed to utter for so long,

He shouts at the top of his voice,

"I'm gay, I like men, not you though Brian don't worry, and I'm out and proud!"

I open one eye to the sudden silence and look at Jason. He stands there in front of me arms held up to the heavens in a very camp hip swaying way with a 'here I am' big smile on his face – centre stage!

Some people in the office had twigged years ago but it wasn't an issue with them so it was therefore not discussed, but for those that go around with their eyes closed, i.e. Karen, and the older ladies and gents to whom it wouldn't occur to question someone's sexuality – this revelation is a shock then seconds later 'shocking'.

I look around the office specifically at the people I know will be affected most and as soon as I make eye contact with each one they look straight down at their desk and pretend nothing has happened, except Brian whose pen is now hanging from his mouth. Karen, who is leaning against the filing cabinets, just looks disappointed but relieved – arms folded with a half smirking and half 'oh well' expression.

Jason looks down at me and simply says,

"Right what was I doing?" looks toward his desk and walks off.

That would have been one of the most surreal moments of my life, if I hadn't already had that bike ride last week, it's like time stood still for a moment then slowly got going, speeded a bit then caught up and returned to normal as though nothing had happened. But something major did happen.

Roxanne comes back and I fill her in on the event. She is devastated that she missed it but misses the point completely. It wasn't so much about expressing himself as getting some sort of life blood into the office or topping their joke.

"I don't really know what Jason expected but I don't think he got the reaction he wanted. I think he wanted some controversy, arguments, name calling or attention but he didn't get it."

"Surely the conservative apron brigade were shocked." she offers.

"Yes they were, but I don't think they are homophobic, they just didn't know what to do with the information. I don't think many of them know any gay men or women, and they certainly aren't used to a massive show of openness like that."

"So, maybe he hoped for a round of applause," she sarcastically replies.

I agree with a naughty glint in my eye.

"That would have been brilliant wouldn't it?"

A quiet pensive moment follows then I remind us.

"Oh well. Back to work."

There is a tension for the rest of the day but it's not aggressive it's embarrassment on everyone else's part, they just don't know how to react.

Jason is disconcerted,

"What do I do now, people aren't looking at me when asking for help or whatever?"

I try to be objective.

"Look, I think it's sort of sweet, I mean really to some of us it's obvious and maybe now they're thinking it makes sense but feel stupid for not noticing. There will be some that have their prejudices but that's life. You will just have to carry on as normal and it won't be an issue after a while. You've been brave.

"I shouldn't have done it, I don't know what came over me … it's your fault."

"What?"

"I got swept up in your euphoria, you owe me."

"What are you on about?"

"Until you tell me what's going on with you I'm sending you to Coventry."

I laugh hysterically as he walks back to his desk. He doesn't look up once and I stand there dumbfounded. I didn't see that coming at all.

I walk over to him and try to diffuse the situation.

"Ok there is something big happening but I can't tell you. I will though … eventually."

He just sits there still writing and doesn't respond at all. I walk away feeling a little sad that he has taken this view but I don't mind being the vehicle for his current dislike of people in general and the need to ostracise in some way.

When everyone has gone home I make my weekly visit to the ladies so I can tidy myself up ready for the next session.

I wash my underarms to get rid of any deodorant and tidy my hair. I look at the person in the mirror and do not recognise the person staring back at me. I am looking at a woman, not a girl anymore and that's the first time I think of myself in that way.

On arrival at the college Anna gets the technology ready to attach to me and as she walks over I realise there are no access points in this dress. It is a strappy low backed clingy dress that is so long it almost trails the ground. She can either go in at the top having to take my dress down or from underneath.

I become very nervous and as she walks toward me she can see my fear.

"What's up Rachel, you look like I'm going to assault you."

"It may come to that. How are you going to attach everything, do you want me to do it?"

"No you can't. What are you so prudish about all of a sudden? I have heard some pretty sensitive and personal things in that room, a bit of flesh isn't going to shock me. We are just girls together."

She's right and I just have to let her get on with it.

She lifts my dress right up and asks me to hold it all aloft while she connects everything.

She steps back,

"You can drop your dress down now."

I do as I'm told then, she remarks,

"You have a lovely body, I've never noticed your figure before. You have a long body and long legs, which is really attractive you know. You should show yourself off more."

I immediately feel very shy and withdrawn but as we walk toward the door of the session room confidence fills me up and I feel loved and adored. I wish I could rewind and immerse myself in the feeling of being looked at and admired by another female rather than the embarrassment, but that moment is lost, I must live in the now, my own 'now'.

I float into the room and Snow Patrol – 'In My Arms' rushes at me from across the room, from behind his tall standing figure, slamming the door behind me and then swirls around my head and body. The strength of it lifts and pulls me over to him and he takes my hand.

Without questioning I follow with his fingers threaded through mine, he stops near a wall and let's go of me. He takes off his coat and spreads it on the floor. He kneels down and holds out a dreamlike arm toward me. I take his hand and sit beside him, he then lays back and I do too.

He pushes his arm under my neck and I turn toward him resting my head in his neck. He folds his other leg and arm across me and covers me in tenderness.

I'm trembling and he rubs my arm to warm me while the music embraces us.

My mural paints itself all over the wall opposite us and spreads the whole way around the room.

"When I touch you Rachel I get a sense of you as a little girl, it's like you have the wonderment and sensitivity of a child in a sensual woman's knowledgeable body. It's a very powerful sensation, what kind of childhood did you have?"

"Not a particularly good one, but the few happy moments I had are very very vivid. I can't remember a lot about it at all, some of it is blocked out so I think it wasn't good."

"I get that hazy lucidity from you. You have very definite self-awareness but there's mystery beneath it. Changing the subject – did you have a weird event today?"

"Yes, you can tell?"

"Mmm."

With that soft reply he holds me closer to him and we lie there together in a perfect moment.

The next thing I know I'm waking up, we have both been asleep and I don't know how long.

"'J', wake up!"

He hugs me to him.

"Have we been sleeping?" he yawns.

"Yes."

The music fades in to my head again; he moves his right arm and strains it down to my ankle, he lifts my skirt and strokes my leg very slowly all the way up to my thigh. He leans across me and spreads his left hand the whole way across the back of my head under my hair and pulls me up to meet him.

The kiss is passionate from the start. Wet, red, round, complete contact.

The alarm goes and he doesn't stop. I don't want him to stop and I kiss him back with total defiance. I can hear Anna at the door and in one quick movement I stand and run to the door, not looking behind me. I can see where I'm going by the crack of light now starting to spread through the room. My dress is bouncing all around me in every direction and as I lunge for the door my boot catches in the hem and I go flying into the corridor wall opposite the door.

The next thing I know I'm waking on a couch in Anna's office with an ice pack on my head.

"What happened?"

"Relax Rachel. You knocked yourself out when you hit the wall," she starts to laugh uncontrollably whilst trying to stop herself, "it was one of the funniest things I've ever seen. I'm sorry, you must be in shock or concussion or something but I haven't been able to stop laughing since."

I am so embarrassed. I went into that room feeling like I was the most stunning creature on the planet and now I feel like I've been pinching sweets in the sweetshop and I've been found out in front of everyone I know with my dress tucked in my pants. I want to be swallowed up in the hole I can see spiralling through the floor right before me; or maybe that's not a trick of my mind and I actually do have concussion or my eyesight's been affected.

I push up onto my elbows,

"Oh Anna, did 'he' see that happen, did he see me?"

"No, don't worry, as you lurched through the door," she's laughing again, "I slammed the door behind you. The most he saw was your enigmatic self, floating in that lovely dress and your long thick wavy hair bouncing behind you, he didn't see the bumbling clod throwing herself at the wall head first."

Her laughter is really nauseating and I lay back into the sofa wondering what he did actually see.

"I think you need a tissue or something Anna, your tears of laughter are ruining your mascara."

"Sorry, but you had to see it. How do you feel now?"

"My head hurts a bit but ok. How long have I been out?"

"Only a minute."

"How did you get me in here?"

"I asked the caretaker to help me. Actually I must go and sort your partner out, he's still in there. I have already told him he'll have to wait a bit but I will just go and let him know it will be a bit longer."

"Does he just sit there in the dark each week waiting for me to leave?"

"Yes, but I offer to put the light on and give him a newspaper but he says he likes to just sit in the dark until it's time for his debrief."

I can understand that, I think I would do the same.

"It's ok, I'll get up and go now."

"Only if you think you're alright. I need to talk to you in depth sometime about the whole experience of the last nine weeks and go over a few other things."

"'Go over a few things?' – Alan you mean?" I offer with a slanted grin.

She smiles but reveals nothing

"If you'll meet me tomorrow afternoon at The Wing Tavern that would be great, about 4 pm?"

"Ok," I sigh as I stand up. I'm half expecting to stagger and fall but I seem to be alright.

Chapter 13

Week 10

Alien Technology
Goodbye

I meet Anna as arranged and we talk generally about the success of the experiment.

The data she has collected, along with the transcript of our conversations, has been a revelation and given her more than enough for a thesis and maybe even one day a book.

She reinforces the need for us to remain anonymous as she sees a possible recall in the future for more in-depth scrutiny. She has considerable interest in our meeting again much further down the line when our lives have taken new and different paths away from each other.

Anna explains to me that if the book thing happens then there would be something in it for me and 'him'. I'm beginning to think there's more to this experiment than meets the eye; a manipulative angle for the sake of a book that I hadn't considered.

"I'm not trying to buy your loyalty Rachel, I just think your efforts to remain anonymous should be rewarded. If we do further experiments they could be very interesting and another book would be an exciting step forward."

Scepticism aside I understand what she's saying but I do feel prostituted in a way. My integrity is for sale!

This whole conversation is making me uneasy. Doesn't she realise how hard it is for me to hear about the impending end of my relationship and that one day I may have to go through all this again? Sometimes I don't understand why I am being so accommodating. Maybe knowing this is all for the greater good is the only way I can justify keeping my promise to her right now.

"Anyhow, I just wanted to tell you all of this before we start the last session. I want to do a debrief as normal at the end, it's more important being the last one, but I have to leave almost immediately on Friday night so I won't be able to hang around too long."

"Why? Hot date with Alan?"

She hesitates and looks down,

"I'm er … going away … on a holiday with Alan actually."

"Oh, why so glum then?"

"I'm not glum."

She sits up-right and smiles

"So what will you do with yourself every Friday?"

I hadn't given it much thought. I haven't even thought about how my jaunting will be affected.

"Probably come here, drink away my sorrows and hit on every man in the place." I reply sarcastically.

"Don't do anything I wouldn't do."

She stands up then leans over to kiss me on the forehead. She turns and walks toward the door, meeting and embracing Alan as he walks in. They both turn and look at me ominously with sad smiles then walk out together.

There was something meaningful in all that but I'll be damned if I know what it is. I hope it wasn't pity, because that would be very hard to swallow considering it's Anna's fault I'm in this situation in the first place.

*

My mum, Elaine, comes to stay.

I have taken a few days off work now to spend time with her and in exchange at this busy time of year have agreed to work over the Christmas period to cover for young parents that want to be at home with their children. I have a feeling I will need something to occupy my mind.

Elaine is something of an enigma. She is a large lady with grace and glamour but not too showbiz. She appears 'with it' and 'having it all together' but she is one of the ditsiest women

I have ever known. She has the elegant look of Helen Mirren, the body of pre-gastric band Fern Britton, the sensibility and kindness of Geraldine Grainger in the *Vicar of Dibley* and the dottiness of Maggie in *Extras*.

I admire her, love her and laugh affectionately with her at her mad, accident-prone and hair-brained antics.

I will be amazed if she leaves my flat without breaking anything or accidently and completely unintentionally, hurts the feelings of any friends we might meet in town.

We do lots of Christmas shopping, knocking over displays and falling over pushchairs which is not unusual and talk candidly the rest of time about my Dad and his strange ways.

"You know Rachel he took me to a fishing village for our honeymoon. His idea of a nice evening in was bringing home a rabbit for me to skin or a pheasant for me to pluck. After twelve years of that, I'm glad he threw us out, I'd plucking well had enough."

"Mum, I don't understand why you married him, what was it that could possibly have attracted you to him?"

"He was very handsome, aloof and interesting in a weird way. All the other young women around at the time wanted to go out with him but it was me he chose. He was different from the others. I just fell in love with him. Despite everything I loved him very much."

"I would call him odd not interesting but I suppose I can understand your fascination with him."

While this conversation evolves I'm comparing their oddball relationship with that of 'J' and I, only ours doesn't have the physical aggression that theirs had or the lack of affection.

She continues, "You know I bumped into him the other day and he told me the oddest thing."

"What could be odder than talking to your antique stuffed birds of paradise artificially posed in a cramped bulbous glass dome case, or placing your bucket of jellied eels next to the twelve bore shot gun at the bottom of the stairs or arranging all your pens and household handy items in a line across the top of your Queen Anne table and getting more than upset if any of them are slightly skewwhiff?"

"You haven't heard anything yet." She says that with a nonchalance as if everything I just reeled off was completely normal.

"What is it?"

"He told me that he was walking through the park the other day and he saw a man looking down and talking to himself. He went over to the man and said, 'Stop doing that you mad man, go back with Zoltan where you belong!'"

I laughed so hard I thought I would choke.

"Mum, he's bonkers"

She laughs, "I know! I think the man was talking on one of those mobile ear phone things but he didn't cotton on."

"You know Mum if we had all stayed under the same roof I dread to think what would have happened, what with your free way of living and let's face it untidiness, along with his compulsive ways and with two young kids underfoot. I think something horrible would have happened."

"Probably. His throwing us out was a mercy then!"

We laugh and talk all week, then an event occurs that I didn't see coming, just hours before she's due to leave, which changes our lives.

Thursday morning comes and while I'm showering Elaine pops out for some newspapers; three hours later she returns.

"Where have you been, I was starting to worry!"

"You won't believe it. I met this chap at the newsagents, well I say met, what I mean is I knocked over a display with my bag and was struggling to pick everything up, those metal card displays weigh a ton, although I could swear the stand seemed to start lifting itself when I reached out to pick it up … odd that … anyway it was taking forever to pick up all the cards and you know they have to …"

My frustration buts in,

"Mum, what about the man?"

"Yes, erm, this man started to help me and then we got talking and to cut a long story short he's taking me out to lunch."

My gulp is audible.

"Don't be so surprised, things like this do happen you know, in real life. You know, weird unpredictable stuff."

If only she knew!

"Yes Mum but not to you, normally. Sorry that came out wrong."

"I know what you mean but things like this happen when you least expect it."

I so want to laugh and tell her about all the events of the last nine weeks but I want to revel in her excitement.

"What's he like?"

"He's very tall and debonair, such a gentlemen. It was an instant connection. We went for a cup of tea and he told me all about himself and was actually interested in me, no family talk or work just my interests and likes. It was amazing Rachel."

"He sounds too good to be true."

"He lives nearby, obviously. All I know is he owns a hairdressers around here."

"Paul, its Paul Channing? He's my landlord." She hadn't even noticed or remembered I live above a hairdressers.

I can't believe it, my mum is actually going on a date with my new found father figure.

"So where are you going? Does he know you're leaving this evening?"

"Yes but we'll just take it one step at a time. Anyway it's only lunch, well a late lunch actually. So he owns this gorgeous building then?"

"Yes, but he doesn't live here. He has another house further down."

"Well that's something else we can talk about then."

"What?"

"… you of course."

I am so pleased now I didn't mention my experiences to Paul or go and look at the loft. He would have told Elaine and then she would have worried about me, which I really don't need.

It's only later when recapping in my mind over what actually happened to my mum in the newsagents that I remember that seemingly insignificant snippet of information she gave me – 'the stand seemed to start lifting itself when I reached out to pick it up.' There is some force at work here, something supernatural is happening and I have no clue what it all means!

I see my mum off feeling excited for her along with mixed feelings for myself. I really don't know what to expect from my final meeting with 'J'.

My Friday morning jaunt is spectacular and moving. I am right in the middle of the Alien Junkyard and have come to a vessel of some kind. The main body shape is similar to that of a squid but has hundreds of twisted and skewed metal dreadlocks instead of tentacles; they are all different lengths and reaching into space in every direction; there seems to be no uniformity to their direction yet the ship on the whole seems to have a natural balance as well as grotesque beauty.

The capacity of the main part of the vessel is about that of the Millennium dome while the hard but fluid metal corkscrew tentacles are about a mile long.

The smooth flawless body is surrounded by thousands of slightly bulging rounded copper strips giving the main body a sort of lantern effect; like those paper lanterns we used to make as kids, we'd cut lines through a rolled then flattened tube of paper, open it out then push the ends slightly towards each other to create a mesmerising 3D decoration.

The mirrored perspex, or whatever space resilient glass-like material the hull is made of, underneath the curved copper, is tinted with lots of different effervescent shades of yellow, orange and red with occasional symmetrical oval copper panels; these panels look like doorways so I decide to take a look inside.

There is a large floating mezzanine that moves around and turns upside down very slowly and in a completely random way. The intricate electronics and machinery that hover on the surface don't dislodge, they just float inches away and glide around with it in a sort of mutual attraction.

There appear to be access points or rather plug in points periodically all around the shell of this great open area and these same junction boxes are also inlaid around the edge of the mezzanine. Perhaps the Alien beings have some sort of wiring or connection leaving their bodies or suits which connect simultaneously with the hull of the ship and power source on the mezzanine. I can only guess, as it would appear that this deserted ship is defunct and left to rot in the Junk Yard.

At first it was hard for me to understand why all this beautifully crafted, precision engineering would be cast aside like this but then some other less advanced non-human life form may think the same of us Earthlings.

Standing at the control centre I look around the vastness of this ship and wonder what kind of life form could use this intimate and interactive equipment, yet still require so much open space. Our own astronauts are cramped into small spaces with every little bit of space utilised without any wastage; why has this been built on such a large scale, how big are these creatures?

On that thought I become a little intimidated and feel the need to leave, this is the first time I have actually felt apprehensive about being out in the universe and I suddenly feel quite alone.

I am back at home quicker than ever.

My last session with 'J' could go one of three ways; it could be emotionless in order to try and soften the blow, it could be full of passion – get as much of each other while we still can, or it could be awkward and meander along the middle not knowing which way to go. Whatever happens it will be dictated by 'him'. I will go along with whatever he thinks is best. His initiatives have always been the most creative and I am happy to respond. It's like being on a committee; I like being directed and doing the donkey work but I'm not very good at coming up with the ideas, I have too much going round in my head and can't organise it properly. 'J' acts on impulse; whatever his instinct tells him he acts on it and suffers the consequences later. I like that about him. The ability to just do something even if it's ultimately completely the wrong decision.

I decide to dress as me, contradictory with my summer clothes in winter.

I have a pretty 1950s button front cotton dress, knee length with very full pleated skirt. Pale Yellow with slightly darker yellow strips. It is fitted at the waist and has capped sleeves. I have a pale blue long cardigan just a bit shorter than the dress with sleeves that widen at the wrist, it fastens at the front at the waist with just one big silver clasp.

This arrangement seems to go nicely with my brown hair and brown mid-calf boots and pale blue woolly tights. I have on my best lacy underwear which won't be seen, as will none of the clothes by 'him' but it all goes towards making me feel young, feminine and stylish.

I lock the door and venture out to the street, feeling confident and ready for a day of torment and delight when something happens to obliterate that self-assurance.

The weather outside is disgusting, it is freezing, sleety and windy. My loose hair, which I would normally have tied up in weather like this, is blown in every direction and my clothes are splattered with black puddle water while waiting for the bus. An umbrella, I soon discover, is useless in this weather and as I try to put it away I drop it in a puddle. I drag my big cardigan sleeves through the sludgy puddle trying to retrieve it then just stand there and sigh at the ridiculousness of me. Finally the bus arrives, ten minutes late!

I walk into work feeling pretty low. I try to dry myself off with old bits of tissue from the bottom of my bag in reception before entering the office space but it's like trying to remove an inkblot or blood stain, I'm just making things worse.

Jason doesn't help my self-esteem, which is now at an all-time low, by saying, "You look like you've had an electric shock then been pulled through a hedge backwards and then dragged in by the cat."

"I think you'll find that lots of women spend hours trying to achieve this windblown look."

"Yes, but they haven't got mascara running down their faces and mud splattered on their dresses. Anyway having hair like a raving lunatic who has just escaped from the asylum is a debatable style choice!"

I disappear into the ladies and try to tidy myself properly but with limited resources it's useless. There's only so much you can do with a hand dryer and toilet tissue. I reapply the mascara then give up and decide it doesn't really matter anyway. The person that matters isn't going to see me.

Roxanne drags her chair round to my desk.

"Listen, while the team leaders are in a meeting I thought we could have a little chat."

I'm not in the mood for work now anyway so seems a good time for a joy ride in Roxanne's head.

"Ok, what?"

"Simon and I finally consummated our relationship last night."

'Consummated', that is definitely not a word I would have imagined Roxanne using, it implies some sort of permanence and commitment, it seems she is thinking differently now, which I'm not entirely sure about!

"It ... was – In ... cre ... di ... ble!" she says mastering the art of mono syllabic gesturing.

I lean in,

"Go on then – details please."

"We were just talking at the dinner table, when he got up mid-sentence walked over to me, pulled my chair out from the table, really forcefully, and swept me up in his arms. It took my breath away."

"Was this at home or the restaurant?"

"Ha ha! My flat of course."

"Then what?"

"He carried me upstairs just looking into my eyes the whole time, then sat me on the edge of the bed. He didn't say a word and neither did I. You know me, I normally like to verbalise everything that's happening during sex, and I like the man to do it too, it turns me on even more normally, but this time it didn't occur to me at all. It's only when I think back now that it was all so graceful and free of stuff, you know, not thinking how to move this way, which position would be better here, would I like my hand to be there. I suppose normally I have sex like I'm being directed in a film."

That makes me laugh, I can just imagine her scripting and directing her love life like that.

"So in essence it's like you imagined it would be, you made love rather than just a sexual act?"

"Exactly. I think back to it now and it was so natural and smooth and poetic but still really erotic, perhaps more so than normal."

"Why is that then, what made it so amazing, you know when you got to the nitty gritty of it?"

"I suppose it was the emotional connection and then the sudden realisation that I was actually being touched, held, kissed and had intimacy with this man that had power over me. I have always felt like the dominant one in relationships. I talked to him about it afterwards which is another first for me and he said the same thing!"

That is amazing. I have a fleeting pang of jealousy but it's short lived and then I'm pleased for her. She has found something incredible with Simon. Something I didn't even come close to with him.

"So Rox, you do realise how lucky you are? What are you going to do next, I mean are you planning on being together or taking it further or what exactly?"

"We're just going to take it slow for a while so we can see whether we really are as compatible as we think we are. He's going back home for a couple of weeks but we'll email, etcetera, then he'll come and stay for a bit and just let it go on like that for a while. We'll see what happens. No real plan. I'm going to miss him so much but he has important work – producing and composing. I just adore that about him."

"Wow, it seems you've got it all!" I say with envious acknowledgement of their perfect relationship.

"I know I'm lucky. You know we've talked about you quite a lot."

Oh no, I don't want to hear any of this.

"Ok. Well you know I really need to get on with this now."

She just smiles and drags her chair back round to her desk.

"It's good stuff Rachel, but it can wait till another time."

'Never', works for me.

Before leaving for college I ring my mum for a quick update on her 'date' (sounds ridiculous and trivial when referring to my own mother). I haven't seen Paul yet and don't think I could bring myself to ask him about it anyway, it may make him feel uncomfortable.

It all went really well and he's going to take her out to the theatre and shopping in the city – lovely! How great for everyone that their lives are sorted at what seems my expense!!

Walking towards that sign outside the college gets my heart racing. Who would think that one insignificant object could bring on such a swell of emotion. One person walks past it and it just tells them something – it's information. Another person walks past and doesn't even notice it even though it's as big as the side of a house. I walk past it and my whole life flashes before my eyes!

Anna is very subdued. She uses one syllable words and only when necessary. I open the front of my dress and she straps on the device. She walks toward the door with only minimum conversation.

I don't know what to say to her, I don't know if she's sad because this is the end of the process, sad because she won't see me on a regular basis any more or whether there is more to it than that.

"You know we can always arrange to meet socially." I say with a comforting smile.

She doesn't say anything to that, just smiles that same sad smile she did when she left me in the pub on Saturday.

I arrive at my door feeling lost. I tie the blindfold and make my last request!

Now I'm the other side of the door, my last request has been permitted, the man I love is only feet away.

I sit, hang the blindfold over the back of the seat and try to hold back the tears as I look in his direction.

He stands towering above me, steps forward then leans over, arms either side of my head clutching the back of my chair to steady himself. He whispers in my ear, *"I love you more than that word allows Rachel, whatever that more expressive and elusive word may be is how I truly feel about you; It's something real, physical, mature and beyond anything in this universe. The word universe doesn't even describe the vast infinite emotional expanse I have travelled to find you."*

He rests on his haunches and brings his head round to face me. Holding onto either side of my chair he kisses me carefully as though we were balancing on a precipice.

I hold his head in my hands and peer through his black veil. I can conjure his face, and project it onto the mask that lies beneath; the enigmatic and quirky eyes and smile of Robert Downey Jnr. In *Sherlock Holmes* – the two combined – handsome, dark, intelligent mystery and conflicting moral awareness.

I'm lost in the moment but brought back to reality as he loses his balance slightly.

I reluctantly and suddenly pull away right into the back of the chair

"I don't think I can do this. Everyone around me has found the love of their life but I feel so empty and dead when I'm not with you. I don't think I can live without you. Before I knew you I was floundering. Lost in my own world and too scared to get involved. I was totally disconnected. You are everything. I admire you, I'm absorbed by and fascinated by your ambiguities. You're so sensitive and gentle and kind yet strong. The love and interest you have shown for me is overwhelming. I like that we've argued, it hasn't been an easy ride but we've always complemented each other. You entertain me and feed me. You're strange but I'm so comfortable with you. I can't go on knowing I will not see you again. It's so unfair."

His response is considered and true.

"I know, I have thought of nothing else in the last few weeks and I've come close on several occasions to ending it, but I have come to a carefully considered conclusion. It is these hard and fast rules and more specifically an actual contract that has brought us together in the first place. That is what made all this possible and I feel strongly that if we mess it up now something bad will happen. I have a strong foreboding … if we don't see this through to its natural end then we're doomed to failure by some outside force. I can't really explain it."

I know he's right! That outside force is fate!

"I understand, I really do. Just hearing it out loud makes sense. It's the main reason I've been able to keep strong until now."

At the beginning of this process it was me holding it all together but now just when my resolve has left me, it's him with the strength and conviction.

"Rachel, you have an interesting temperance that brings out the best in me, it's not old fashioned or naïve, as I first thought before I got to know you, it's a part of your nature, an attractive hold over me.

"You are able to make me feel calm and introverted in a way that no woman has ever been able to and it's not even deliberate on your part. Shyness is seen as a negative debilitating weakness but when it's just with one person, one part of your life, it can be evocative, sensual; it brings life to my core. I love the surges of 'not knowing' and I now embrace the modesty that now inhabits me when I'm with you − that little bit of intimidation. It makes me light headed and creative, a need to do more to hold onto you. It's really quite something!"

I am light headed myself now, those thoughtful dreamy words are almost more than any one person can respond to. How can I be so lucky to experience my fantasy like this?

I melt into his arms. He then stands and takes a step back pulling me up with him.

Ludovico Einaudi's 'Le Onde' envelopes us. So poignant. A piece of simple piano music inspired by Virginia Woolfe's *The Waves*. The notion of individuals and their spiritual collective now creeps and grows along these walls with tendrils that reach out and wrap around us. I ask him to acknowledge the music. It's important to me that he can hear it or imagine it.

"Yes, I can hear it!" he whispers with a little surprise.

The subtle key changes ignite something primeval in me, a love without paraphernalia and attachments – a pureness.

"I do want to break one last rule though." He murmurs.

"Which one?" I reply but knowing full well what he means. I just want to hear him say the words. Sex has played no part in our growing relationship. I don't deny longing has drifted in and out of my mind but it has not dominated or influenced me or him. If we made love now though would it be because we really want to or because it may be a lost opportunity? I hadn't considered this happening at all.

"I need you."

My limited response doesn't reveal how much I want this to happen.

"I don't know if that's a good idea. I want you too but I'm scared!"

"I'm scared. I feel nervous like it's my first time."

"But is that because you're breaking rules. You don't even know what I look like – is that the excitement?"

"You know that's not true. I have so enjoyed getting to know you and feeling the way I do around you. I'm so in love with you Rachel, it's only this last couple of days I have felt that I can't go on after this ends without experiencing the intimacy that would live on with both of us for ever. To physically play out the emotional passion I have for you. To be able to remember a moment when we're both completely joined together!"

"What if it's just clumsy and bad? I don't want that to be my last memory. Our first time could be so special in the right circumstances."

"This is the right circumstances, our circumstances. You'll instinctively know how to respond to me, just as you always have, I just touch you Rachel and I'm somewhere else, somewhere strange and peaceful. You could just stand there like a statue and I'd be aroused by you. Do you even know how you smell to me?"

"I shouldn't smell of anything."

"That's one of the many amazing things about all this. To me you have a natural aroma of marzipan, it's a sort of vanilla essence on every part of you, and it evokes happy memories of being a boy, devouring cake and enjoying parties – cherished memories."

"You have such a way with words. I'm yours, even if this is a deliberate seduction?"

"I don't want us to make love if you're not ready. Don't say yes if you're unsure. It's got to happen only if we both feel exactly the same."

"I do… I really do, I just don't want to disappoint you."

"But you couldn't disappoint me. I don't want to do it because I need satisfying, I want to do it because I love you so much. If it's any consolation though, I don't want to disappoint you either."

That makes me smile and relaxes me. It's not really a matter of disappointing each other, were not in it for the endorphin rush, we're in it because of a deep and meaningful connection, something not of this earth.

I love, adore and cherish this man so much that my chest compresses and the warmth embraces me.

This whole time, we've been stood talking and have had no contact.

He then takes my hand while sitting back in his chair. I stand before him while he unties my boots. I place my hands on his shoulders to steady myself while he pulls them off from my heels forward to the toes. Each heavy boot drops like a dead weight to the ground.

He glides the palms of his hands along the backs of my legs right to the top and then pulls the tights and underwear down to the ground. I step out of them kicking them away.

I straddle his legs and sit facing him. His head is level with my neck and he kisses my throat while undoing the middle five buttons at the front of my dress and then he pushes his arms through and inside. My arms just dangle without purpose, allowing my torso to feel every breadth of his fingers.

His fingers softly glide up and down my back while he kisses me tenderly and thoughtfully along my collar bone, throat and mouth. I'm kissing him softly, tender and arousing at the same time. His hands then press and span the width of the small of my back and I can feel every slight movement rippling through me.

Matt Johnsons 'Beyond Love' now ripples into the air, the lyrics capturing our sincere attachment and constancy;

> 'Move away from the window ... and into the light.
> There are some things in this life, that you just can't fight.
> It's as if the spirits above, have cast a little spell upon us.
> It's as if heaven above. Is beckoning us.
> So let us take off our crosses and lay them in a tin,
> and let our weakness become virtue... instead of sin.
> Our bodies stand naked as the day they were born,
> And tremble like animals... Before a coming storm.
>
> Take me beyond love.
> Up to something above.
> Upon this bed, between these sheets.
> Take me to a happiness beyond human reach.
>
> The force of life is rushing through our veins.
> in and out like the tide. It comes in waves.
> The drops of semen and the clots of blood.
> Which may, one day, become like us.
> With outstretched hands reaching beyond love.
> And up to something above.

Before our juices run cold and our flesh grows old.
Let me feed upon your breast and draw closer to your soul.
Let me stay with you tonight, and I'll offer you my world.
I'll take you to the angels...
...If you'll take me to yourself.

Beyond the grasp of lust.
Beyond the need for trust.
Beyond the gaze of the sick & the lame.
Beyond the stench of human pain.'

The feel of the expensive heavy material of his trousers against my naked legs provokes a sensual lift and I pull him closer.

I open his shirt and feel the contours of his chest and stomach with the back of my hand, the sensitivity of 'back of hand skin', enables me to feel the softness and detail of the epidermis stretched across his abs and ribs.

Stroking down to his waist, I feel along the ridge of his belt. I then push my index finger between the trouser band and his abdomen, he moves slightly and pulls me even closer. I like the pressure of his trousers pushing against my finger as it slides right around his hips, the tightness of his trousers dictates how my finger moves, and then I undo the buckle along with the zip.

I ease onto him, clean and flawless. I have never experienced calm quiet eroticism before; it's not reticent or reserved, it's gentle and all it needs to be. With everyone else it seems to have always been a case of 'go as hard as you can for as long as you can' to get the best out of the situation.

He groans hard into my neck; it's like he's held it back for a while and then can't help letting it out in a powerful throaty gasp – the sound he makes begins my decisive moment and in turn his!

We are hardly moving together but inside we are at the highest point of motion and in total synchronicity; colours, music, heartbeats and rain splash the room and drench us with every sense. Smells of happy memories past and present waft through the luxurious, richly precipitous air around us.

Just as the climax starts to diminish, the second wave begins I become aware of the position of his hands.

He has lifted my skirt and his palms are now wrapped around the underside of my thighs, supporting my whole weight, with the backs of his hands laying on his knees. The index finger on each hand is lodged along the length of the crease at the top of my leg; he's discovered an erogenous zone; he's hardly moving his fingers but there is a slight stroking that heightens the sensation even more.

My hands continue to glide around his muscular back and stroke his soft neck.

We journey into another place; not space – it's another dimension, another time. We didn't jaunt. It seems to be a combination of what we are both now able to do – a new achievement – this is rapturous eternity, exquisite and unknown.

We're kissing passionately now, with full force and my hands clasp his hair at the back of his head. I don't ever want to let go of this man. This man that makes me feel complete and needed.

He pulls me close and tight to him. He then pulls his arms out of my dress and wraps them lovingly around me.

I sit astride him in that same position loving him and holding him, not wanting to let go for what seems only seconds but I fear it is a lot longer than that.

It's me that breaks the silence

"You're trembling!"

"I can hear your music in my head, the world doesn't exist when I'm with you, I become invisible, none existent, and nothing matters. I'm so in love with you." He replies with sadness tinged joy.

Those words tear into me. They mean so much to me but can mean nothing given our pre-ordained future; pain and longing split me in half and splatter me against the now dead walls around us.

When I leave this place I will no longer be a solid mould, my broken pieces will knit together and I'll be a pitiful frankensteined woman with hurt in my eyes.

His alluring, rich manly voice brings me back to the present, the place I need to be.

"*Rachel*, I want you to know that even though we may never meet again, you are, and always will be the biggest part of me – like an organ. You're inside my head and body and influencing my senses. I see the world differently now. I know I can be positive about myself and perhaps even relax within society, perhaps even trust it again. You did that!"

I lift myself away from him and button myself up, "I needed you to say something like that but is it enough to sustain me in a life without you?"

"*Rachel*, you embrace sensory stimulae and gain strength from it, not as part of the masses but from the energy the masses create, while I have rejected it and wanted it to disappear. You seem to blend into the background while I stand out. We are two completely opposite and contrary people yet we connect in a way I never would have thought possible. The bond we have can never be broken even if we never meet again. Come here and just lay with me."

I shuffle along the smooth cold blackness then feel the edge of his coat on the floor with my bare feet.

I lay my head into his neck and my left leg across him. The edge of his loose shirt lays carelessly on my leg. My left arm rests across his bare stomach with my hand nestling in the middle of his bare chest.

His voice guides me into his world,

"I am relaxed in this blackness with you and the permanent sickness in the pit of my stomach always leaves when I walk into this room. Your presence then takes me through the feeling of contentment and comfort to a happy excitement and belonging." He continues by quietly singing Peter Hammill's 'Vision' to me;

'I have a vision of you, locked inside my head;

It creeps upon my mind and warms me in my bed.
A vision shimmering, shifting
Moving in false firelight;
A vision of a vision,
Protecting me from fear at night,
As the seasons roll on, and my love stays strong.
I don't know where you end, and where it is that I begin.
I simply open my mind and the memories flood on in.
I remember waking up with your arms around me;
I remember losing myself
And finding that you'd found me,
As the seasons roll on, and my love stayed strong.
Be my child, be my lover, swallow me up in your fire-glow.
Take my tongue, take my torment, take my hand and don't let go.
Let me live in your life,
For you make it all seem to matter.
Let me die in your arms,
So the vision may never shatter.
The seasons roll on; and my love stays strong.'

He kisses me softly on my forehead and holds me even tighter to him.

'Le Onde's solitary piano now reverberates around the room echoing from wall to wall and our lying here together in a perfect quietness and understanding gives me what will become a special memory of love and hope.

"When this is over, early next year some time, I'm leaving the country. I may never return and if I do I don't know if I will ever return to Brailsford but none of that matters because we are reconciled to our fate. Who knows what the future holds but we can't manufacture it; our destiny relies on that and I've never been so sure of anything in my whole life."

The alarm pauses the music and the moment in a dead stop.

We get up and as the link of our hands breaks he stuffs something into my hand, I act quickly and push it down my dress and then he utters the words that will forever cover me in a film of him,

"I am in all that you generate, produce and create, every idea, concept and piece of art no matter how small, I'm in everything you love and hold dear. I will know when you have been inspired and whether you have acted on it."

I manically pull on my underwear and then my boots (laces left undone); all done within the blink of an eye and without hesitation or deviation – now second nature.

The door opens as I tie my blindfold. Anna grabs hold of me, yanking me through the opening, then spanks my new-born bottom with her resuscitating words of supposed reassurance.

"What a great ending to a very productive and fulfilling ten weeks; really satisfying, bravo!"

I look up at her with contempt and she responds, "Well what else should I say?"

"I know, but 'bravo' is a little insensitive don't you think?"

We walk along the corridor while she explains herself.

"Look I was trying to draw your attention from him to me and it worked didn't it."

I put my head in my hands while walking and have to admit,

"For a few seconds, yes, Anna, you're right … again."

Now though I'm numb; I don't know how to feel. I can't cry or feel anger, the other extremes of happiness or euphoria … nothing! I must be in some sort of shock!

"Come on, we'll go for a quick drink after I've spoken to 'J'."

Just uttering that one innocuous letter of the alphabet can now turn my stomach over and make my legs fail beneath me. I stumble and stutter along the passage into the doorway of her office.

She leaves and I have a moment alone to reflect on my predicament; it's probably now or never. Do I ruin everything and get what I want or do I respect the process that brought me to this point and lose everything that made me who I am today – powerful and happy?

I have five minutes to decide!

Anna returns and thrusts a cheque into my hand, I don't even look at it, it doesn't interest me, and I have half a mind to give it back to her, but then 'J's words pop into my head about 'rules bringing us together' and then my mind is made up. It would be bad karma to reject the money and I have to see this through properly, according to the contract.

I can't go to the pub and talk though, I can't pretend my heart isn't breaking.

"Do you mind if we meet another time Anna. I'm quite tired and just want to get home."

What I really want to do is remember this last hour over and over again so it becomes a permanent part of my brain. A nodule with its only little medical name – the 'Supramarus' attached onto the Amygdala in the Limbic system!

"…er, I really need to ask a few questions now if you don't mind!"

"Please Anna."

"I should get some responses from you now while you're still emotionally charged and in the moment, its more accurate data if I do it now." She pleads.

And that's the problem for me, my outpourings in that room are just data

"I beg you Anna, another time please!"

She hesitates with a look of wanting to grant my wish, but there's something else behind those perfect almond shaped eyes, something she's not telling me

"Well …" She can see my tears welling up, I can't fight them back any longer and to make me talk now, even here, would be too cruel. "Ok Rachel".

I quickly force my hand into my dress and yank the small pads from my body and throw them in her direction. I look into her eyes which say goodbye to me without any need for words then I run.

*

It's only when I finally arrive home, which seemed to be an endless journey, that I remember the note he gave me which

I had stuffed down my bra. I quickly and clumsily grab at it and open it out.

It's just a plain white piece of A4 paper. In the middle is the drawing of the handmade fireplace in my apartment. I am sat facing it now and a chill runs through my body as I compare the accuracy of the detail. One word is written beneath it,

Magnificent

- The song that was playing when I followed him through the lonely back streets of Brailsford.

How does he know these things? Did he sense me? Has he manifested into these rooms before? My brain is going into overload ... stop thinking, stop questioning!

All this stuff doesn't matter, he's here with me now, I know it, so I just lay down and close my eyes ... sleep takes over.

*

I wake and not only is it the next day but it's evening and I have slept for a solid twenty-four hours.

After eating I check my mobile, which has been switched off, and my landline for messages, I discover that I am supposed to be going to Jason's tomorrow for film club – the last one before Christmas next week.

I'm really not in the mood and besides I want to have my memory time and think about what happened yesterday. Also I need to take in the fact that 'jaunting' is now a thing of the past and ask the question – am I a different person now?

There are going to be a lot of jollities at work this week and I can't face a full day of engrossing in films; I have my own head film to watch – my own story to relive.

I arrange to postpone film club until after New Year, after a ridiculous amount of questioning from Jason, and then stow away in my own world of 'him' for the next twenty-four hours.

Work is ok and I'm glad the experiment came to an end at this time. I can enjoy the parties and laughter which help to take my mind off things but as Friday looms and what would have been our time together I start to feel differently about the contract and our law abiding self-proclaimed adherence to the rules. It's then that I change my mind.

Very suddenly Thursday afternoon I have an epiphany and desperately want to find him. I don't want to be part of this experiment anymore. What's the point of keeping to these rules if I'm so unhappy and no one else is hurt if I break them? What if we were wrong and trying to find each other is our destiny?

Everyone around me is happy, in love, settling down and sharing while I'm forced to give up 'him' and for what?

I haven't cashed the cheque, I haven't even looked at it, it's still in my coat pocket. It then occurs to me that Anna hasn't contacted me to ask for a further meeting yet which is strange.

I run into one of the interview rooms to use the phone so I can have some privacy and ring the college. Someone answers but she's only a temp and isn't familiar with who anyone is and they've all gone out for Christmas dinner anyway.

Everyone gets Friday afternoon off, goodwill for all the hard work, so I make a beeline for the college.

I run into the building and there is scarecrow woman. I'm just explaining, as I walk towards Anna's office that I need to see her urgently about something when she stands and interrupts me,

"You can't go in there, it's someone else's study room now."

"Well where is Anna then?"

"Didn't she tell you?"

I'm impatient now

"No, what?"

"She's left the country, indefinitely!"

I remember now

"Oh no no, she's just gone on holiday."

"Er, no she hasn't. Is that what she told you?"

"What?"

"Yes, she took all her files and stuff yesterday. She's gone for good."

"Where has she gone?"

"Dunno. She just cleaned out her office and said she was going abroad for the foreseeable future and didn't leave a forwarding address."

My head is my hands. I don't believe it

"No, no, no. That can't be, you must have got it all wrong."

"Oh" she laughs, "But I don't think so. Now do you mind I've got to finish these nails before I leave for a party in ten minutes."

I walk out without uttering a word and stand with my back to the college, incredulous of this news. What is my next move?

Alan!

I jog all the way to his house which takes me a good hour because I keep getting lost in the rabbit warren of the new estate he lives on.

Eventually I find it and the 'For Sale', sign looms and grows as I stand below it. It's like a giant axe that's about to decapitate my head from my body, which wouldn't be a bad thing at the moment. I can see from here that the house is completely empty!

I stand staring at the shell of the building and decide there is no point spending time looking for 'him' it's not meant to be. I have no idea where he's based and he could be anywhere in the world. Fate is refusing me and pushing me in a certain direction and I have to submit.

Why have Anna and Alan eloped and why didn't she tell me? It now becomes clear why they looked at me in that peculiar way the last time I saw them together – it was goodbye. It also explains why Anna's look was so forlorn and pitying when I left last Friday.

Back home I lay on my sofa staring at that fireplace with his drawing in one hand and a glass of wine in the other.

The radio is on, which I haven't been taking much notice of, but then Andy Burrows – 'If I Had A Heart' cuts through the air spinning like a disc and lands in front of me, Pow – why did 'J' let me go like that, was it so easy for him?

The tears dribble down the middle of my cheek following a perfect path to the corner of my mouth and as they flow faster and faster my desperation turns to salty fear, bitterness and recriminations; how could it be so easy? Was he lost in the moment? Is it so much easier for men to control themselves emotionally even when they are supposedly madly in love with someone? Why didn't he fight for me?

It's easier now for me to feel anger rather than loss. It's easier for women to get lost in their emotions and find new ones to aggravate the situation.

I could spend days thinking about this but I can't – I need to talk to someone about this but now I realise I wish I had kept Sarah in the loop about all this, it would be easier now. I can't relay the whole ten weeks to her or tell her 'J' and I did the deed, it's too much to go over before we can get to the bit I need to discuss right now.

I have to talk myself round, make myself understand that what happened was not a sham. I have to access that new part of the brain 'the Supramarus' (supernatural love) that I have created for this very reason.

As I remember the words he gave me and look again at the drawing and immerse myself in that perfect moment where we laid together, I realise 'it was what it was' and I have to move on and learn from him. I must resist the feeling of loss and emptiness. I have to stop over-analysing my current situation and flitting back and forth from anxiety and remorse to gratitude and acceptance.

I mustn't give in to any feeling of settling for an ordinary life. I have to start a new meaningful life!

I must remember and trust his words about being with me when I create!

Dido – 'Girl Who Got Away' now plays on the radio. this song reflects my emotions and I now cry away my loss and smile with resolve.

Chapter 14

Pregnant!

A new year and a new beginning.

The soundtrack of the first chapter of my life is complete and overtures the next one, 'Le Onde' – a continuous theme that now plays and follows me wherever I go.

This baby is a part of him. I don't feel anger or abandonment, only love and thankfulness. I know our paths will cross again someday, somehow, and until then I will keep our future safe, nurtured and loved.

I remember that perfect love and moment that changed my life and created the four week old baby inside me that now symbolises that; a living breathing entity – a moment in time never to be lost. Unconditional love forever more and without boundaries.